Books by John Migacz

The Dieya Chronicles

Currently Available
Incident on Ravar
The Beginning

Future Dieya Chronicles
Earth

Due 2016
A Second Chance

A Busman's Holiday

By

John Migacz

A Busman's Holiday
Copyright 2016 by John Migacz

www.johnmigacz.com

ISBN 978-0-578-17587-4

Printed in the United States of America

Acknowledgements

I'd like to thank Marcia Migacz, and the Greenville SCWW gang for all their help in editing this novel. I'd especially like to thank Marcia for her love and support, and Prem Rawat for the courage and inspiration.

busman's holiday

noun | bus - man's holiday |
/ˈbəs-mənz/ /ˈhälə-dā/

a holiday spent in following or observing the practice of one's usual occupation, as a bus driver taking a long drive

Chapter 1

I yanked open the barroom door and stepped in out of the cold wind and the harsh sunlight. Darkness and warm air wrapped around my body like a soft baby blanket. An old Wurlitzer in a corner spun a bluesy tune, filling the near-empty bar with more laidback ease. Layers of old smoke and whiskey wormed their way into my nose and into my consciousness. A sigh of pure pleasure escaped from my mouth as I skirted the half-dozen dark wood tables and limped to the bar. Tuck a cot into a corner and I could live here.

Glad to get off my leg, I slid onto a barstool and pulled out my cigarettes. I stared into the pack of Luckies and a single wrinkled cigarette stared back at me. Nothing looks so forlorn as a last smoke in a rumpled pack. I shook it loose from the white container with the big red dot in the center, then crumpled the empty pack and dropped it on the counter. I like to think of it as a red dot, instead of a red bulls-eye, as most folks referred to it. In my business, having a red bulls-eye on you wasn't a good idea.

The bartender, a cute blonde in jeans and a worn Star Wars sweatshirt with a hole in the elbow, finished talking to a middle-aged guy sitting at the other end of the bar and headed my way. Ponytail swinging with each step, she got sexier as she neared. The spray of freckles across her face didn't hurt either. She wasn't as young as I first thought, probably just a little younger than me, but she had the kind of lean body that always got my attention. Eyes, a little on the hard side, flashed with humor, intelligence, and a touch of innocence.

Interesting.

My hands patted my pockets for a match as she leaned on the counter.

"Need a light?"

"I need everything," I said.

She slid a hand into the front pocket of her tight jeans and pulled out an old Zippo. Her long fingers flicked the striker and I cupped her hand, leaning forward to accept the light. I kept my hand on hers, closed the lid with my thumb and read the inscription on the lighter.

"Born to Kill?" I released her hand and blew smoke out a corner of my mouth. "You don't look born to kill."

"Maybe." A smile teased her lips. "But I could if I wanted to."

I inhaled more smoke deep into my lungs and returned the smile. Nicotine and a cute woman. My world was looking up.

She glanced at the lighter, then returned it to her pocket. "It's just a souvenir from an ex-boyfriend."

"Was he born to kill?"

"No," she snorted. "He was born to lose."

Her hand scooped up the crushed pack of Lucky Strikes and threw it in the trash. "If you need more cigarettes, there's a machine in the corner."

"Yeah, but I'm trying to quit."

Her blue eyes roamed over me, taking in the beat-up leather jacket, the worn shirt, and faded jeans. They rested a moment on the scars on my hands, then she looked back into my eyes. "Can I get you something else?"

She gave me the once-over to see if my pockets held the price of a drink. Her eyes said she didn't think so. With a chuckle, I pulled out a wad of bills, peeled off a twenty and tossed it on the bar. "Johnny Walker Black. Neat."

She glanced at the twenty and left it on the counter. "Coming right up."

At the other end of the bar, the middle-aged guy with the red-rimmed eyes waved an empty bottle. "Hey, Becky. Can I get another beer sometime this year?"

Becky walked to a cooler. "Keep your pants on, Ralph."

The drunk grinned. "Maybe you don't want my pants on."

"If your pants were off, you wouldn't like how I opened this long-neck." She popped the top on a Coors and slid it down the bar.

Ralph snagged it and saluted her with the bottle.

Becky hefted a Johnny Walker Black half-gallon bottle from a row of liquors and headed back my way. She slapped a glass down in front of me.

I stared at the whiskey as she poured two fingers. With a twist of her wrist, she finished pouring and raised the bottle. The motion brought my eyes to hers and I reached out and gently held her arm. Her skin felt warm, soft, and very alive.

"Don't go away," I said and lifted the shot. Liquid fire poured down my throat and I set the empty glass on the counter. "Again," I said, and released her arm.

"Twelve-year-old whiskey should be sipped and enjoyed."

"That's what the second glass is for."

"The first?" she asked.

"Take the edge off."

"Must be a hell of an edge," she said, and poured another.

I slid a hand under my jacket and rubbed my aching side. "It is today."

I sipped the amber liquid and glanced around the bar. Besides the drunk, there was only an old guy in a corner booth, nursing a beer. "When does the crowd come in?" I asked.

Becky glanced at her watch. "Oh, about quarter past three years ago."

My eyebrow raised and she shrugged.

"Since the plant closed, this place has had less business than an Easter chick sale in August."

"Why stay?"

She leaned on the bar and looked around the room, her gaze touching on everything. "Good memories. Plus, I own it. The bar, the stock, and the rooms upstairs." Her eyes met mine again. "It's not much, but the little business I get keeps me afloat."

"I've never met a woman with good memories of a bar."

Becky took a rag from her back pocket and scrubbed an imaginary spot on the gleaming mahogany. "I grew up here. My dad owned this place."

"We have something in common. I've always wanted to live in a bar."

"Then I'm living your dreamed-of life," she said.

"Wanna switch?"

"Lives?" Her blonde head tilted in thought. "Maybe." She jammed the bar towel into her back pocket. "But first I'd have to know a lot about yours. What do you do?"

I stared into the dregs of my glass, swirled the contents, and thought about how to answer. The realization hit me that I really didn't know anymore. "Nothing at the moment."

She glanced down. "From the size of that wad in your pocket, I'd say nothing pays pretty well."

The door opened behind me and I watched her eyes flash with fear, then go stone cold. She may not be born to kill, but whoever came in was certainly on her wish list.

Looking into the mirror behind the bar, I assessed the two men who had just entered. Long overcoats and suits couldn't dress up these slimeballs. One was tall and dour-faced while the other was short with a smug, arrogant attitude. I labeled them "Runt and

Puss." From their size difference, I could have labeled them "Mutt and Jeff," but that would have afforded them too much dignity. The tall one flicked off the red neon "Open" sign.

The men sauntered to the old-timer in the booth and stood there, not saying a word. The oldster looked up, and without finishing his beer, hurried out of the bar.

Of all the gin-joints in all the world... I sighed, wondering if I was in the wrong place at the wrong time or the right place at the wrong time.

I silently cursed karma and finished my drink. The glass clicking down on the bar drew Becky's eyes back to me. "Once again, please."

She blinked twice, glanced up at the two men, then poured another round. "This one's for the road," she said.

"I'm not driving."

Her eyes flitted once more to the men who were approaching the oblivious Ralph, then back to mine. "You'd better go." She started down the bar.

The slimeballs flanked Ralph. The taller one poked him in the back – hard. Ralph turned to argue, then his drunk-red face paled. The smaller one yanked him off the bar stool and propelled him toward the door. Ralph used the added impetus to hurry out.

Becky wiped her hands on her jeans as she walked toward the pair.

The smaller one grinned. "Well, sweetcakes. We're here as promised."

Becky placed her hands on her hips. "I told you. I don't need, or have the money for insurance."

Runt leered. "A slick piece of ass like you needs all the insurance she can get." He glanced at Puss. "If she doesn't have cash, maybe we can take it out in trade." Puss's lips raised in what might have been a smile, but looked more like a bad bout of gas.

Hate burned in my belly more than the liquor. How many countries had I seen this in? Once again, the strong prey upon the weak. In nature, the strong kill and eat to survive. In humans, the strong prey on the weak just because they can. I idly wondered which category I fit into.

I chugged down the scotch, knowing it would help numb me after, and slammed the glass down on the bar. "Hey! How about a little service here."

Runt and Puss turned from Becky, glanced at each other, then strolled along the bar toward me. "New around here, huh?" said

Runt, a smile plastered on his smug face. They stopped two feet away from me, Runt standing in front of Puss.

I stood.

Runt leaned closer. "You don't want no trouble with us."

"Oh? Why's that?"

He opened his jacket to expose the .45 caliber 1911 Colt Automatic hanging under his arm and grinned.

"Nice vintage technology," I said, not even attempting to keep the derision from my voice. I held my jacket open to show the twin 9mm Sig P-228s in speed rigs, one hanging under each arm. "I prefer modern." I let go of my jacket and gripped the edge of the bar.

Runt's eyes widened and he reached for his weapon. I launched and head-butted him. The blow staggered him back into Puss. My hand snaked out, yanked Runt's .45 from its holster and whipped the heavy barrel around into Puss's temple. Puss crumpled in a heap and Runt fell back over him. I dropped a knee onto Runt's chest as he struggled to rise. His breath whooshed out, and he gasped for air.

I felt movement behind me, turned and leveled the .45. Becky had come around the bar hefting a Louisville Slugger. "You going to use that on me?"

She lowered the bat. "I thought you might need some help."

I grinned. "My hero." Layers of outrage, relief, and fear painted her face, but she still stood straight and strong – I liked that.

"Ex-boyfriends?" I asked as I stood and pointed to the two men.

Her face crinkled with disgust. "No." The word spat from her in an automatic response as she gestured to the slimeballs. "These are two of Teddy Tedesco's goons. Tedesco moved in when the unions left town. He runs all the rackets on the east side." She closed her eyes for a moment and inhaled deeply. "There'll be hell to pay when he hears about this." She eyed the men on the floor, then placed a hand on her hip. "Listen, I'd like to thank you for the help, but I think you should leave."

"What? Just when we're getting to know each other?"

Puss moaned and lifted his head. I held up a finger. "Excuse me a moment." I leaned over and smashed the barrel of the .45 down onto Puss' head, twice. "I hate when someone rudely interrupts a pleasant conversation."

Her hand jumped to cover her mouth and her wide eyes stared at Puss, then snapped back to mine. "Oh shit!" She grabbed onto the bar, then straightened. "Listen. I can't leave this place. It's all I have." She looked down. "They'll kill me."

"Tedesco plays that rough?"

She nodded.

"Well, I guess you'd better get out of town."

"No!" Eyes filled with anger burned into mine. "I won't be run off."

"So you're in all the way?"

"I won't be run off."

"It will get uglier than this."

"I won't be run off."

She said it more softly this time, and I knew she repeated the words more for herself than me.

I shrugged. "Well, maybe I can talk him into playing nice."

Runt had rolled over on his side and was struggling to sit up. I pushed him down and replaced my knee on his chest.

He cursed. "You're a dead man! Dead man! You hear me?"

"Yeah. I hear you." I stripped off his neck tie, rolled him onto his stomach, then whispered in his ear. "I'll tell you a secret. We're all dead men. We just haven't quit moving yet." I bound his hands, then rolled him onto his back and placed my knee on his chest again. "Now... Let's chat. Tell me all about Teddy."

"Screw you. I'll kill you!" He squirmed under me, but I just added more weight to his chest. I turned and looked up at Becky. "You might wanna go upstairs or back behind the bar for this."

She shook her head, then those long fingers swept back the few tendrils of hair that had escaped from the ponytail. She stared hard at me. "I'm sticking."

"Suit yourself." I pulled the Ka-Bar tucked into a sheath sewn into my scarred motorcycle boot, and held it close to Runt's face. "Now. Where should I begin?"

I placed the knife edge between his teeth and turned the blade. A gargle popped out his open mouth. "Should I begin by cutting out your tongue?" I withdrew the blade. "No. That wouldn't allow you to talk. Counterproductive." The blade touched Runt's earlobe then slid up to the ear hole. With a slight turn, blood flowed. Panic flushed over Runt's face, and he clenched his teeth. I held the bloody knife tip in front of Runt's face. "No. Not the ears. You need to hear my questions."

I tapped the bloody knife on his nose and watched for fear to loosen his tongue. It was close, but it needed more. I smiled down into his face. "I got it. You don't need to *see* to answer questions."

I put the point of the knife on his lower eyelid and applied slight pressure. He squirmed and his feet drummed on the floor. Blood trickled like tears and I increased the force, waiting for fear to overcome the blocks of loyalty and pride.

"All right! I'll tell you what you want!" screamed Runt.

I lowered the knife. "Good. Let's start with some addresses."

Five minutes later, I had all the information I needed about Teddy Tedesco. I rolled Runt onto his stomach and cracked the .45 on the back of his head.

"You must like hitting people with guns," said Becky.

I looked at her for the first time since I had drawn the knife. She was sitting on a bar stool, writing on a pad.

"Is it a macho thing?" she asked.

I jammed the .45 into my belt and rose. "No. Think of it as a pacifier. It keeps the kids quiet and is less noisy than a bullet in the head." I gestured at the pad. "What are you writing?"

"I kept notes in case you forgot something that creep said."

"Admirable." I searched her face for traces of fear, disgust, hatred, anything. I only saw that stone-cold determination. "How you holding up?"

Her shoulders crunched together and she doodled on the pad. "I'm... fine." She looked up and her eyes blazed. "I'm just trying to get by, and those thugs think they can hurt me and take everything I have." Her narrowed eyes studied the prone men. "I hate them! I hate them, and all men like them."

"That's good. But remember, unbridled passion can overcome reason and lead to tragedy." I took a step toward her, then grunted in pain. I reached inside my jacket and my hand came away bloody. "Shit."

Becky leaped off the stool. "You're hurt! I'm sorry. I didn't even see them touch you."

I leaned down and wiped my hand on Puss's jacket. "They didn't."

"Come with me. I've got a first-aid kit in the storage room."

"It'll hold 'til we clean up this trash first." I grabbed Runt's arms, and with Becky leading the way, dragged him around the bar to the storage room. By the time I had Puss piled on top of Runt, she had the kit out and was ripping off strips of tape. "Take off your jacket and shirt."

"I thought you'd never ask," I said and took off my jacket.

Her eyes widened at my two-gun rig. "You need two guns?"

I carefully slipped out of the harness. "I'm ambidextrous." I took off my shirt and checked the bandage on my right side. It was seeping blood but didn't look that bad. I hoped I hadn't broken open too many stitches.

"You were hurt before," she said.

"Yeah. But I'm trying to quit." I took a deep breath, gripped the bandage, and ripped it off. "Ouch! Shit! Damn!" I reached for the fresh bandage but Becky brushed my hand aside.

She staunched the bleeding and applied butterfly band-aids to the area that had broken open. She peered at the deep wound and bruise along my side. "What did this? Knife?"

"AK-47."

Her hands hesitated a moment, then continued taping the bandage. "A bullet wound?"

"Yeah. And I got one just like it on my left thigh."

She stopped and those blue eyes peered into mine. "What the hell are you into? And who are you?" Her eyes narrowed. "You know, I never heard your name."

"I thought busting up those hoods was enough of an introduction, but I guess not." I reached out a hand. "Jack. Jack Daniels. At your service."

"Jack Daniels?" She just stared at my hand, then shrugged. "If you don't want to tell me your name that's all right, but you should have gone for Johnny Walker."

I sighed. "It's Jack Daniels. Honestly."

She continued taping the bandage as her brows furrowed. "What kind of parent names their kid 'Jack Daniels?'"

"An asshole drunkard named Jake Daniels."

"I see..." Becky reached for more tape, then stopped and eyed her work. "I think I'll wrap gauze around your chest to apply pressure to the bandage."

"Where did you learn first aid?"

Her hand rummaged around inside the kit. "Growing up around here you get to see the aftermath of a lot of bar fights." She found a roll of gauze and tore open the package with her teeth. "Especially during playoff times." Becky stared at my chest, eyes roaming over the many scars, then back to my face. "You've got a nice physique and a nice out of season tan, but I could do without the scars."

"I'm trying to quit."

She placed the end of the gauze roll against the center of my chest. "Hold this here and turn around." I did as she asked, then heard her gasp. I knew the crisscross of old scars on my back wasn't pretty to look at. I just hoped it didn't repulse her too much.

"Jesus Christ, Jack! What the hell did that?"

"A barbed-wire whip."

She gently laid a hand on my back. "Barbed-wire?"

"Yeah," I nodded. "The nuns were really strict."

She inhaled deeply. "Oh, Jack…"

Her hand felt warm and gentle and I stifled a smart-ass remark to savor the feeling. The compassion in her voice had touched me.

Becky's hand slid up to my shoulder and squeezed it once, then she began to wrap several layers of gauze around my chest. When she finished, I turned to face her. She was almost as tall as I was and I studied the cute spray of freckles across her cheeks.

She stared into my eyes a moment as if looking to see who was inside, then looked down to examine her work. "That's the best I can do."

"Thanks. Nice job."

Becky glared down at the two thugs still out cold on the floor. "This is such a mess. What am I going to do?" Her last words faded as worry displaced action. She hoisted herself up and sat up on the short counter that split the room in half.

"I think these sleeping beauties should be taken home to their mommy, don't you?"

Becky reached out and placed a hand on my arm. "Why are you doing this?"

"I dunno. Maybe it's because I'm the only one who can." I stroked a knuckle down her cheek hoping to dispel some of the worry etched in her pretty face. "And you have nice eyes."

"There has to be a better reason." Disbelief and a hint of suspicion coated her words.

There was a better reason, but I damn well didn't know what it was. "Let's just say it's what I do."

"Is that where you pick up your scars?"

"Yeah. They might mark me, but they never touch me."

I grabbed my shirt and finished dressing, then slipped into the speed rig. I squatted by Runt and Puss, emptied their pockets and placed the contents on the counter. I hefted the .38 revolver Puss had carried. "Wow, these boys are old school." I pawed through their wallets and removed all IDs and cash. "Nine-hundred and fifty-three dollars." I split off six hundred, stuck it in my pocket and pushed the rest at Becky. "It turned out to be a better day than you were having."

She pushed the cash back at me. Outrage peppered her words. "I don't want their money!"

"Why not? They wanted yours."

"It's not the same."

"OK," I said, and scooped up the cash.

"How come you get the bigger share, anyway?" she asked, her voice laced with a bit of humor.

I chuckled. "I knew there was a mercenary heart in there somewhere." I spun Runt's set of keys around on my finger. "Their car must be parked close." I pushed the button and heard the chirp outside the delivery door.

Becky slid off the counter and stepped to the delivery entrance. "They must have parked in the alley." She turned the locks and swung opened the door. A gray 1990's Mercury was parked next to a dumpster.

"What a piece of crap," I said. "I guess the plant closing hurt their business, too."

"What's next?" asked Becky as we stepped back inside.

"What's next? No hand-wringing? No tears or admonishments?"

Her eyes hardened as she looked down at the pair. "They came into my bar. They threatened me with robbery and brutality. I'd say they earned the same treatment they would have given me."

Becky didn't cringe or slump as most women would. She was leaning forward as if ready to spring. I thought she just might do.

"Well, first off, let's get these sweethearts into the car. Got any duct tape?"

She reached under the counter and pulled out an almost full roll. A tough woman who uses duct tape. This could be love.

I spun several coils around Puss' hands and feet, then put a large "X" over his mouth. I stuffed the roll in Runt's overcoat pocket.

"Take Puss' feet if you will."

"Puss?"

I grinned. "Yeah, when they came in I labeled them Runt and Puss."

She lifted the tall man's feet. "It fits."

We wrestled Puss through the doorway and into the trunk and placed Runt in the passenger seat. "Let me have that bar rag."

She snatched the cloth from her back pocket and I wiped the blood from Runt's face and untied his hands.

"Got any cheap whiskey?" I asked.

Becky nodded and was back in a minute with a half-empty bottle. I studied the label, then looked up. "Old North Bend?"

"Something I keep for the freeloaders."

I opened the bottle, sniffed, and my head jerked involuntarily. "God. That reeks!" I smiled at her. "Perfect."

I got into the driver's seat, dashed a liberal quantity on Runt's clothes and hair, then handed the bottle out the window. "If I'm successful, I hope we'll celebrate with a little better quality than this." As I started the engine, Becky laid a hand on my arm. "I'm coming with you."

"No. You're not." I started the car

"I told you I was in this all the way. Besides, this is my fight." Her stance said it all. This was a woman who wanted to confront her enemy.

"Okay. But I need to reconnoiter first, and a lone sneak and peek is best." I placed my hand over hers. "There is something you can do."

"What?"

I reached into my pocket, withdrew my wad of bills and the cash I took from the slime-balls. "Hold this for me." I forced it into her hand and closed her fingers around it.

She looked down at the money. "Jack. I can't..."

"Oh, and if I'm not back in two hours, use it to get out of town."

I slammed on the gas, sped down the alleyway and glanced into the rearview mirror. Standing with arms crossed, stood a lovely, strong-willed, really pissed-off woman.

Chapter 2

Tedesco's headquarters was near Seventh and should only take me a couple minutes. Runt had explained the layout and said a max of three people would be there at this time of the day. I hoped he wasn't lying.

With the heater turned high, my thoughts drifted to Becky. It might be nice to have an extended relationship with a woman who didn't seem to think me strange. On the other hand, she didn't know how really strange I was.

I cut over on Frontage to the run-down industrial area. Most warehouses were closed, with more than a few rusting away. I turned into Peize's Warehouse and followed the faded sign to "Receiving." The building had a raised dock with three bays and crumbling stairs that lead to an office door. I pulled close and exited the car. I hadn't gotten halfway to the stairs when the office door banged opened and a big man walked out. According to Runt, this had to be Silvio.

The big man stood at the top of the short flight of stairs and curled his sausage-sized fingers into fists. "This is private property. Go away."

I held up a hand and put on my sincerest look. "I'm sorry, Mister, but the guy in the car paid me fifty dollars to bring him here." I gestured back to the car. "He's passed out."

Silvio glanced at my passenger, then did a double-take. "Joey?" He rushed down the stairs like a rock avalanche and yanked open the door. He leaned in for a moment, then jerked his head back. "Phew. What the hell was he drinking?"

"I don't know," I said. "Let me give you a hand."

We hauled him out of the car and with Runt between the two of us, carried him up the stairs. Silvio certainly could have done the job by himself, but I wanted to get inside the building.

The small receiving office contained a door to the warehouse, a desk, a phone, and a metal chair. A game of solitaire was splayed out across the desk. We dumped Runt into the chair and Silvio leaned over, grabbed Runt's chin, and looked closely at his face. "Hey, he looks – "

Whatever brilliant diagnosis Doctor Silvio was about to render was cut short by my Sig pressed up against the back of his neck. "Sit on the floor." I grabbed him by the collar.

Silvio tried a bluff. "Listen, smart-ass, I can whistle and twenty guys will be here in two seconds."

"Maybe, but in the first second my bullet will make a real mess of your brains." I pulled him into a sitting position on the floor and reached into Runt's pocket for the duct tape. "Put your hands behind your back."

Silvio did as I asked, then looked up at me. "You're dead, you know."

I spun the tape around his hands. "That's what everyone keeps telling me. Now, get on your stomach." Silvio complied and I taped his ankles together, then tethered his hands to his ankles. I did a quick pat down and pulled a .38 snub-nosed revolver out of his pocket.

"Wow, this must get lost in your hand. You should think about getting a bigger gun."

"I'll think about it," he said. "Maybe a real gut-puncher. Just for you."

"Thanks, Silvio." His eyes narrowed at my use of his name, and I patted his cheek. "I gotta tape your mouth. I'm sorry we can't continue this conversation, but I don't want you whistling."

He scowled as I taped his mouth with a strip of duct tape. "You're all right, Silvio. I'm glad I didn't have to put you down."

Silvio nodded once, and I stood. Runt chose that moment to groan. "Hey, Joey," I said. "Thanks for moaning. I almost forgot about you." I thought that whacking him in the head again might ruin his chances for a Nobel Prize, so I taped his hands behind him, ran a strip over his mouth, and taped his legs to the chair instead.

I walked to the office door and peered through the window into the warehouse. Wooden crates stood on either side of the door, leading into a large dim area. I nudged the door open and stepped inside. Shoving Silvo's gun into a crack between the crates, I drew my own weapons.

Sig in each hand, I crept next to the crates. To the right, I heard talking and sounds of machines running. I crouched low and thrust my head out for a quick peek.

Twenty feet away, an overhead bulb hung low over two men cutting coke on a long table. From the pile of plastic bags, I'd say business was good. The machine noise I'd heard was a washing machine and a dryer, both running. I hadn't realized that today was wash day or I'd have brought my undies. I'd have to settle for hanging Tedesco out to dry instead.

A fluorescent-lighted, small prefab glass office stood behind them, with one man seated in an office chair behind an old wooden desk. He was on the phone, leaning back, feet propped up on an open drawer. From his fat belly, fat cigar, and fat diamond pinky ring, I figured this had to be Teddy Tedesco.

I holstered my Sigs and sat back on my heels to give this some thought. Killing all three of them would be simple, but for some reason I didn't want to. I searched, once again, for my conscience and didn't find it. But something in the back of my brain nagged at me. It took me a moment to realize it had something to do with Becky, and her opinion of me.

Huh! Was I going soft? Was it because I was tired? Or was it because of that mess in Angola? I realized I was massaging my wounded side and dropped my hand.

I pushed away that ugly memory and studied the uniform wooden crates that lined the wall. Each three-feet square and stacked three high, they formed two columns along one side of the warehouse. Most were labeled *peças para veículos automóveis*. Portuguese for car parts.

The steel roof girders had pulleys and hoists attached to them in several places. Teddy's business must include chopping cars and selling the parts to South America. In today's uncertain economy, I guess Teddy wanted to diversify his holdings. Smart business acumen. It would be fun to discuss his portfolio.

I climbed to the top of the crates and crawled along the flat surface until I was even with the cutting table. From the shadows, I had a good view of the entire warehouse. Below me, the two men packed the drugs and discussed last Sunday's game; off to the left, skeletons of cars were neatly lined. The washer and dryer humming below me lent a soothing, homey air to the room – and covered any noise I might make.

As I pondered the best way to take the two men out, the dryer buzzer below me howled. I dropped flat and tried to slow my racing heart. Damn machines.

Keeping well back in the shadows, I peered over the edge. The two men had peeled off their latex gloves and were squatting by the dryer. The smaller man pulled handfuls of old issue twenty-dollar bills from the dryer and tossed them into a basket. The other arranged the bills into neat stacks. Talk about money laundering.

With barely a thought, I leaped, landing with a knee on the back of each man. I drove their heads together at the same time. They went down in a heap, their bodies breaking my fall nicely. I lifted my head and checked on Teddy but he was still sitting, talking on the phone. The two under me were out cold, but I nevertheless pulled out the trusty roll of duct tape and trussed them up and patted them down. Never leave anything to chance was something I'd learned the hard way.

I examined two of the twenty-dollar bills, knowing what I'd find. Yep, all the bills had the same serial number and an issue date of 1974. Tedesco must have come across some old plates. Washing and drying newly printed bills gives them an old, used look. But they couldn't distribute them without drawing a lot of heat. I sat back on my heels and the Portuguese writing on a crate caught my eye. Ahhh… it made sense. I bet the auto parts headed to South America were loaded with the fake twenties.

I grinned as a tale of bullshit and bravado swirled around in my head. A story that would confuse everyone and take any heat away from Becky.

I stood, straightened my jacket, and headed to Teddy's office. The overconfident ass didn't even look up as I opened the door and stepped in.

"Yeah. No problem," he said into the phone. "I'll have it to you by Thursday."

I walked to the side of his desk and clicked the disconnect button.

"What the – " Teddy looked startled, then dove for the open drawer and reached inside.

I let him get his hand in the drawer then slammed it shut and held it closed. I grabbed him by the throat with my other hand as he yelped. I squeezed hard and watched his eyes pop wide. His other hand tried to force mine from his throat, but that wasn't going to happen.

"*Ola, Tedesco. Voce foi um menino impertinente.*" I grabbed the hand in the drawer, yanked it out, and groped for the gun inside. It was a nickel plated .32 revolver. Christ, these guys were old school. I dropped it into my pocket, pulled out my Sig and released the chokehold. "*Eu sou aqui para cortar suas esferas,*" I said with my best Portuguese accent.

Teddy leaned forward in his chair until I pointed the Sig at his head. He fell back, rubbed his throat, and glanced at the door. "Tony! Bobby!" he yelled.

I perched on the edge of his desk, shook my head and put on my best Portuguese accent. "Dead, Teddy. Tony. Bobby. Silvio. Joey. The rest. All dead."

The blood drained from Teddy's face. "Who – what?"

"Oh. Sorry for the Portuguese before. Let me translate that message from Muñoz. Teddy, you've been a naughty boy. And I'm here to cut your balls off."

He grabbed the arms of his chair. "I don't know what you're talking about!"

"Sure you don't. I'm sure you didn't think passing all those counterfeit bills to our rivals would hurt our organization either."

Tedesco said nothing and I watched his eyes dart from side to side, the rat looking for the rat-hole. I reached down and pulled the Ka-Bar from my boot. "Muñoz was quite clear. He wants your balls." I put the Sig away and cleaned my nail with the knife. "Rodriguez, on the other hand, left it to my discretion."

Beads of sweat formed on Teddy's forehead and cheeks, and rolled down onto his cheap, plaid polyester suit jacket. I wondered how many folks he had made sweat the same way.

"Listen," he said. "I don't know who these people are, but I'm sure we can come to some kind of understanding."

I shook my head. "Muñoz may be crazy-mean, but no one crosses Rodriguez." I widened my eyes. "I certainly won't."

Teddy lifted a hand. "Look, I have money."

"Yeah. Some just came out of the laundry."

"No. No. Real bills. New dollars. We can work this out."

I paused a moment, as if thinking it over. "Rodriguez wants the plates. There's no negotiating that one."

His head bobbed up and down like a bird. "Sure. Sure. No problem."

"Good. Now pull up your feet and cross your ankles in a lotus position."

"Why?"

I pulled out the roll of duct tape. "'Cause you'll look like a big fat Buddha and you need to be doing some praying." He hesitated and I stabbed the knife into the desk. Teddy watched it quiver until it stopped, then his eyes found mine. Whatever he saw there made him pull his feet up onto the chair and cross his ankles. As I taped them together I asked, "Are you right or left-handed?"

He looked confused. "Right."

"Where are the plates?"

"In my safe."

"Where? What type of safe?"

He shrugged. "In a cutout apartment in a Liberty floor safe."

I taped his left forearm down to the chair arm and rolled him closer to the desk. "Now." I pushed a pad and pen to his right hand. "You're going to write down the location of the safe and the combination."

Teddy stared at me for a moment, then wrote down the information.

I picked up the pad. "I'll have my men verify this and…" I re-read the combination then dropped the pad. "Tsk, tsk, Teddy. What did you hope to gain? More time? There's no one coming to your rescue."

Sweat rolled into his eyes, making them red and puffy. He swiped his face with his jacket sleeve. "Wadda ya mean? Let me go."

"Liberty safes have a minimum of four combination sets. You've only written three." I yanked the knife from the desk and stared down at his spread-open crotch. "Maybe Muñoz has the right idea." I leaned forward and put the point of my knife on his crotch.

"No! No." He clutched at the pen and scribbled a different address and combination on the pad. "This is it! I swear!"

Fear dilated his eyes wide. He was telling the truth this time.

"Thanks, Teddy." I taped his right hand down then taped his mouth. Just for fun, I spun his chair around and around. On every revolution I slid the knife closer to his eyes. I stopped when I could hear him screaming through the gag. Sometimes I really love my work.

The knife went back into my boot and I searched the office. In the top drawer of his desk was a ledger with payments for thugs, drugs, money in, and money out. Extortion payments and due dates. I turned a page and grunted. It listed employees and payoffs to cops – complete with names and dates.

I looked at Teddy. "Sloppy. Very sloppy." I dropped the ledger on the desk. "I'm glad I'm not working for you. Rodriguez at least runs a neat organization." I hunched my shoulders. "I could never work in America anyway. It's too damn cold here." I opened a file cabinet drawer. "I can't wait to get back home where the weather and women are hot!"

I found nothing more of note in the filing cabinet until I opened the bottom drawer. A mass of cash filled the drawer to overflowing. I squatted and flipped through several stacks of fifties and hundreds still in bank bands. These were very real.

Nice.

I emptied a box of office paper and filled it with the cash. I couldn't tell how much there was, but it was a hefty sum. I dropped the box on the desk and gave Teddy's chair another spin. "You just keep spinning 'til I check out your info."

I stepped out of the office and closed the door behind me. I pulled out my cell and dialed. The phone rang three times, then a voice answered, "Yeah?"

"Yeah? Is that any way to answer the phone? A highly paid civil servant such as yourself should be better mannered, even though you're ugly as a monkey's ass."

There was silence for several seconds. "Who is this?

"Had me dead and buried in your mind already, Charlie?"

More silence... then, "Christ! Jack, is that you?"

"Yep. Listen, I need a favor."

"What you need is to come in. We need to know what the hell happened."

I felt my teeth clench and had to relax my mouth to talk. "Well, here's what happened. Your intelligence was shit. A lot of people died including half my team. We extracted and I quit the business."

"Come in. We'll talk. We still owe you for the job, botched or not."

"Botched?" My hand squeezed the phone so hard I thought it would shatter. "The only thing I botched was agreeing to work for you assholes again in the first place. The poorest warlord clan in Nigeria has it more together than you clowns." I took a breath to calm down and push out the ugly visions running through my brain. "I'm done, Charlie. Good luck when you want to hire more mercenaries – good ones, anyway. The word is out."

I heard a big sigh on the other end of the phone. "Sorry, it went down like that, but..." Another sigh. "What was the favor you needed?"

"I need the Gary Indiana Secret Service." I could hear the wheels spin in Charlie's head.

"What – "

"Not to worry. It's about funny money, not the Man."

More silence. "OK. Call John Warner. But let me call him first and give him a heads up. Give me five minutes."

He gave me the number.

"Listen, Jack…"

"Forget it Charlie. And forget me." I punched "end" and slipped the phone back into my pocket.

I waited five minutes, then called John Warner. I don't know what Charlie had told him, but he was full of "Yes, sirs" and "Will do's" as I told him what I needed.

I re-entered the office. Tedesco had finished spinning and was facing the wall. I turned the chair around. "My people are checking out your safe. Lord help you if you've lied." I hefted the box of cash under my arm, gave his chair another spin and walked into the warehouse. I checked on Tony and Bobby. They were awake, had really nervous looks on their faces, but were still secured. I walked toward the shipping office to check on Silvio and Joey.

The unfamiliar weight tugging my coat had me pulling out Teddy's .32 revolver. The gun even had a pearl handle. How sad, I thought, and stepped into the shipping office.

Silvio was still on the floor but Joey was standing and pulling a gun out of the desk drawer. Our eyes locked for a second. His eyes filling with hate caused an instant of hesitation as he lifted the gun. I didn't hesitate, but fired three rapid shots. Joey pitched backwards, hit the wall, and slumped to the floor. Keeping the gun on him, I glanced over to check that Silvio was still bound securely, then advanced. Three holes about a half-inch apart were centered on Joey's chest and his blank eyes stared out at nothing.

"Nice shot grouping," I said and looked down at Silvio. "Maybe a thirty-two isn't such shit after all."

I checked Joey's wrists, wondering how he'd gotten loose. Tape still wrapped his wrists, but was frayed apart where they'd been connected. I checked the chair he'd been tied to and found that the outside corner of the steel edging was coarse. Probably from rubbing on the cinder-block wall. Bits of tape still clung to the edge.

My luck must have really changed. If I'd entered the office a moment later, it wouldn't have been pretty.

Teddy's prints would be on the gun as well as mine so I judiciously wiped only the parts that I'd touched, then dropped the gun near Joey's body to add to the confusion. I switched the box to my other arm, propped open the office door and walked outside to the Mercury. I tossed the box onto the passenger seat, started the car, and pulled away.

I slammed on the brakes before I got five feet. "Where's my head today?" I got out of the car and opened the trunk. Puss' eyes blinked in the light. He looked cowed and fearful. Evidently the stay in the trunk had sucked out some of his arrogance. "OK, Puss. No more loitering." I yanked him from the trunk and tossed him down onto the ground. "You stay right there. I'm going to back up over you and crush your legs, then your head."

He made a little whimpering sound deep in his throat.

I got in the car and revved the engine several times, then slammed it into drive and peeled out. I wish I could have seen Puss' face.

A block from the warehouse I pulled the Mercury over to the curb and waited. John Warner was true to his word – in less than fifteen minutes, two Ford Crown Vics zoomed past and pulled into the warehouse parking area.

Counterfeiting, drugs, car theft, bribery, extortion and who knows what else. Teddy and the boys were going to be locked up for the next couple dozen years.

I wiped down the Mercury of my prints, abandoned it downtown, then caught a cab.

"Where to, buddy?" asked the cabbie.

I gave him the bar's address.

The cabbie gave my worn clothes the once-over. "No offense, pal, but you got the fare?" He stared at me in his rearview.

"Sometimes paying your fare can make life fair."

"Huh?"

"Yeah. I got it." I leaned back and patted the box. I thought about Becky's blue eyes and smiled. "Yeah. Could be I got it all."

Chapter 3

The cabbie dropped me off in front of the bar. The neon "Open" sign was still turned off so I walked to the back alley and rapped on the delivery door.

"Who is it?"

"Becky, it's just me. Jack."

"Just a minute." I heard locks snapping, then a moment later, "Come in."

I eased the door open.

Becky stood behind the counter. Surprise flashed over her face for a moment, then she looked behind me. "You're really alone?"

I closed the door and threw the bolts. "Yep. Just me."

She let out a big breath and her rigid stance sagged.

I waggled my finger. "You're very trusting when you open doors."

She nodded. "But I was only expecting you, or Teddy and his thugs."

"And if it was Teddy?"

She lifted her hands from behind the counter and slapped down two guns. "I wasn't going to let them take me."

A grin crept on my face and stayed there. I gestured to Runt's and Puss' guns. "You know how to use those?"

Becky lifted the .38, stared at it, then put it down. "I've seen enough TV to have figured this one out." She tapped the .45 with a nail that had been chewed to the nub. "This one I can't figure out if the safety is on or off." She lifted her attention from the gun and leaned forward over the counter. "I'm glad you're back in one piece. How'd it go?"

Her words were casual, but tension, worry, and fear wreathed her face.

"Teddy and his goons are getting ready for a long stay in the penal system as we speak." I placed the carton on the counter. "All except Runt."

"Did he get away?"

Her eyes slid away from mine when I shook my head.

"Did you… did you kill him?"

"No. I shot him. The bullets and the fall killed him."

She closed her eyes, then buried her face in her hands. Her breath came out in a shudder. With the counter between us, the only comfort I could offer was a shoulder and a stroke of her back. "It's over. Finished. Everything is going to be alright."

She tugged at my jacket to get closer. I pushed her back for a moment and slid over the counter. "If we're gonna hug, let's do it right." She threw her arms around my neck and buried her head in my chest. I didn't know if it was her presence of mind or just luck that kept her away from my wounded side, but I preferred to think it was her awareness.

She felt good. She might have a lean build, but everything wrapped around me felt soft and wonderful. Her hair smelled of woodsy flowers and the rest smelled all over like a woman. I rocked her a little and she lifted her face.

"Thank you, Jack."

I cupped her face with both hands and brushed my lips over hers. "You're welcome."

Gratitude, coupled with sexual vulnerability and uncertainty, stole over her face. I could have her if I deepened the kiss, but this wasn't the right time for her – or me. "I'm sorry." I slid my hands down to her shoulders. "Let me take a rain check on that. I'm too hungry to do it justice."

Becky took a step back but kept a hand on my left arm. Probably for some human touch, and partly to make sure I was real. She smiled and shook her head. "You're an odd man, Jack Daniels." She glanced at my side. "How's the wound?"

"Fine. You're a good medic."

"Thanks." She kept the hand on my arm. "Can I make you something to eat?"

"We'll go out later. Right now we have some business to take care of." I opened the carton, dumped the money on the counter and chucked the box into the corner.

Becky's eyes widened at the sight of the banded stacks. "My God, Jack. Is it real?"

"Real as indigestion." I took off my jacket and tossed it over a stack of Bud Lite cases. "Get something to write with and I'll show you how to count banded cash."

She opened a drawer in the counter and took out a pen and paper.

I grinned and ran a hand down her arm. "I just love your efficiency." I parted the cash into two mounds. "Pile the banded hundreds, fifties and twenties in their own stacks. Then we count the stacks, and multiply by the denomination." I frowned. "There's more twenties here than I would like."

"I don't mind," she said, her eyes glued to the mounds of cash. "I like all denominations."

"Ah, an unbiased money lover."

We began combing through the piles. Becky worked with a deftness and organization I admired.

"Wow, Jack. Did you ever see this much money before?" Her hands never slowed.

"Yeah, I have, to tell you the truth. I once shoveled twelve million in English pound notes into a blazing furnace."

Her hands stopped and she stared at me. "You burned it?"

I shrugged. "It was bad-guy money. They would have used it for bad things."

She started sorting again. "I don't know if I could have withstood that much temptation."

"I wasn't the least bit tempted." I leaned toward her and spoke out the side of my mouth. "I had already stashed as much as I could carry."

Becky shook her head and sighed. "I think I'd like to learn more about you, Jack."

I stopped sorting through the cash while I sorted through her words. "Maybe." I resumed stacking. "Maybe you wouldn't like what you learned." For some reason, I felt embarrassed.

Becky's bright smile wiped that away. "I already know everything I need to about you, Jack. I'd just like to know more."

We finished sorting and converted the ticks on the pad into dollars.

"...carry the one." I put down the pen. "It looks like two-hundred and fifteen thousand dollars. Teddy certainly was an up-and-coming entrepreneur."

Becky looked at me, eyes gone cold. "Teddy Tedesco was a pig. This is money he stole from honest people."

"Not all. Most are payoffs from Brazilian gangs."

The hardness left her eyes, replaced by apprehension. "Are we in trouble having this money?"

"Well, no one will come looking for it, if that's what you mean. I threw Tedesco enough red herrings so it wouldn't lead back here. But you must be careful when spending this kind of cash, or the real nasty gangsters – the IRS – will come looking for you."

Becky stared at the money and I could see the wheels spinning and the gears clicking into place.

"Now I'm real hungry," I announced as a distraction.

"I know a great little restaurant. It has the best Italian food outside of Italy."

"Actually, 'Italian' food in Italy isn't very good. The food of Italy is wonderful, but not the Italian food."

Furrows lined Becky's forehead.

"If you get my drift…"

"No. But there's a wonderful place down the corner that serves the best spaghetti and meatballs this side of – well, heaven, if not Italy."

"Great." I slipped into my coat.

Becky gestured at the cash. "We can't just leave this on the counter."

I nodded. "Good point. Do you have a safe?"

"Yes. But it's not big enough to hold all this."

I glanced around the room, my eyes stopping on the garbage can. "Do you have any more plastic trash bags?"

Becky nodded, reached under the counter and pulled one out.

"Hold it open for me." She did as I asked, and I scooped the cash into the plastic bag. I lifted the half-filled trash bag from the garbage can, placed the bag with the cash in the bottom, then put the garbage back in over the top.

"There you go. Safe as Fort Knox – unless the thieves have read Poe."

Becky's eyes narrowed and she glanced at the ceiling. "'Nothing is more hateful to wisdom than excessive shrewdness.'"

My eyes popped open in surprise. "You've studied 'The Purloined Letter'?"

"Sure. English 201. Poe was my favorite of the old writers."

"Humph!" I grunted. "Efficient, organized, and educated. I think I need to learn more about you."

She shrugged. "Scholar, I'm not. But I aspired to be a poet as a teenager."

"Ahhh, poetry. Here's my favorite." I cleared my throat. "There once was a girl from Nantucket –"

Becky's eyes rolled. "Let's go eat, Jack."

Chapter 4

We walked two blocks down from the bar to a small restaurant. In the window, *Migliano's Restaurant* blazed in neon red. The restaurant was tucked in between two brick office buildings. The only attempt at ambiance was Chianti-bottle candleholders on red-and-white-checked tablecloths. A marvelous aroma created the real atmosphere with the extra spice of Mr. Migliano's gregarious nature. He greeted Becky like a long lost-daughter with a kiss on both cheeks, and shook my hand like I was a best-loved son-in-law.

"How's it going, Mr. Migliano?" Becky asked.

"Eh, we're getting by." He glanced at the door. "With certain... rising costs lately..." He shrugged, his shoulders and hands moving as only an Italian can do, then led us past a few other customers to a corner table. "Little Becky, how are you getting along?" We sat and he handed us menus. "I know it's hard for you since your poppa passed."

"Well, things are looking up." Her eyes asked me if she could share the information.

I nodded.

"Tedesco is finished," she said with a grin.

"Eh?" Migliano wiped his hands on his apron and leaned forward. "What you say?"

Becky looked to me for an explanation.

"Mr. Migliano, she means that Teddy and his boys were arrested today for a multitude of crimes. They won't be collecting any longer."

The permanent frown lines in Migliano's face softened and he demonstrated what an ear-to-ear grin looks like. *"Meraviglioso! Semplicemente merviglioso. Quella è le migliori notizie."* He clapped his hands together. "It's a celebration. I'm gonna give you the best dinner you've ever tasted." He kissed his fingers to heaven, then hurried back to the kitchen shouting, "Gino! Some Chianti for Becky and her new boyfriend."

I raised an eyebrow. "New boyfriend." I grinned. "My status grows." I nodded to Gino as he filled two wine glasses, left the decanter and scurried back to the kitchen.

"Have many boyfriends?" I asked.

"Jealous?"

"Well…" I thought about it for a moment. "I've never been in a relationship long enough for jealousy to develop, but I don't think I'm the type that would be."

Becky looked at me over the edge of her wine glass. "Well, I'm the jealous type. A real green-eyed monster." She tapped her fingernail on the table. "I wanted to rip Mary Beth Jablonski's eyes out after Bobby McNamara walked her home instead of me."

"Tell me about it."

"It happened right there." She pointed to a large corner booth. "A bunch of us met here after an ice skating party. As a fifteen-year-old, it was hard for me to understand why cute, wavy-haired Bobby preferred her to me."

"Sounds traumatic."

"Yes. Later, even after my dad pointed out that Mary Beth had big breasts, it still rankled."

I chuckled. "Your dad sounds like he was cool."

Her eyes focused on her wine glass, but she wasn't seeing the Chianti. "He was," she whispered.

Gino stepped out of the kitchen with dishes lined up like soldiers on his outstretched arm and headed our way. He plunked down a plate of bruschetta, two veal parmesan entrees, a huge bowl of spaghetti and meatballs, and a plate of ravioli. "The bread just come out of the oven. I be right back." He eyeballed the level in the decanter and rushed to the kitchen.

"My God!" Becky grabbed her fork. "Mr. Migliano must have given us everything that was ready in the kitchen."

I reached for the appetizer. "Did you ever get back at Mary Beth Jablonski?" I bit into the bruschetta and my taste buds sang.

"Sort of," Becky said, scooping spaghetti onto her plate. "She married Bobby four years later. They have six kids. He's almost bald and weighs at least two-sixty."

"Ouch. Sounds like a horrible revenge."

"Little did I know Mary Beth was saving me from a fate worse than death."

"So…" I piled ravioli onto my plate. "Was he your last boyfriend – until me, that is?"

"No. I've had several men in my life. Tried to fall in love with all of them, but couldn't. And what makes you think you're my boyfriend?"

I waggled my fork toward the kitchen. "Mr. Migliano's pronouncement makes it a done deal."

"Ha!"

"Any current beaus' backs I need to step on?"

"No need for macho shit. I'm not seeing anyone." Becky sighed and leaned forward. "Listen, Jack. I know we've gone through some... emotional trauma in the last few hours, but..."

I reached over and held her hand. "Yes... Look, I came into your bar looking for a place of refuge. A place where I could just forget about things for a while. Maybe think about a new career." I leaned forward and gazed into her blue eyes. "My goal here isn't to climb into your panties. Sex is wonderful, but sometimes it has too high an emotional cost." I released her hand and resumed eating.

Becky's lifted her fork, but it stopped halfway to her mouth. "Do you always let your head lead instead of that little buddy in your pants?"

My lips pulled into a grin. "I've learned to go with logic first, unless overridden by gut instinct."

"What about passion?"

"Passion that doesn't look beyond the moment of its existence is a dangerous thing." I waved my fork at her. "But if you follow your bliss, doors will open that wouldn't otherwise."

"Did you study at ECU?"

"ECU?"

"Yeah. Existential Crap University."

That dragged out a laugh from deep in my belly. It felt good. "No. I once had a Hindu cellmate. He followed every bit of advice with a sage adage." I shrugged. "I guess some stuck."

She lowered her eyes and pushed a scrap of spaghetti around on her plate. "You were in prison?"

"If you're thinking I'm a hardened criminal, you can stop. This was a little rathole of a jail in the Sudan. It was back in my salad days, before I let logic rule."

Becky put down her fork, perched her elbows on the table, and intertwined her fingers. "Who are you, Jack? Really?"

Truth and lies swirled in my mind and I shrugged. Truth always sat easier in the stomach, even if it stuck in the craw on the way down. "OK. If you want it, here's the Cliffs Notes version of Jack's life."

I sighed and decided to start at the beginning. It might even help me make sense of the current state of my life. "I was a poor kid. Mom died when I was little. Did real well on my SATs. Didn't have the money to go to school so I looked into joining the military. Walked into a recruiting center and enlisted, but didn't wind up in the service." I swirled the last of the wine at the bottom of my glass. "Did you know that the SATs have a psych test buried in them?"

Her eyes flooded with skepticism, then insult. "That can't be!"

"It be, my naive little friend." I finished the last of my wine. "Seems my test answers tripped a flag somewhere, and the next thing I know, I'm an eighteen-year-old kid being trained in Israel."

"Israel? Trained by who?"

"One of many three-lettered agencies... Anyway, I worked for them for several years until futility and inept management ground me down, then I tried other things." I glanced down at my hands and decided the next part of my bio was better left off. "I decided to forget about the problems of the world and stepped into your bar to think about a career change."

"And I dragged you right back into trouble." She laid her hand over mine. "Sorry."

I flipped my hand over and our fingers curled together. "Naahh. That wasn't trouble. That was merely a brief excursion into compulsory negotiation."

"A much appreciated one – and I'd like to talk to you about the money."

"And I'd like to hear it, but let's enjoy this excellent food without the specter of filthy lucre to upset our appetite."

She agreed, and while we ate, Becky talked about the neighborhood and the good people in it. Part of me felt a little pride in taking Tedesco off their backs. The other part of me wondered why I felt any pride at all.

After doing serious damage to the food, I leaned back and dropped my fork. "God, that was good."

"Mr. Migliano's food is the best," said Becky, and pushed away her empty plate.

"And we did a fine job of polishing off most of it," I added.

She nodded. "For me, it was probably nervous eating from today's incident." She sat forward. "Speaking of which, I have some ideas about the money."

I held up a finger. "I'd still like to hear them." I glanced up. Mr. Migliano was headed our way with a loaded tray. "But over coffee and tiramisu."

Becky held her stomach. "I just couldn't."

"I could." I greeted Mr. Migliano with a smile. "*Grazie, signore. Il pasto era magnifico. Nessun migliori hanno potuto essere trovati sull'intero continente.*"

"Ahhh... *Parlate Italiano! Meravigliosa. I'la ve ha provato ad insegnare a Becky la nostra bambina per gli anni senza successo.*"

We spoke a little more and Mr. Migliano strolled back to the kitchen, glad-handing and chatting with other customers along the way.

"You speak Italian." Becky pursed her lips. "I'm impressed. I only know a few Irish phrases."

I smiled. I couldn't wait until we ate Chinese. "Ordering food is a survival skill, quickly learned." I shoveled sugar into my coffee. "Now, tell me about yourself. You can start with your last name. I never did hear it."

"Oh, I'm sorry. It's Quinn. Rebecca Quinn." She shrugged. "I'm just a local girl whose dad owned the local bar."

She reached out and I thought she wanted to shake hands. Instead she grabbed the tiramisu and slid it to her side of the table.

"I thought you couldn't."

"I'm not eating it," she said as she took a big bite. "I'm just savoring the aroma."

"Well, be careful you don't savor the plate." I sat back and drank my coffee, happy to watch her eat. "You wanted to talk about the money."

She nodded and finished swallowing. "Yes. We have a lot of money."

I tilted my head and stared at her. "We?"

Her gaze lowered and red crept up her cheeks. "Oh. I thought... I assumed..."

I chuckled. "In this case, your assumption is correct. What do you say we split it − seventy, thirty."

Her embarrassed look was replaced by a cunning countenance I hadn't seen on her before.

"No. It should be fifty-fifty," she said. "I wouldn't feel right accepting seventy percent."

I jerked in my seat. "Ah... I..." My eyes fluttered as her words sunk in. I grinned and eased back down. "Nice move. Where did you learn your financial negotiation skills?"

She placed both elbows on the table and sipped her coffee. "From you. Back in the storeroom."

"You're a quick study." I nodded. "Fine. Fifty-fifty. Do you want company traveling to Acapulco, Tuscany, or wherever?"

She shook her head. "Forget travel. I'm a homebody. Every time I've gone on vacation, I couldn't wait to get back." She lowered her coffee cup and leaned forward. "No. What I was thinking about was this." Becky took a deep breath before continuing. "The people in this neighborhood, they're like my extended family. When my mom died, they were there for me. Caring, nurturing – and scolding when I needed it.

"Now, times here are hard and the money Tedesco stole from them could be the difference between living and just existing."

"I thought I saw that 'Maid Marian' look come into your eyes back at the bar."

"The what?"

"That 'Let's play Robin Hood' look."

With a little huff, Becky straightened in her seat. "Well, it's a good idea."

I tilted my head. "I'm not belittling your intention." I sipped my coffee. "Not too much, anyway…"

"You're way too cynical, Jack." She waved a hand and fingers in front of my face ala Obi Wan Kenobi. "You don't need to be cynical. You need to go home and rethink your life."

My laughing inhale had me choking on my coffee.

Becky chuckled.

"Damn it!" I wiped my mouth. "You almost made coffee come out my nose!"

"That's how I gauge the success of my quips," she said.

I looked into her smiling face. Wow. A tough, organized, woman who uses duct tape and can quote Star Wars.

This really *could* be love.

I patted for my cigarettes, then remembered I was out. I folded my napkin instead. "How were you figuring disbursement?"

Becky shrugged. "Just ask people how much they paid and give them back that amount."

"Are you that naive or that trusting?"

"Folks here wouldn't lie to me." She stirred a few tiramisu crumbs around on her empty plate. "Except Dowd's Cleaners on Eighth. That bastard would lie."

"I sense a story."

"Just my favorite green dress and a stain I didn't put there. Anyway, I'm going to return the money." She sat back and looked at me. "I could use your help."

"My help? Why?"

"Because you have nice eyes, too."

I snorted.

"And I think if you do this, it would make them even nicer."

I looked down at the table, wondering if Becky could see the piece I felt was missing in me. "Let's go," I said, then stood and reached into my pocket.

Mr. Migliano was there in a flash. "No. No. You no pay. You give me the best news and I must repay with my cooking. Prego. Prego."

"Then thank you for a wonderful meal, Mr. Migliano." I reached out my hand but he ignored it and wrapped me in a bear hug.

"It's good." He released me and enveloped Becky in another hug. "You come back again soon, bambina."

"Thanks, Mr. Migliano," she said from somewhere within the folds of his arms.

With the tinkle of a bell, we left Migliano's and strolled down the street. The street lights flicked on and I glanced up at the stars. The sky looked empty compared to an African sky, but that made it somehow more peaceful.

It grew colder by the minute and I stuffed my hands into my pockets. We walked side-by-side, with Becky matching my stride as if we'd been walking together forever.

"That was really nice of Mr. Migliano to give us a free dinner," said Becky.

"Yeah. It saved me from embarrassment, for sure."

"Embarrassment?" she asked.

I shot Becky a sideways glance. "Yeah. You have all my cash."

Her hand flew to her mouth. "Oh, I forgot."

She reached into her purse and I put a hand on her arm. "Don't pull it out here. Wait until we get back to the bar. There could be a mugger around here. After all, this area is a villainous hive of scum."

"It's a 'wretched hive of scum and villainy.' If you're going to quote from Star Wars, get it right." She shot me a look. "And it's not. This is a fine neighborhood."

"Really?"

"Well, it is now that Tedesco is locked up."

We walked another block in silence.

"You know, I gotta ask," I said. "Why do you know Star Wars so well?"

"It's my favorite movie. Why? Princess Leia. She's a take-charge woman who can shoot, spy, fly, she can do it all. She's the best role model for women since…"

"Since Raquel Welch in a fur bikini?"

"I said role model, not pin-up model for prurient teenage boys' fantasies." She shifted her purse and looped her arm through mine. "What's your favorite movie?"

"Raiders of the Lost Ark."

"Hunk Harrison Ford was in both." She looked over at me. "You kinda look like him."

"Yeah, he's my stand-in. I use him when the shooting starts."

"Funny. Why Raiders?" she asked.

I had never thought about it, so we walked in companionable silence for a few minutes while I analyzed.

Becky didn't rush me. I appreciated that.

"Well… I guess it's the way Indiana Jones takes a beating and never seems to get seriously hurt – and he always wins and always gets the girl."

"Is that so important?" she asked.

"Winning is most important."

"I meant getting the girl."

"That's secondary to getting paid."

We had arrived at the bar's delivery door. Becky dug in her purse for her keys, then turned to me, her back to the door.

"But without the girl, there's nothing to spend your money on," she said.

"You're right. I guess the girl is important." I ran my fingers up and down under her coat lapels. "But a statement like that should really be verified." My fists tightened on her coat, and I yanked her against me. Her eyes popped wide for a moment, then I crushed my mouth against hers. I eased off on the pressure and turned the kiss into a soft, gentle touch. My tongue teased her lips and I swallowed the moan that escaped from her throat.

Her keys tumbled to the ground as her arms wrapped around my waist. I cupped her face in my hands and pulled away. Eyes closed, pleasure radiated from her face. The pounding pulse I'd thought was hers was really my own. The kiss that started off as a smart-assed response had weakened my knees. I shook off the feeling by taking a deep breath and slipping back into my glib jacket.

"Becky. I need something from you."

She still hadn't opened her eyes. "What do you need?"

"I need... my cash."

Her eyes flew open and she blinked several times. Then those soft blue eyes filled with angry storm clouds. "Don't screw with me, Jack!"

I retrieved her fallen keys, unlocked the door and turned to her. "I wasn't."

She reached into her purse, withdrew my wad of cash and slapped it into my hand.

I grabbed her arm as she pushed past me. "I wasn't."

She stopped and I released her arm.

"I'm just not... for some reason I don't want it to be..." I shrugged. "Sorry. I didn't mean it. Sometimes being an asshole just overwhelms me."

Those cold, hard, blue eyes stared at me for a second longer, then melted and warmed. "I can see that." She looked at me for another moment, then smiled and quick-kissed the corner of my mouth. "Come by in the morning for breakfast." She patted my arm. "I know a great little pancake place."

"You're on."

She shut the door and I heard the locks turn.

I sighed and headed down the alley. I couldn't decide if what I was feeling was frustration fighting with right, or confusion fighting with sanity. Either way, I felt lighter.

Maybe I didn't need just a career change.

Maybe I needed a new life.

Chapter 5

I sat at the end of the bar on what'd become my personal bar stool, nursing my first Johnny Walker Black of the evening. Becky stood at the other end of the bar and called out over the crowd noise and the Pistons' game on TV.

"'Nother one, Jack?" I smiled at her and shook my head.

Ralph sat next to me, slumped on his stool. "It's a good thing what you and Becky did, Jack." He took another long pull on his Coors. "A good thing."

"I don't know what you're talking about," I said.

"Sure you don't." Ralph stared at me through red-rimmed eyes. "Right after Becky found out how much money that scum Tedesco hustled folks for, it gets returned."

I shrugged.

Ralph turned and studied the bottle in his hand. "It must have been Santa Claus, then."

"He *is* a jolly old elf."

Ralph snorted, finished his beer and waved the empty bottle at Becky.

Even though we had returned the money anonymously, people knew that Becky had a hand in it. The amount turned out to be less than a third of what I'd picked up from Tedesco. Extortion must have been one of Teddy's newer enterprises.

I scanned the barroom. The place was hopping – if a dozen people in a bar could be called hopping. Maybe folks now had more money to spend, or perhaps it was the neighborhood's way of saying thanks to Becky.

It had been an interesting week since I first stepped into this bar. I'd shaken off most of the bitter brood that had infected me, and surprisingly found the glimmer of a new beginning. My nicely healing wounds added to my upbeat attitude as pain wasn't my constant companion anymore.

Even before Tedesco's money, I had enough cash to sit comfortably on this bar stool for the rest of my life, but I knew in a month I'd be bored and squirming from butt blisters.

The problem was where to invest my time. Becky had been right about returning the extortion money to the neighborhood. It did something to my insides that reminded me of a feeling that I barely remembered. I wasn't sure what to label it, but it felt good.

Part of that good feeling was Becky.

I watched her fill two beer mugs from the tap, appreciating her economy of movement and dancer's grace. That electric sizzle of sex still bounced between us, but we'd yet to act on it. I tried to chalk up my reluctance to non-interest, but I knew that was pure bullshit.

It was fear.

My friendship with Becky was growing and I enjoyed our time together. Pushing sex might just screw that up.

Her reluctance I chalked up to a level of trust I hadn't given her. I just wasn't letting her in. Again, I recognized my reason as fear.

I couldn't see myself married with kids and a house in the 'burbs. I'm not sure if that was something Becky even wanted, but somewhere I assumed it was something all women wanted. I guess society's sinister stereotyping had done its wicked work on my biddable brain.

The basketball game ended. Becky switched the station to a soccer game in progress and turned off the sound. Someone dropped a quarter into the jukebox and a bluesy tune pumped out into the air. I watched Becky fill orders, smile, joke, and lend a sympathetic ear when needed.

Bending at the waist over a low shelf, she filled several small bowls with pretzels, and placed them on a tray. While she worked, I enjoyed the view. She headed my way and handed me the tray.

"Make yourself useful."

"I was."

She rolled her eyes. "Useful doesn't mean checking out my ass."

"It does to me," I said.

"Would you put these on tables that need refills?"

"Say please."

She leaned close to me, lifted the hem of her T-shirt, and balled it up into the middle of her chest. Her taut stomach muscles flowed down into her low-cut jeans. She placed a thumb in her jeans and pulled them outward slightly while she fanned her T-shirt. Visions of the road to paradise filled my eyes and saliva pooled in my mouth.

"It must be hot in here," she said.

"Please," I groaned.

She dropped her hands and the vision ended. "I thought I was supposed to say please."

I tugged on my collar to let out some steam. "You were. And you win."

I picked up the pretzel-laden tray and headed out, dropped off full bowls, collected empties, and made small talk.

Dwayne's bowl was empty and I headed his way. He was the neighborhood mailman who drank three Bud Lites every night, talked with anyone about any sport, and laid an occasional bet with "Willie the Book" who had made a nest in a back booth.

"Pistons look good this year," said Dwayne, never taking his eyes off the TV.

"Yeah. They'll look good until the playoffs, then choke."

"Come on, Jack. Have some faith."

"Faith makes a poor point guard," I said, and continued on my Becky-appointed rounds toward Sam and Bernie. Sam and Bernie were two grizzled Vietnam vets who sat at the same booth from six to nine every night and drank copious pitchers of beer. They were completely opposite in appearance – Sam dark and wiry, Bernie light and beefy. Becky mentioned they'd been fixtures at that booth since she was a little girl. Both wore black baseball caps covered with pins and miniature medals as old Vets are prone to do. On the front of Sam's hat was a 1st Marine Division patch. On Bernie's was a Combat Infantrymen's Badge encircled by the phrase, "Dysfunctional Veteran – Leave Me Alone."

Sam and Bernie's pretzel bowl was half full, and I started to slide on by, but I heard the words "get rid of that stupid Goryunov gun" and it stopped me in my tracks.

I turned and stared at the two men. Both looked sheepish and wouldn't meet my eyes. I slid into the booth next to Bernie. "A Goryunov? As in an SG-43 Goryunov machine gun? That's a real collector's item." I swapped out their pretzel bowl. "And illegal as hell."

Sam and Bernie exchanged looks and Bernie shrugged. "You know, Sam, Jack might be able to help."

Sam evaluated me from behind his thick, black-rimmed goggle glasses, then nodded. He glanced behind him and leaned toward me, his face as serious as if he was about to tell me who had whacked JFK.

"I was a supply sergeant." He held up a forearm, tattooed with a map of Vietnam and glanced around again. "I came into possession of some interesting hardware over there. Shipped it home thinking it might come in handy someday." He shrugged. "Now, it's just heavy crap."

Bernie snagged a pretzel and crunched. "Sam's dying and doesn't want that 'hardware' to fall into the wrong hands."

"Jeez, Sam." I placed a hand on his shoulder. "I'm sorry to hear that."

"Nah. Don't fret, Jack," Bernie said as he lifted his beer. "Sam's been dying since '73."

"Hey!" blasted Sam. "Have a little respect for the soon to be departed."

"The only thing that's departed is your sex life," quipped Bernie.

"Asshole."

"Jarhead."

Sam turned toward me. "As I was saying, I have some stuff I'd like to sell, or just get rid of. My kid wants no part of it." He snorted. "Says he's a pacifist."

I nodded. "Yeah, we're all pacifists until we see that the other guy has a gun."

They grinned at me and clinked glasses. "You got that right," said Sam, and finished his beer. "I knew you'd understand."

It was my turn to lean closer. "Tell you what." I glanced over my shoulder, playing into their game. "Give me what you want to dispose of. I know a few guys."

"That's great," said Bernie. "I thought you might be someone who could help."

I stood and glanced around again. "Let's keep this strictly between us."

"I'll drink to that," said Sam and eyed his empty mug. "Well, I would if you'd get us another pitcher."

I grinned. "Coming right up."

Chapter 6

During that first week I fell into a serene routine. I flopped at the local YMCA, had breakfast with Becky, and plopped onto a stool the moment the bar opened. The dream life of living in a bar seemed to be coming true. My favorite time of the day was just after the bar opened. Perched on a stool, I'd drink coffee, peruse the local paper and bask in the quiet of the room. To me, Becky's bar smelled of hope and tradition, and I'd inhale the scent of old forgotten dreams layered in the old wood. I leaned back and sighed.

Becky stepped out of the storeroom, clipboard in hand and pencil jammed behind her ear. "Gotta delivery coming in soon. Heavy kegs. Wanna help unload?"

I nodded.

She eyed the back shelf, slid out the pencil, and made a check on the clipboard. "Thanks," she said, then stared at me and grinned.

"What?" I said.

"Nothing. You're just handy to have around."

"I'm glad to be around."

"I like that, too," she said, and stepped back into the storeroom.

At times when she smiled, Becky looked like a twelve-year-old kid. It did something good to my insides, and I found myself wondering what to do about it. My introspection ceased when the front door opened and a woman entered.

I could only stare.

The woman had soft red hair that flowed to her shoulders. Her electric blue eyes captured my attention like a sunset you couldn't look away from. Such open innocence filled her eyes that I wondered if she was real or newly born. Though dressed casually in jeans, sneakers, and a navy pea coat, she walked to the bar with a ballet dancer's grace. The poet's line "alabaster skin" floated through my thoughts. I'd read the line many times before, but this was the first time I'd actually experienced what it meant. She was the most feminine, yet child-like, woman I'd ever seen. There wasn't a sexual attraction, just a blossoming awareness of something calm and beautiful.

I stood and stepped closer, eager to hear her voice.

She placed her purse and a folder on the bar, then smiled. "Is Becky in?"

Her voice didn't disappoint. It was soft yet clear. Her ethereal smile made me think she lived on another plane and had just drifted down to ours. I shook off the feeling that a fairy queen had just dropped into a bar in Gary, Indiana, and found my voice. "Uh, yeah."

Becky saved me from any more embarrassment by stepping out of the storeroom. "Angel!" she cried as she saw the woman. She ignored the pass-through and plunked her butt onto the bar, swiveled around and leaped down. Within seconds, she and Angel were hugging, kissing, and giggling like schoolgirls. I couldn't help but grin along with them.

Becky held Angel's arms and stepped back. "It's so good to see you."

"And you." The smile left Angel's face and she stroked long fingers over Becky's cheek. "I didn't hear about your dad until Father Dombrowski mentioned it yesterday. That's why I stopped by. Connor Quinn was a fine man and a good father."

"Thanks, Angel."

Compassion and understanding flowed between them, and as the silence lengthened I felt compelled to break in. "Ahem…"

"Oh, I'm sorry." Becky released one of Angel's arms and gestured to me. "Angel, this is a friend of mine, Jack Daniels. Jack, this is my friend, Angel Anderson."

I took her extended hand in mine. It felt warm, soft, and gentle. "Pleasure to meet you, Angel."

"And you, Jack."

Her gaze touched mine but I felt no judgment, no sizing me up or attempting to stick me into a box, just acceptance. That rarity had me forgetting to release her hand.

Becky cleared her throat. I glanced at her, then dropped Angel's hand.

Angel picked up the folder from the bar and handed it to Becky. "When Father Dombrowski heard I was coming over, he asked me to deliver this. It's the information sheet."

"Ah, thanks." Becky accepted the folder and tucked it under her arm.

A honking horn jolted me back into reality.

"That's the delivery," said Becky.

"I'll take care of it. You chat." Becky's smile was reward enough for any labor.

I walked into the storeroom and out the back door. The driver had the truck's motorized tailgate raised to the level of the dock. A beer keg lay on its side on the tailgate.

"I got four kegs and ten cases for you."

"Got it." I stepped onto the tailgate, took a deep breath, and hefted a keg. Legs and back straining under the weight, I muscled it onto the dock. "Christ, these are heavy."

The driver stared at me, his face saying he was looking at a moron. "Yeah, they're heavy! That's why we roll 'em off!" He reached over and tilted the next keg onto its side and rolled it onto the dock with his foot.

I puffed out a breath, closed my eyes, and shook my head. "Damn. A woman's fine face just took me right out of my game."

The driver grunted, then grinned. "They can do that. That's why I only look at them from the neck down. That way, they're all the same and you can deal with it."

"Sage advice, friend," I answered. "Sage advice."

I rolled off the rest of the kegs and used the hand truck on the cases of Bud. When finished, the driver pushed a clipboard at me and I signed the delivery slip. "Thanks," I said.

He reached up and the truck's overhead door rattled down. "Remember. Neck down!"

We both grinned and I walked back into the bar determined not to have my wits stolen again. Angel Anderson would get an evaluation that didn't include fantasy.

Becky and Angel sat on barstools, heads huddled together. As I walked to the pass-through, I tried to give Angel an assessment from the neck down, but I was drawn back to her face. Pretty, delicate features, striking blue eyes, totally female. On the surface, she'd gain a second look from me, but not a third. What caught my attention again was that aura of innocence and otherworldly attitude. The term "full of grace" slipped into my mind.

Angel seemed to be true to her name.

"All done," I said at Becky's raised eyebrow.

"Thanks, Jack."

Angel glanced at her watch, stood and slipped into her coat. "I've really got to run. I'm teaching a class at Bromleys."

Becky smiled. "Of course you are." She rose and they hugged. "It's good to see you. Stay longer next time."

"I will. We'll hang out at St. Mike's Festival. I'll help you work the booth."

"Sounds good," said Becky.

Angel turned to me. "It's nice to meet you, Jack."

I nodded.

With a wave, Angel was out the door and gone. It felt like a light had been turned off in the room.

"Wow," I said. "She is something!" I turned and looked into Becky's narrowed eyes and thrust up my hands. "Jam that green monster back into its cage. I don't date outside my species." I glanced back at the door. "She'd only be dating a fairy prince."

"Fairy prince?"

We stood side-by-side and I draped an arm around Becky's shoulders. "You know, someone who's like she is – a pure, beautiful flower come to life."

Becky snorted. "Angel's very human, believe me." She wrapped her arm around my waist. "But I know what you mean." Her gaze drifted to the door. "Angel is the kindest person you will ever meet."

"Bromley," I said. "Isn't that the school for deaf children?"

Becky nodded. "Yeah. Angel's a part-time volunteer. She learned to sign just so she could teach those kids. They say the children respond well to her."

"I bet. It's not every day you get to be taught by a fairy princess. Known her long?"

"Forever. Angel and I went to St. Teresa's together, from K4 up." She shrugged. "We lost touch after she went off to college."

"She's a school teacher?"

"Yes and no. She's doing office work downtown until a teaching slot opens up."

I turned Becky toward me. "And what's the St. Mike's Festival?"

Becky pushed herself up and perched on the bar. Her shoulders scrunched with excitement and she smiled. "It's our great street fair! Kind of a post-Easter Fat Tuesday. The proceeds go to the church's youth organization. It's along First Street and the mall parking lot. We have carnival rides, local rock bands, carny games, street vendors and this year, Jimmy Palma and The Elegants are giving a free show."

I had spent many Mardi Gras in New Orleans, but primed by Becky's excitement, this one sounded like more fun. "Will you have a booth as well?"

She raised an eyebrow. "Of course. Right next to Mr. Migliano's. His coils of pork sausage, onions and peppers smoking on the grill draw people like free beer."

"Which there won't be."

She shook her head. "Nope. But those people will get plenty thirsty after eating hot sausage and," her shoulders raised and she opened her hands, "we'll be right next door."

"Handy."

"Yeah, and close to Mr. Migliano's cannolis as well." She held her stomach. "Ugh. Last year I told Dad I deserved a cannoli after every fifty beers I sold. I had to force down the last two 'cause my dad ragged me about it."

"Sounds like fun. Do you sell bottles or cups?"

"Plastic cups of draft only."

"That means we'll have to roll a bunch of kegs into the van."

"Of course," she said, with a tilt of her head. "It'd be stupid to lift them."

I nodded. "Certainly would."

.

Chapter 7

It was a fine, fine Saturday. The mixed aroma of sugar, onions, and smoking hickory charcoal floated in the air. A cacophony of noise filled the street. Carny barkers' spiels lent a staccato undertone to the music from live bands and street vendors' boom boxes. Somehow, the sounds of Rock, Italian, Irish and a touch of Reggae music lent a perfect tuneful background to the milling crowds at the St. Mike's Festival.

Bright spring sunshine coated the event and people responded to the warmth with smiles and laughter. Becky said the festival had done well in the past, but this would certainly be a banner year. I weaved slowly through the crowd, enjoying the flavor of the multicultural neighborhood and accidently locked eyes with a carny barker. He broke into his shtick.

"You there, sir. Win a prize for your best girl. Three throws for two tickets. Just knock the bottles off the stand."

I walked past and just waved a hand. "No thanks. They never did anything to me."

"They're saying mean things about you now!" he yelled to my back. "Come teach 'em a lesson."

I kept walking. Tossing softballs at lead-weighted bottles was a sucker's bet. Besides, I had to get to Becky's tent. I had promised to help her serve beer.

It's funny, though I dreamed of living in a bar, the thought of serving people drinks wasn't in my fantasy. I'd promised to help out Becky because...

That was the million dollar question. I shook my head, trying to rattle the pieces together in my mind. I'd slid into Becky's life and liked being there. My attraction to her was growing along with my fear. In the Philippines, armored in only my boxers, I'd once faced a hopped up, machete-waving religious fanatic. I had felt less fear then.

This was an untraveled road and the threat of rejection stood arm-in-arm with my past, both looming like a two-headed Godzilla over any relationship I might develop with Becky. The image made me grunt with displeasure. I hated anyone trying to strong-arm me – even if it was me.

Ten feet away, a thin-faced guy in a long coat bumped into a man holding his little daughter's hand. "Excuse me," he said, bringing a finger to his flat cap. "Sorry."

He walked away and I moved to intercept him. I pretended to gawk at a vendor and bumped into him. "Oh," I said. "Sorry." I had picked his pocket as cleanly as he had picked the little girl's father. I took two steps then turned and held out the wallet. "Say, is this yours?" I asked.

With a look of surprise, the pickpocket patted his coat then smiled. "Yeah, thanks!" He reached out his right hand.

I pretended to hand the wallet back then clamped my hand on his wrist and yanked him toward me until our chests bumped. "Not here. Not now."

His eyes said they didn't know whether to bluster or be angry. His face said he chose anger.

"Say buddy, what the hell are you –"

Wrong choice. I jerked his pinky upward until it snapped. As his eyes widened and his face filled with pain, I whispered in his ear. "If I see you around here again, I'll stomp you into the sewer and let the rats chew your balls off." I released his wrist and shoved him away. It was his move.

Mouth agape, he stared at his injured hand, then turned and fled.

I hurried to the man and the little girl. "Excuse me, sir. I believe this is yours." I handed him his wallet and smiled at the little girl. She answered with a sweet grin that showed two missing front teeth.

It was indeed a fine, fine day.

Chapter 8

The lines in front of Migliano's and Becky's spoke well for business. Mr. Migliano waved his tongs at me as I passed. "Jack! I gotta sausage and peppers witha you name on it."

I held up a hand. "Can't right now, Mr. Migliano. Becky is working me too hard."

He laughed and I skirted the lines at Becky's tent. The sight of Becky and Angel handing out plastic cups full of beer stopped me in my tracks. The two of them joked with the customers, wise-cracked with each other, and grinned the whole time.

Angel caught sight of me and I flashed "How are you?" in American Sign Language.

She quickly signed back, "You can sign?"

"Yes," I answered the same way. Then I added, "Shouldn't everybody?"

Angel giggled.

Becky had caught the exchange and shook her head. "Figures." She waved her fingers and hands around in a horrible pantomime of sign language, then yelled, "Jack, that means get your butt in here and relieve Angel. She has to leave."

I signed to Angel, "Don't you hate wannabes?"

Angel laughed, took off her apron and reached under the counter for her purse. She waved to Becky and signed, "Good to see you again" to me, then left.

I stepped behind Becky. "You guys seem to be having a lot of fun."

"Too busy to have fun." She held up an apron and an ID badge. "Here, put these on."

I took the apron but tossed the ID back under the counter. "Badges? We don't need no stinkin' badges."

Becky chortled as she took tickets from a customer. "Start pouring and I'll hand them out."

The next couple hours were a blur of foam, hands, and tapping kegs. One keg tap went awry and a stream of beer shot four feet into the air to the applause of the crowd.

Becky plugged the leak, brushed away a strand of hair with the back of her hand, and smiled. "Half-hour to go."

"Closing early?"

"No. The permits only allow us to sell alcohol until seven."

I nodded. "Then you open the bar?"

"Nahh. Why bother? Everyone will be here." She handed out two beers and jammed the tickets into a bag. "Besides, it will give me a chance to take in the festival. So far all I've seen are thirsty street walkers."

"Street walkers?" I grinned.

Becky rolled her eyes. "You know. People walking in the street, milling around and—" She jammed her fists on her hips and blew that same wayward strand of hair from her face. "You know what I meant. Cut me some slack, Jack. It's been a long friggin' day."

Becky and I strolled along a street filled with noise, people, and energy. Night had fallen and the darkness hid the dirt and wear on the carnival tents. Flashing neon painted the street with a patina of fun and frolic.

Becky twined her arm around mine. "Win me a teddy bear?" she said, as we passed the bottle and ball toss.

"Will they let me shoot the bottles?"

She shook her head. "The police frown on shooting, unless they're doing it."

I glanced at her. "You don't seem like the teddy bear type."

"I do if they're two legged and very rich."

"Oh, Pooh."

Becky snorted. "Let's get to the bandstand. The Elegants are playing right after the glad-handing and back-slapping speeches."

"Speeches?"

"Of course. Mayor Croft and Councilman Douglas would never miss a chance to hear their own voices."

A squeal from the loudspeakers interrupted my next question. A balding, thirty-something, whip-thin Latino tapped the microphone. His beaming smile seemed pasted on his lips. "Welcome all to St. Michael's Festival."

A smattering of applause and whistles greeted his words. He cupped a hand to his ear. "I can't hear you!"

This time, the response was focused and louder.

"I hope you're all having a good time. The city, Mayor Croft, and Councilman Douglas thank you for your continued support."

I leaned toward Becky. "Who's the dullard?"

"That's Councilman Douglas' aide and perpetual ass-wipe, Diego Sanchez. He says he's a man of the people as he came from the streets, but I think he wants Douglas' job – for a start."

"Lord deliver us from self-serving politicians masquerading as public servants."

Becky nodded and I blotted out the next twenty minutes of speeches by watching the crowd. Enterprising vendors wove through the mass with trays of soft drinks, cotton candy and popcorn. One audacious vendor hawked pretzels stacked twenty high on a long skewer. A brisk business greeted each seller and their wares were long gone before the speeches ended.

Six men, wearing black pants and gold sequinned jackets with black velvet lapels, climbed up the side stairs and stood at the back of the bandstand. This had to be Jimmy Palma and The Elegants. The man standing in the center sporting the largest pompadour had to be Jimmy himself. One of the men sat behind his drums and twirled his drumsticks. The crowd surged forward.

I tuned back in as the mayor intoned, "…all for the good of the people!" The drummer for the Elegants emphasized the mayor's words with a ba-boom-boom-crash on his drums, much to the delight of the crowd. Diego Sanchez rushed to the bandleader and spoke urgently in Jimmy Palma's ear. Jimmy just tilted his head, smiled and shrugged. Sanchez turned away, lips tight and eyebrows furrowed.

Mayor Croft acted deaf to the drums, but he wasn't dumb when it came to losing his audience. "So, without further ado, I'd like to present Jimmy Palma and The Elegants, brought to you by the city council!"

"City council, my ass," said Becky over the cheers. "They're here 'cause Father Dombrowski got Jimmy's DUI swept under the rug."

"And they say people have lost their compassion."

"Hey. We Saint Teresa graduates stick together."

Jimmy Palma approached the microphone as the band began the first strains of "Stardust." I grinned at the choice as Jimmy began singing. His voice, somewhere between Nat King Cole's velvet and Billy Joel's baritone, was pleasant and he did well with the tune. I scanned the mixed crowd to see their reaction to a forties song when the band switched into the chorus of the Beatles "All My Loving."

After a short snippet, they followed up with the bass player strutting on stage doing a fair rendition of Eminem's non-explicit "The Real Slim Shady."

"These guys are pretty good!" I said.

Becky squeezed my arm. "Told you."

The band slid right into Van Halen's "Jump" without missing a beat.

I glanced to the left and watched Sam and Bernie drift through the crowd toward us.

"What kind of crap music is that?" said Bernie as they neared. "In my day–"

"You never had a day," said Sam.

"Ha! This from a guy –" Bernie's retort was halted by The Elegants' version of the fifties hit "In the Chapel in the Moonlight." Bernie smiled. "Now that's music!" He turned toward Becky, bowed, then extended his hand. She curtsied and took it. Bernie did a quick two-step then turned her into a spin.

"He'll be rubbing on Sloan's Liniment tonight, that's for sure. " Sam looked over his shoulder, then leaned toward me. "We still on to dump my collection?"

I nodded. "You bet. Monday looks good. I'll let you know what time. "

"Thanks, Jack. I appreciate it."

I smiled as Bernie lowered Becky into a dip. "My pleasure, Sam. My pleasure. "

They danced toward us and Bernie spun Becky's back into my chest. "Your turn, Jack. She's blistered my toes."

"Come on, Bernie," said Sam. "Let's leave these kids so they can dance the night away."

Bernie nodded and they waved goodbye.

Becky leaned back into my chest. "Do you dance?"

I wrapped my arms around her and whispered into her ear. "I've been known to crush a few toes."

The Elegants began "Don't Be Cruel" with Jimmy mimicking Elvis fairly well.

"Is this our song?" I asked.

Becky grabbed my hands and we danced. "Nope. Our song is Toby Keith's 'I Love This Bar.'"

I grinned and nodded. "It's my kind of place."

Chapter 9

I set a clandestine midnight meeting with Sam and Bernie for the weapons pickup. Actually, high noon would be a less conspicuous hour, but these two old Vets needed a little juice in their lives. Bernie's beefy hand raised Sam's garage door. After I backed in, he quickly yanked down the overhead door and locked it. An old army canvas covered a large lumpy pile in the corner and a black plastic bag was taped over the garage's side door window.

I jumped out of the van. "Hey, guys. You ready?"

"I'm sorry." Sam's face flushed and he paced in small circles. "I didn't remember how much crap I had." He swiped his wrist over his brow and pulled the canvas off the pile.

My blood froze.

It looked like a weapons drop for a merc mission. Dozens of Chinese pistols, AK-47's, the Russian SG-43, and two 82MM mortars littered the floor. "Damn, Sam!"

Sam's eyes darted over the pile and back to mine. "Too much?"

Supply sergeants never change. I dropped a hand on his shoulder. "Sam, if you were in Hannibal's army I bet there would be elephants sitting here in your garage." I laughed and opened the van's rear doors. "Let's load up."

I put the word out to friends and a few collectors, and waited for the responses. I was determined that Sam's entire collection would go, even if I had to buy it myself. Dying or not, he didn't need a stash of old weapons to worry him. Then again, being human, he'd only find something else to worry about.

Within three days I had sold off all of Sam's armaments. He had taken good care of the weapons and I got top-dollar for the pristine collection.

Chapter 10

On Saturday night the bar was almost full. Word of mouth had brought in new customers and they were making the place their own. Dwayne chatted up a young guy about soccer, Ralph was sucking down his Coors, and Sam and Bernie sat in their usual booth, downing pitchers of beer. I was making the rounds with bowls of pretzels.

How that had gotten to be my job was something I'd have to take up with the owner. I grinned when Becky laughed at something Ralph said. Yeah, I'd have to take it up with the owner real soon.

I walked to Sam and Bernie's booth and placed my tray on the table. "I have something for you, Sam." I let the edge of a thick envelope peek out from under the tray.

Sam slid it out and gave me a quizzical look while hefting it. "What's this?"

"If you open it here, open it under the table," I said.

Sam did as I asked and his eyes bugged. "Jesus Christ, Jack! What's all this?"

"I sold your collection, and it's a seller's market."

Sam stared at the cash. "So much?

"Yeah," I said. "The Goryunov alone brought in big bucks."

Bernie leaned over and tried to see. "Just how much?"

Sam looked up and grinned. "More than enough to take that Tahoe trip we've talked about for years and travel first-class all the way!"

Bernie shot me a look. "Got anything for me?"

I plopped a bowl on the table. "More pretzels."

"Hell. It's always the REMF's that make out."

"Up yours, Bernie," said Sam. He stood and gripped my hand, hard. "Thanks Jack. I hope you took out your commission."

"It's taken care of." The look on their faces was payment enough for me. "Have fun at Lake Tahoe, guys." I picked up the tray and strolled back to what was becoming my personal barstool.

That had been enjoyable. Maybe this "random acts of kindness" thing did work, as Becky kept telling me.

I glanced at Becky, put down the tray and held up a finger. She was wearing the dark blue T-shirt I'd given her, the front proclaiming in bold white letters: "I don't have a license to kill, only a learner's permit."

She wiped her hands on a rag and walked toward me, snagging a glass and a bottle of Johnny Walker Black on the way.

"You seem to have made Sam and Bernie's day." She poured the amber liquid into the glass. "What's up with that?"

I looked back at Sam and Bernie, big grins still plastered on their faces, then turned and propped both elbows on the bar, hands cradling my face. "Will you still love me when I'm old and gray?"

She placed the tray under the bar and squinted her eyes. "Who says I love you now?"

I snorted. "Listen. How about we go somewhere tomorrow? It's Sunday and we can hang out." God, that sounded really lame. "I'd like to talk to you."

Becky's eyes studied my face before answering. "Sure. But first we have to stop at church."

"Church?" I put on a worried look. "I don't know if I'm ready for that kind of commitment."

She jammed her hands on her hips. "Have you just been stringing me along, then?"

My fake worried face turned real as panic rushed down my spine and splashed into my stomach. I answered her with the cleverest retort I could muster at the moment.

"Uhh…"

Becky slapped a hand over her mouth and stifled a giggle. "Well, that was fun." She leaned on the bar. "Don't worry. I have to talk to Father Dombrowski over at St. Mike's about something."

I collected myself and slipped my brain into smart-ass gear. "But, sweetheart. We haven't done anything to confess… yet." I ran a hand down her arm.

"Get a grip, loverboy. It's business."

"Supplying the church with holy wine?" I asked. "Or having him bless yours?"

"Come with me tomorrow and see," she said, and flashed a smile.

Thoughts of trust and honesty in relationships buzzed through my mind. "OK. I'll drive."

"The van?"

I shook my head. "No. My car."

She tilted her head and raised an eyebrow. "You have a car?" A man slid onto a stool at the other end of the bar and Becky glanced his way. "All right. Pick me up at nine a.m." She walked down to the new customer, polishing the bar with her ever-present rag.

Tomorrow.

Was it cards on the table time? A churning stomach crushed the butterflies in my belly into a sour mash. Why did I want to do this? Was it just something new to do, or did I feel that Becky had earned a position of trust? I inhaled deeply and then I knew.

It had to do with my fear. I hated any feelings of fear and the only way I knew to conquer them was to yank them out into the light, face them square on, and kick them in the balls.

Even if the balls were my own.

Tomorrow then.

Chapter 11

Sunday morning arrived with a brilliant blue sky and a tantalizing taste of spring.

The Mercedes SL-65 hummed along the Interstate. Though I was doing seventy-five, the car screamed at me to open her up and let the twelve cylinders roar, but I knew better than to listen to a machine.

I exited at Fifteenth Street, geared down, and pulled into the alley behind the bar. The dashboard clock read 8:59. I waited until it rolled to 9:00, touched the horn, and then got out of the car. The delivery door locks were turning as I walked up the stairs.

Becky stepped out and we each halted in our tracks. She stared at my black suit jacket, dress pants, and white turtleneck shirt, and I at her dark blue satin dress with white lace at the collar and cuffs. Gone was her ponytail and she'd done something curly to her shoulder-length hair.

"Damn!" I said.

"Damn, back at 'cha."

I slouched off my surprise. "You look incredible."

"You clean up pretty good yourself." She smiled, then gaped at the silver Mercedes. The smile disappeared and she slammed a fist into my arm. "Damn it, Jack. You stole a car!"

A backward step and raised hands avoided another slug. "No. It's my car. Honestly. The registration's in the glove box if you want to check."

Her eyebrows furrowed and she stared at the car again. "Did you spend your share of Tedesco's money on it?"

I almost grabbed at the lie she'd inadvertently thrown me, but today was a trust day. "No. I've had this for about a year." I walked to the passenger side and opened the door for her. She gave me a dubious glance, then settled into the seat. I closed the door, rounded the hood, and slid behind the wheel.

The glove box was open and Becky was studying the registration card. I started the car and said nothing.

She put the card back, closed the glove box, and stared out the windshield. "Sorry."

I placed a hand on her arm. "No. I'm the one who's sorry. I haven't been very forthcoming with you. Sharing my life with someone hasn't been my style, and it's a tough habit to break."

Her eyes found mine and she smiled. "I understand. But I really am your friend." She placed her hand over mine and looked down at our joined hands. "I've wondered why you haven't... let me in. Whether you care enough about me to share yourself."

"I – " Honesty time. Trust, I told myself and swallowed the fabrications that automatically came to my lips. "I do care about you. I like our friendship. I'm afraid if you know too much about me it will spoil that."

"Oh, Jack," she said, looking up. "I already know you're a putz."

I grinned. "Well, fuck you very much."

She patted my hand. "Maybe later. Right now we've got to get to church."

I dropped the Mercedes into gear and hit the gas. The acceleration pushed Becky back into the buttery soft, leather seat.

"Wow," she said. "Power." She glanced around at the interior. "Is that why you chose this macho baby?"

"Actually, this is a thank you gift for a favor I did for a German industrialist."

She dropped down the visor and checked her face in the mirror. "Nice thank you. That must have been some favor."

"Yeah." I flashed on Max and his son's tear-stained faces as they clung to each other after the rescue. The kidnappers told Max not to call the police. He didn't.

He called me.

"St. Michael's is over on Twelfth, isn't it?" I asked.

"Yes. Pull around to the side entrance. Church services will be going on and I don't want to get in the way."

"So we're not going to kneel and smell incense?"

"Well, you can if you want to, but I have to meet with Father Dombrowski. I'm funding a CYO little league team."

"Oh." The depth of Becky's neighborhood loyalty still amazed me. I wondered how it felt to be so solidly rooted.

"So..." I said. "That means the kids will have 'Tavern' stenciled on their uniforms." I turned a corner and glanced over at her. With her hair down she looked... different – and really, really, sexy. I cleared my throat. "I've been meaning to ask. How come the neon sign outside the bar just says 'Tavern?' The top part of the sign looks like it's broken off. Is there a story there?"

A small grin lit her face. "Yeah. It's a Dad story. The sign used to say '6th Street Tavern,' then 2nd Street got eliminated by the mall, and the city in their infinite wisdom and infinite taxpayer dollars, re-numbered the streets. My dad thought having a bar named '6th Street Tavern' on 5th Street was confusing, so he decided to change it." She shook her head and smiled at the memory. "He and a couple of buddies borrowed a ladder and a hacksaw, and cut off the 6th Street part."

"Oh, God."

"It gets better. They didn't brace the sign and when they were halfway through, it broke off and crashed through the front window."

"Professional job."

"Yeah, my dad was a real professional – at serving drinks. And that's what he was doing when I came downstairs to see what was going on. The broken sign was still laying half in, half out of the shattered window. Glass was scattered all over the room and Dad was pouring drinks and toasting with three of his cronies like they had accomplished a moon mission."

"Your dad sounds like he was a good guy."

Her eyes focused on something only she could see, and a little smile blossomed on her face. "He wasn't your typical father, but he was a great dad."

"You loved him very much."

She nodded. "Yes. Even though he's gone, I feel him in every part of the bar, every time I look around."

That explained much about her love of the bar. "How about renaming the tavern?" I said.

"I've been thinking about it, but can't come up with a good name."

We pulled up to St. Michael's side door and exited the car.

"I have a great name," I said. "How about 'The Duck Inn'?"

"Corny."

"Fu Bar?"

"I think something simple would be best," she said.

"OK. I can do simple."

She glanced over as we walked up the steps. "Do, or are?"

"Nice. How about 'Becky's Bar?'"

She shook her head. "I don't want my name on it."

I opened the church side door and we stepped into a darkened alcove. "Since this is Indiana – how about 'Hoosier Daddy?'" She shot me a bad look as we walked to a door labeled "Office." I tried again. "Tune Inn? Stumble Inn?"

"Not very original."

I opened the office door for Becky and she stepped inside. "Original? How about 'Big Dick's Halfway Inn'?"

Becky turned to her left and smiled. "Hello, Father."

Father Dombrowski stood against the wall by a bulletin board, paper in one hand and pushpins in his mouth. His black-garbed, six-four frame was immense. He was giving me a look that my grandmother had termed, "The Stink-Eye."

"Father Dombrowski, this is Jack Daniels," Becky said by way of introduction – or blame.

The priest continued to stare a moment longer from under gray, bushy eyebrows, then removed the pins from his mouth and offered me his hand.

After I checked to see which hand held the pins, we shook. "Nice to meet you, Father."

"Likewise." He turned to Becky and his hard face cracked into a big smile. "It's good to see you, Rebecca. How've you been?"

"Real good." She reached out and placed an envelope into his hand. "Here's the money for the team and a little extra."

"Thank you, sweet girl. This will help many more children."

"We've been discussing possible new names for the bar," she said.

"So I heard." The priest's intense, dark eyes darted a sideways look at me, then turned back to Becky. "We can hold off on printing the name on the uniforms until you decide on a proper one." He spread open his arms as if to encompass the town. "Gary may be a large city, but our little parish here is really just a small province." He lowered his arms. "I hope you will choose something that reflects that."

"How about 'Hope's Province'?" I said.

They both turned to me.

"Hope," Becky said.

"Province," said the priest.

Grins widened their faces.

Father Dombrowski kept his smile, covered Becky's hand with his paw, and extended the other to me. "Nice to have met you, Jack." He released his grip. "Now you kids run along. It's too nice a day not to be out in the sunshine."

Becky twined her arm through mine as we walked back to the car.

"'Hope's Province,'" she repeated. "I like the sound of that." She patted my arm. "And that was a real nice recovery in front of Father Dombrowski."

"With a big man like that, you have to be fast on your feet."

"He's the runt of the litter, from what I hear. He's one of five brothers, from Scranton, Pennsylvania. Being the smallest, he was sent to seminary school and the rest worked the coal mines."

"Tough job."

"They both are. He says his brothers' work warms the body, and his work warms the soul."

I opened the car door and Becky climbed in. I skirted the hood, sat in the driver's seat and started the engine.

"Father Dombrowski and my Dad were relentless opponents." She clicked her seatbelt.

"Religion or politics?"

"Chess."

"Chess?" The picture I had built of the elder Quinn shattered like his plate glass window. "Your dad sounds like a complex man."

"Not really. He always described himself as having a sharp skull and lazy bones." She glanced up at the interstate sign. "Where're we headed?"

"I thought I'd show you my place, then we'd do lunch."

Her brows furrowed. "Why would I want to see a crappy cot in the YMCA?"

I shrugged. "That's just where I was sleeping to be nearby. I have a place in Crown Point."

She stared out the windshield, the furrow never leaving her brow. "I don't know which I find more unsettling, that you slept at the 'Y' to be close, or that you have a place in exclusive Crown Point."

The answer wasn't an easy one for me, so we drove in silence for a while.

I reached over and clasped Becky's hand. "This is hard for me, but – "

Becky held up her other hand to stop me, and stared out the passenger window. "I think I've just figured it out."

I slid into the right lane under the "Crown Point" exit sign.

"What have you figured out?"

She sighed and kept her face turned away. "You're married."

"What?" I squeezed her hand. "No! Never have been."

She turned and looked at me. "Engaged?"

"No!"

A little smile played over her lips. "Gay?"

"No. None of the above." I ran a hand through my hair in frustration. "Jeez!"

Becky turned her body and leaned toward me. "Then what's the hard part? I know you killed that pig who worked for Tedesco. I know you stole his money." She threw open her hands, then dropped them into her lap.

I patted my pocket for a cigarette, realized it was a nervous gesture, and gripped the wheel harder instead. "I never finished giving you my bio." I pulled off the exit and worked my way down Rt. 231. "After I left the government's employ, I formed my own independent company, so to speak."

She folded a foot under her leg. "Doing what?"

"Well, the only thing I knew how to do. I decided my skills could be useful to others."

Her eyebrows bunched together like cars on a freeway. "So what are you saying?"

I took a deep breath, then let it out. "I'm a mercenary. *Was* a mercenary. I hired out to those who could afford my price. Did whatever they paid me to do."

Her eyebrows were still bumper-locked. "You went to war for people who paid you money?"

"Not war." I rolled my shoulders. I was comfortable with what I'd done in the past. I hoped she could be. "We were advisors, soldiers if a quick strike was needed. Men you called when the people in power wouldn't or couldn't help."

Becky mulled over my words for a moment. "But the people you fought, they were all bad people, right?"

I shook my head. "Right and wrong mostly depends upon your perspective. I let myself believe that the right side was the one who paid the most."

Becky stayed quiet until we turned onto Greenway Street. "I'm having trouble wrapping my mind around this. My image of you as just a local tough guy has shattered." She clasped her hands. "Now I find you destroy people for money."

"Sorry, but I had to let you know." My revelation might have tumbled any further relationship we might build, but I felt she had to know.

She stared down at the floor. "It would almost be easier if you were married."

"Would it?"

She looked up and sighed. "No. Not really." The hands in her lap were still clasped, but now the knuckles were white. "But you said 'was.' Does that mean you don't do that anymore?"

"Yeah. I'm done."

I slowed, pulled into my circular drive, then shut off the car. "That's something you can count on. Never again."

The clicking of the car's cooling engine sounded loud against Becky's continued silence. Her head bobbed slowly as if trying to force in the information. Then her hands unclenched.

"Now it's my turn to say 'this is hard for me.'" She hesitantly reached out and touched my arm. "I have to know why you quit."

The deep breath I sucked in didn't release the stress in my chest. "Well... I got tired of crawling through the cesspools that the press calls the 'Third World.' The job that made me reconsider my career choice was when we were hired to take out a small-time African dictator. A really nasty one. The things he did to his own people bordered on insane evil. Turns out, he was the one we helped put in power three years earlier."

"You realized you weren't making a difference," she said.

I smiled. "Yeah. I fooled myself with that line for a long time."

Her eyes had relaxed a little. She didn't look like she was struggling with a calculus problem any longer.

"Our last job went sour." I hesitated and tried to blot out the visuals that streamed into my head. "Our op had us blasting into the guards' barracks and neutralizing their threat." I inhaled and let it out. "It wasn't the barracks. It was a nursery." I chanced a quick look at her face, but couldn't read her. "It was bad. With the guards still functional and outraged at the mess in the nursery, the operation when to hell real fast. People died who shouldn't have." I relaxed my hands from their death grip on the wheel. "That's when I quit."

She stared out the passenger window for several minutes. "I'm sorry, Jack."

I didn't know if she was sorry about the job or sorry she'd ever met me, but I found myself waiting anxiously for her next words.

"I'm sorry you had to go through that." She straightened a fold in her dress. "And I can't imagine how you live with it." She unhooked her seatbelt and turned toward me. "I know the world isn't a bright tidy place. I fool myself into believing it is, most times. There are many types of people in the world. I'm the type that hopes for the best and wears blinders when I can't see the good."

"Well, in my experience there're only two types of people in the world." I glanced over and tried a smile. "Sheep and wolves."

"No!" Her hand gripped my arm and I stared down at it. "No," she said again, and shook her head. "Some are sheep, some are wolves." She waited until I met her eyes. "But a few are shepherds. When a shepherd has to become a wolf to hunt a wolf, it's time to leave the shepherd business."

I smiled. "I'm no white knight."

She returned the smile. "I know. You're a putz. But a smart enough putz to know when to let it go." She squeezed my arm and stared deeply into my eyes. "Let it go, Jack."

I had told myself that it didn't matter. That whatever she thought of me didn't matter. When I felt the weight lifting from my chest, I knew I'd been full of shit.

"Well..." I gestured to the house to break the mood. "Welcome to Jack's place." I got out of the car and walked to the passenger side.

Becky stared at the ivory and stone two-story Neocolonial home, and eased open the car door. I reached in for her hand and helped her out.

She stood and gazed up at the second story.

"Four bedrooms, two-and-a-half baths. Sits on a half-acre... Fireplace..." I was waiting but Becky still hadn't said a word. Then she turned to me.

"Is this really yours?"

"Yes. Free and clear."

She shook her head. "This is like a dream. One of those lousy reality shows that swap people's lives."

I wasn't sure if that was good or bad. "Let's go inside. I'll give you the two-dollar tour."

We climbed the steps and I unlocked the door, pushing it open for her to enter. The place wasn't huge, just spacious enough so I didn't feel hemmed in. The stairs were several strides ahead to the right, and the living room and dining room split to either side.

I dropped my Sig, keys, cell phone, and wallet on the foyer's Chippendale table. She placed her small clutch purse next to my things and I led her into the living room.

The entire house had been furnished by Prétentieux's top designer, Susan Boyér. She liked subtle, comfortable furniture, all in shades of eye-easy creams, tans, and greens, and I agreed.

Souvenirs from my travels decorated the walls and tables. Crossed Zulu Iklwa spears here, a bronze reproduction of Canova's *The Three Graces*, there. The fireplace was ready with logs and kindling, but it was too warm for a fire. Perhaps tonight.

A quick vision of entwined naked bodies rolling around in front of the fireplace flashed through my mind. I squashed that thought with an image of Laurel and Hardy from *Babes in Toyland*. I found that worked better for me than thinking of dead puppies.

"The furniture is comfy, if you'd like to sit," I said.

Becky had stopped to study a painting on one wall. "Monet?"

"Yeah. Water Lilies. Done in 1904. It's my favorite."

She peered closer at the brush strokes. "This isn't a litho." She turned to me. "A reproduction?"

Her eyes narrowed when I shook my head.

"A forgery from one of your jobs?"

"No. Well, it's from one of my assignments, but it's not a forgery."

Her eyes widened as the realization hit home. "You have an original Monet?"

I joined her in front of the painting. "It's just something I picked up along the way."

"Jack. You don't just pick up something like this along the way." Her hands fisted on her hips. "This was stolen."

I nodded. "Yeah. From the Museum d'Orsay in Paris in nineteen-forty-three." I looked at the painting and was struck, once again, by Monet's shadings, brushwork, and skill. "Two years ago, we were hired to track down a former Nazi official living undercover in Geneva. We turned him over to the Israelis who promptly stiffed us on most of our fee. This and several other stolen art works were stashed in our man's hideaway. I thought we might have trouble collecting payment, so I didn't report his art treasures. I sold off the others to pay my team and expenses, and kept the Monet as my recompense." I smiled. "Besides, I like this painting."

She stared at the painting, as rapt at Monet's genius as I was. "This should be shared with the world."

We stood there, both gazing at the work of art. "Yeah. I'll turn it over to the world some day." We turned and faced each other. "But not today," I said.

"That's wrong, selfish and inconsiderate." She looked back at the painting and her voice softened. "But, yes. Not today." She placed her arm through mine and gave me a smile that lit the room. "Now, show me the rest of your house."

I took her through the library, the kitchen and den.

"Let's see if the master bedroom is as well decorated as the rest of your house," she said.

"We've yet to see the solarium."

She stood with her hands laced behind her back and swayed from side to side. The smile on her face was coquettish yet shy. "Is it near the bedrooms?"

"Uh, no." I wondered if Becky was thinking about rolling around naked in front of the fireplace. Not wanting to push, I brushed off the feeling as wishful thinking, and led her to the solarium.

Scents of a dozen species of flowers greeted us as we entered the glass room. Sunlight streaming in through the windows coated the carefully placed plants with a glowing nimbus. A table, couch, and chairs sat near the north end, facing the backyard. "Nice, but too warm," she said and continued out a side door.

She stopped and stared at the pool. It wasn't Olympic size, but big enough to do strong laps.

"You have a pool," she said and walked to the edge.

I strolled to her side. "Yeah. I like to swim."

"An indoor pool."

"Yeah. I like to swim in all seasons."

She slipped off her shoes and touched a toe in the water. "You have an indoor, heated pool."

"Yeah. I like to be comfortable when I swim in all seasons."

"You have an indoor, heated pool, but no bedrooms."

The comment was so strange my mind ground to a halt and I felt my brows furrow. I certainly wasn't on the same page as Becky. Was I reading too much into this exchange or not enough? Looking into her eyes I realized I didn't have a clue. "Uh, the bedrooms are upstairs."

"Then let's take a swim."

"I'm sorry. It's an oversight, but I don't have a bathing suit for you."

Her eyes rolled. "I guess I'm going to have to take matters into my own hands." A grin spread over her face. "So to speak." She crooked a finger. "Jack, come over and stand right here." She stepped back and pointed down.

Puzzled, I stood in front of her at the edge of the pool. She leaned forward, her lips a whisper from mine. The blood immediately left my brain for a better option.

"Jack," she said. "Close your eyes."

I hesitated. She placed her hands on my shoulders and her lips by my cheek.

"Just for a moment." She sighed, her breath tickling my ear. "Please…"

My eyes closed, then flew open as a hard shove knocked me backward into the warm water. A quick kick brought me to the surface and I pushed the hair out of my eyes. "What was that for?"

Becky looked down and smiled. "That was for being obtuse." She reached behind her and slowly pulled down the zipper of her dress. With a roll of her shoulders, the blue satin pooled at her feet. She stood there, a blonde goddess in thin wisps of lacy-white bra and panties. My body temperature heated the surrounding water several degrees as the power of speech deserted my brain.

Her hands reached to the front of her bra and with a snap, it fell away. "You've been keeping me waiting, Jack." She slid her panties down and they fell to her feet. She stepped out of the circle of lace. "Maybe I should keep you waiting."

Her body stunned my senses. Taut, firm muscles accentuated the all-over feminine softness. Her breasts were larger than I'd imagined, with full pink nipples that sent a craving to kiss rippling down my spine. She was as real a blonde as a heartache.

Becky walked to the water and curled her pink-painted toenails over the pool's edge.

"How's the water?" she asked.

"Umm," I moaned and grasped the edge of the pool. I stared up at her, unable to engage my brain.

She smiled down at me. "I'm glad to see that something can stifle that glib attitude of yours." Becky dove over me with a quick spring, and entered the water with barely a splash.

With the vision of loveliness gone, some blood managed to seep back into my brain. I heaved myself out of the pool. My jacket tugged at me and I pulled it off and staggered to a nearby shelf.

I toed off my shoes as I pulled out armfuls of towels and dumped them near the pool. My hands hurriedly yanked off the rest of my clothes, almost of their own volition for I couldn't take my eyes off Becky. She treaded water in the center of the pool. Her hair, floating on the water, spread in a lazy circle around her shoulders. Her lips curved in a beguiling smile.

"Come on in. The water's… warm and inviting," she said.

I dove in and headed for the bottom. Thoughts of taking revenge for pushing me into the water disappeared as I gazed upward at this beautiful water nymph. With a quick kick, I surfaced next to her.

Her smile was seductive. "Glad you could join me."

We clasped hands and hot desire flashed through me. A burning need said take her now. Take her fast and hot, and release the pressure and hunger building in my body. I dragged her toward me and crushed my mouth against hers.

"Now," I muttered into her mouth. "Now." The rational part of me pushed away a corner of the lust and calmly notified my brain that if I acted on the need, we'd both drown. I broke the kiss and found I was panting. Her eyes reflected the same fire that burned in mine.

I grabbed her arm and dragged her to the edge of the pool. My hands found her waist and heaved her onto the scattered towels. In a second, I was out of the water and Becky was under me. She felt gloriously hot and deliciously wet. She wrapped her arms around me and her nails dug into my back.

"Yes." Her voice was a harsh whisper. "Now, Jack. *Now!*"

I stared into eyes glazed with passion, and dove into her. There was no finesse. It was body to body combat as we each took what we needed. Cooled from the water, our bodies quickly heated and grew slick with sweat. Our moans mingled as dozens of blazes shot through me, spurred by her wildfire response. It was frantic, blind sex, with the hard slap of flesh against flesh echoing off the hard tiles. Her back arched and her feet braced on the floor to gain leverage. She matched my hard thrusts with the hard force of her own. Hot passion flashed through my body as we drove each other over the edge. At the battle's end, our cries of surrender numbed each others' ears and we collapsed, casualties of the clash.

Slowly, the scent of spent passion mingling with chlorine brought me to awareness. I levered myself up on my elbows. "Sorry. I'm crushing you."

Becky didn't open her eyes. "No. You're not." She pulled me back down.

I stroked her hair and nibbled on her earlobe. "You okay?"

"I'm better than ok," she replied. She turned and looked at me. "Are you okay?"

I rose up to see her in focus. "I'm better than okay." I smiled and ran a finger down the side of her face. "I'm totally satisfied, but strangely, want more."

She stretched her arms over her head and sighed. "Well, I'm totally relaxed and limp as a noodle." She glanced downward. "I guess you are, too."

I grinned. "Give it time."

I shifted to get off her, but she pushed me over and lay on top of me. Arching her back, she stared down at me, her hands on my chest. "Jack, that was... powerful."

"Sorry it lacked artistry."

Becky shook her head to free the wet hair clinging to her face. "Screw artistry. It was wonderful." She pushed the matted hair away from my forehead and looked into my eyes. Her hands spread over my chest. "You're a wonderful lover."

"I haven't made love to you yet."

Her eyebrow raised. "No? Then what the hell was that?"

I ran my fingertips gently over the tips of her breasts. "Just the overture."

She shifted her legs and straddled me, then placed her hands next to my head. As she leaned over, her hair made a wet blonde curtain around her still-flushed face. "God, I love musicals," she said, and lowered her soft, giving lips to mine.

Chapter 12

Becky sat in my kitchen chair, legs curled under. Her wet hair hung over the collar of the thick, white bathrobe. In my oversized robe she looked small and very young. Serenity radiated from her. Though we had made love again on the couch in the solarium on our way to the kitchen, I wanted her again.

I banked the fire and poured champagne into a flute half filled with orange juice. "Mimosa?"

"I'd love one. Thanks."

As I watched her long slender fingers wrap around the glass, the fire flared to life again. I made my own mimosa and considered pouring the rest of the cold champagne onto my crotch.

What the hell was going on? I hadn't been this horny since the aftermath of my first firefight. Those three days in that Moroccan bordello had been a release and a celebration of being alive.

But this was different. This was a desire to get as close as possible to Becky. A desire to melt into her and make her part of me.

I stared into my drink and felt my brows furrow. What the fuck was happening to me?

"Problem, Jack?"

Becky's question snapped me back to the moment. Looking again at her glowing face, I smiled. "Not at all. Ready for some food?"

"God, yes."

I got down some coffee cups.

"Let me guess the menu," she said, as she pulled her chair closer to the table. "Black coffee, dry Coco-Puffs and potato chips."

"Please," I said. "I may be acting like a horny teenager, but my palate is a trifle more sophisticated." I arranged bagels on a plate and placed them on the table. "Fresh bagels, three different types of cream cheese, fruit…" I opened the refrigerator door and pulled out a plate and set it on the table. "…and fresh smoked lox."

Becky's nose crinkled.

"Not a lox fan?"

She shook her head. "I always thought fish on a bagel was a travesty, two things that shouldn't be eaten together. Like calamari and peanut butter."

I shuddered at the thought and poured her coffee, jumping when she ran a hand up the back of my leg under my bathrobe.

"Are you really acting like a randy teenager, or is this your usual seduction scene?" she asked.

I walked back to the 'fridge and pulled out the artfully arranged fruit plate, then joined her at the table. "Must I remind you that you seduced me?"

"Doesn't fly, Jack." She gestured to the bagels and fruit. "You had this ready." She speared a strawberry and waved it at me. "I may have pulled the trigger, but you loaded the gun."

I nodded. "Guilty." She had rolled up the sleeves of the bathrobe above her elbows and I ran a finger down her bare arm. "But you can't blame me for wanting to make love to a beautiful woman like you."

She patted my hand. "Easy, cowboy. I'm hungry and need something in me besides you." She set to work slathering up a bagel. "Tell me, is this your normal method of getting a woman into your bed? Give her a tour of your very fine house, get her naked then show off your very excellent – Monet?"

I smiled. "Actually, you're the first person I've ever had over. And I haven't gotten you in bed – yet."

"Put that on hold until I'm finished eating. You can't just have your way with me then not allow me to keep up my strength." She looked at me over a piece of pineapple. "Am I really the first person you've had over? How long have you owned this house?"

"About four years, now." I bit into my bagel, then realized just how hungry I was. "I guess I've been building a sanctuary for myself without being aware of it." I shrugged. "My subconscious must have been ready to quit the business before I was."

"Your old career must have taken its toll somewhere besides that magnificent, macho body of yours." Becky placed a hand on mine. "Now that you're finished with that, what are you planning to do with the rest of your life?"

The question had been buzzing in my mind like a mosquito and I flicked it away.

"Spend a leisurely Sunday..." I rose, picked up the thick Sunday paper and plopped it down on the table. "...scoffing at the doomsday pundits, and reading the comics."

Becky ignored the paper and my comment. She stared at me as if looking for the answer, then nodded. I'm sure she sensed that I didn't have a clue as to what to do with my life.

"So…" She pulled the paper to her. "We're going to sit around like an old married couple doing their Sunday morning thing." She looked up. "Does the image frighten you?"

Frighten me? The problem was, it didn't frighten me at all. The question had flashed over me in an instant and the answer felt good. As I stared into Becky's blue eyes, I had a slippery inkling of what the fuck was happening to me.

Whoa, big time there, Jack. I'd have to think about this later – if something like this could be analyzed.

"There are many things that frighten me." I laughed to ease out of the seriousness of the question. "But that isn't one of them." I sipped my coffee and leaned back. "How about you?"

She took a deep breath. "Scares the absolute pee out of me." She looked down. "Glad this is your robe."

My eyebrows sprang up. "It really scares you?"

"Well, I have a bad track record with relationships." She shrugged. "As you once told me, I like our friendship and don't want to screw it up."

"Well that's easy then," I said. "I'll trust you, and you trust me. That way we won't screw it up. If something's wrong, we tell each other. No holding back."

She nodded, snagged her coffee cup and sipped. "What was your longest relationship?"

I remembered a week I spent in Paris with a woman named Monique – a week where we never left the hotel room. I thought back over my trysts and realized Becky was probably looking for something more substantial. It bothered me when I came up blank.

"Uh… I don't think I've ever been in a relationship."

Her lips curved downward. "Too busy or not the type?"

"Too busy. Too lazy. I don't know." I shrugged. "I was never in one place long enough to go through the rituals of dating and the rest. How about you?"

"I dated a bit. Was engaged once. It lasted about two months. Dick thought an engagement meant he could change the way I dress, my hair. God… He even wanted to change the bar into a yuppie fern place." She shuddered.

"Dick?"

"Actually, that's a devolved name. I called him 'The Prick,' then 'The Dick'." She sipped her Mimosa. "Now it's down to just, 'Dick'."

I smiled. "You're a tough one." I toasted her with my glass. "I like that about you."

Becky smiled, split the comics off the paper and slid the rest over to me. "Do you think 'Peanuts' is funny?"

"'Peanuts' hasn't been funny in thirty years. It's just a rehash of fifties psychobabble."

"Ouch. I was just testing your comic sense of comics." She opened the paper, then peered over a corner that had curled down. "I wouldn't give it any more thought than to say it sucks." With a snap, the corner rose again. After a second, she allowed it to curl down and looked at me. "Superman or Batman?"

"Superman."

She nodded and snapped the corner up again.

"But Batman as a dark avenger has some merit," I said. "As a kid, I never realized he was seeking vengeance for the death of his parents. I just thought he was a superhero who couldn't fly but had really neat toys."

"I was a fan of Wonder Woman," Becky said from behind the paper. "A lasso that commands men to tell the truth. What woman wouldn't want one of those?"

I swallowed a hunk of bagel before answering. "Actually, most people already have a built-in bullshit meter." I shrugged. "Most times they'd rather not use it."

Becky lowered the comics to the table. "Possibly true. But it's a skill that needs to be developed as a teen." She leaned forward, peered hard into my eyes and said nothing.

"What?"

She stared for a few moments longer, then leaned back and raised the comics again. "Nothing. Just activating my bullshit meter."

I laughed. "I deserved that."

"Yep."

I picked up the front section of the newspaper, scanned the headlines, then opened to page two. A story on Rwandan rebels caught my eye and I shook my head at the US press once again putting their own spin on the conflict. My mind churned with ideas about how to get involved in the conflict until I remembered I didn't do that anymore.

At a gasp from Becky, I lowered the paper. She reached across the table, yanked the paper from my hand and plopped it down. With eyes glued to the front page, her mouth opened in shock. As she read, her eyes filled with tears.

"What is it?" I stood and stepped around to read the article. At the bottom of page one was a picture of a very familiar, lovely, red-haired young woman. Under the snapshot splashed the horrible tag line, "Woman Found Murdered."

"Oh, my God!" Becky's hand flew to her mouth. "Angel."

I quick-scanned the article and felt my throat tighten. Becky didn't need to read any more. I flipped the paper over. When Becky reached for it, I held her hand. "You don't need the details."

She stared at me a moment, then wiped her eyes with the heel of her hand. "It can't be Angel!" She shook her head. "She's too…"

"It's her. She's been identified." Bile and sickness clenched my stomach. I was familiar with death, but destroying something as pure as Angel was beyond just the cycle of fate. It was an abomination.

Becky's head shook again as if to rid her mind of the thought. "How could someone hurt Angel? She's…"

"Yeah. She was."

Becky's eyes hardened. She pulled back her hand and curled it into a fist. "How could anyone do something like that!"

It wasn't a question. Just a statement. I knew how someone could do something like that – it's because they could. And it was something that was done all the time. I found my fists clenched as well and forced them open.

Becky stood. "I need to make a call."

"You're cell's in your purse. I'll get it."

While Becky placed a call, I retrieved her clothes and brought them to the downstairs bathroom. I fingered the lacy whites and thought about what Becky and I had shared. I was in her life now, and what touched her, touched me. Angel's innocent face flashed in my mind and the shock in my belly turned slowly to ice. I jogged upstairs to change.

I dressed in my usual jeans and leather jacket. Becky needed to see the normal and the familiar. Violence usually doesn't bother anyone – until it hits home. Then mortality and vulnerability paint a very different picture on what we perceive as reality. It's a shock to the system as our carefully crafted universe gets shattered.

Becky was dressed and waiting for me as I came downstairs.

"Angel's folks didn't answer their phone, so I called Father Dombrowski. He said Angel's parents are in shock as we all are, and he'd be in touch when I could be of help."

"I'll take you back home," I said.

The ride back was quiet, punctuated by occasional small talk. The grief and disbelief still poured off Becky's body like rain from a downspout. My questions about the neighborhood were given monosyllabic answers. We pulled up in front of the bar and got out of the car. I placed an arm around Becky's shoulders and looked up at the broken "Tavern" sign.

"Hope's Province will look good up there."

Becky glanced up and some of her grief fell away. "It's a good name." She unlocked the door and we entered the bar.

It felt different inside. The quiet silence made me think of a church. Hope's Province was indeed a good name.

"I have a suggestion for the bar –"

Becky rounded on me before I could finish. "Et tu, Dickay?"

I didn't react, knowing her anger was misplaced. I laid my hands on her shoulders. "I was just going to say that maybe we should swap out that fat old fuzzy TV and get a big flatscreen."

Her head fell against my chest. "Sorry."

I wrapped my arms around her and held her tight. "Show me your bedroom."

She nodded and I held onto her as we walked to the back and up the stairs.

Becky held my hand and led me past the tidy living room and kitchen to her bedroom. I ran a knuckle down her cheek, then undressed her and laid her down. I stripped and joined her on the bed.

There was no speed and need now, no savage drive of sex. Our lovemaking was slow and peaceful in her small bed.

Afterward, I held her while she cried.

Chapter 13

Monday was rainy and business at the bar was slow. Becky went about the job of running a tavern, but a patina of pain overlaid her actions. I sat on my barstool and thoughts of Angel Anderson swirled through my head like the Johnny Walker in my glass.

Last night, after leaving Becky's, I had scoured the web to find out any information on Angel's death, but there wasn't much. The papers said Angel's beaten body was found in a park near South Street. Ligature marks on her hands and feet suggested she had been tied. The police had little to go on.

Becky waded through her grief as she went through the motions of bartending. Her sorrow would soon turn to anger, and dull her sweet shine. I didn't want that. I wanted to see a smile back on that pretty face.

I stared into my glass as if the amber liquid held the answer. Maybe I didn't need to stop a horrible dictator to make a difference – just stop one asshole at a time.

I downed the rest of my drink, slid off the barstool and dropped a twenty on the bar. "I have to go out for a while," I said.

Becky marched over and stared at the twenty. "Since when do you pay up front around here?"

"Pay?" I looked down at the twenty. "Oh." I shoved it back in my pocket. "Sorry. I guess I was distracted."

"I'm wearing a baggy sweatshirt and baggy pants. I don't think I was what distracted you." She placed a hand on my arm. "What's up?"

I looked around the bar, a little unsure of myself, then nodded as the answer filled my brain. "I need to get something."

"What?" she asked as I walked to the door.

"Direction," I said without turning around.

Chapter 14

The 12th Street Precinct was a typical cop shop. I climbed the five concrete stairs of the old brick walkup, and held the door open while a policeman took a scruffy, handcuffed man out to a waiting squad car. I entered and glanced around the room. The place had needed a coat of paint a decade ago. The path to the raised front desk was a brown streak worn into the yellowing linoleum. Notices papered the walls and one large fading sign warned me that spitting was illegal. A few cubicles and desks littered the room. The row of chairs against the wall were empty with the exception of a drunk handcuffed to a pipe. The place smelled of dust, sweat, piss, and fear. I walked to the front desk.

The gray-haired sergeant shuffled papers around before peering at me over his half-glasses. His expression said that everyone who came to his desk hammered his hemorrhoids.

"Yeah?" he growled.

"I'd like to talk to the detective in charge of the Angel Anderson murder."

"Well, you can't. He's gone home." He picked up a folder and scanned the contents.

I drummed my fingers on the desk a moment. "What's the detective's name?"

"Rocco Rinaldo." The sergeant dropped the folder to the desk and he leaned forward. "Any other questions?"

"Yes." I stepped back from the desk. "Where's the men's room?"

With a dismissive grimace he pointed down the hall and picked up the folder.

I'm a fair man. At least I like to think so. In any human interaction I return smile for smile, politeness for politeness, or bullet for bullet. If the sergeant had been the least bit friendly, things might have been different.

As I walked down the hall, I snagged a black magic marker off a desk. Passing another, I grabbed an empty 9x12 brown envelope.

In a stall in the badly-needed-to-be-cleaned bathroom, I wrote "Detective Rinaldo" in big letters on the envelope and stuffed some of what we used to call John Wayne toilet paper inside. It's rough, it's tough, and it won't take shit off nobody.

With the envelope tucked under my arm, I left the bathroom. I waited until the desk sergeant's head was turned, then bounded up the stairs to the detective's area. The dingy, gray, high-ceilinged room was an improvement on my senses – it only smelled of dust and burned coffee. A few tired-looking men sat behind desks that filled the room. They stared at papers or talked quietly into telephones. One pudgy cop, wearing a stained paisley tie and a white shirt one size too small, stood next to a coffee station. He poured black sludge into a cup and looked up.

"Help you?"

I waved the envelope. "The sergeant downstairs told me to leave this on Detective Rinaldo's desk."

He pointed to a desk in the far corner. "Back row. All the way on the left."

I nodded and headed in that direction. The cop took his coffee into a side office and closed the door. The rest of the detectives ignored me.

Good. My luck was holding.

I wound my way to the back, hoping the detective had left Angel's file on his desk. My luck ended with Rinaldo being a neat freak. His desk was clear with only a picture of him and his family in a studio pose. The faded picture had probably graced his annual Christmas card a decade ago.

I glanced around the room. All the cops had their backs to me. I dropped the envelope on the desk, bent down and opened the lower desk drawer. Under the "A's" I found the Anderson file. I yanked it out, and spread out the sheets on the desk. After one look at the pictures, I knew that Angel had been tortured as well as raped and murdered. I quick-scanned the report, then concentrated on Rinaldo's notes. I let the typed words flow over me. My earlier training hadn't been for naught. I would be able recall anything on the page later.

At the sound of an opening door, I dropped the file back into its slot and closed the drawer with my knee. I picked up the envelope and stood next to the desk. The pudgy cop was staring at me, and I gestured to the desk on either side of me, raised my shoulders and put on a questioning expression. He frowned and pointed to the one on the left. I smiled, dropped the envelope on the desk, and walked to the door.

"Thanks," I said, and headed down the stairs.

Chapter 15

Sweat rolled into my eyes as I pushed hard at the weights. My stereo speakers belted out Long John Baldry's tune, "It Ain't Easy," and I did bicep curls to the backbeat. Although my exercise room held all the latest equipment, I still drifted back to free weights as one would to a first love.

I was putting in the punishing workouts I usually do before a mission, and that's how I saw my current direction. This one felt personal, and was a bad way to approach any operation. I concentrated on locking down my feelings.

Long ago I learned there's a switch inside me. It allows me to put a bullet into someone's head and never think about it again. A switch that can be turned on or off with a flick. I felt my imaginary hand hover over the switch and mentally reviewed Detective Rinaldo's notes.

An early-morning jogger had found Angel's body in the park. The autopsy report said that cause of death was strangulation. Besides the battering, the broken arm, and cigarette burns, there were several human bite marks on the body. The killer was a sick, evil bastard for sure, and I hungered for an intimate one-on-one interview between him and the sharp end of my Ka-Bar.

The neighborhood canvass had turned up no witnesses. Rinaldo had the name "Digger Phells" circled with question marks on the sheet, but nothing else about him. The rest had been a list of Angel's acquaintances, her employment history, and other small details about what looked like a normal woman with a normal life. Her ex-fiancé had an airtight alibi and Angel hadn't been seeing anyone else according to her friends and family.

I wiped down with a towel and slid on a t-shirt and my dual Sigs. A hidden door in the back of the closet in the exercise room led to my underground shooting range. I ran down the fifteen stairs, turned, then ran back up. I continued the loop until I had counted two hundred steps. At the bottom, I pulled on my eye and hearing protection and activated my target program.

This ingenious urban combat program, written by a friend of mine, not only popped out random target figures of bad guys and bad guys holding hostages, but also flashed a laser spot on the floor that I had to reach before shooting.

Still puffing from the stairs, I raced to the red spot, dropped to a knee, and fired three shots from each weapon into the head of a raghead target. The spot changed to the other side of the room and I rolled into position as another AK-toting, raghead target popped out.

The ten minute program ended and I checked my scores. I had missed twelve percent of my shots and blown the ear off a hostage.

I needed more practice.

As I replaced the targets too chewed up to be used again, I thought about changing the pictures to urbanites wearing crooked baseball caps and gold bling. It would be more in keeping with what I was seeing as my current assignment. Photos of Angel's battered body flickered through my brain and I felt my imaginary hand slam down on the switch.

It was time for action.

Chapter 16

After a hundred dollars in payoffs and two hours of searching in the freezing-cold night, I found Digger Phells in a rundown section of town. This industrial neighborhood was another victim of the recession. Boarded or broken windows from old brick buildings stared down like blind eyes at the potholed street that no longer saw traffic. Weeds thrust up through the sidewalk cracks in a forlorn effort to bring life to this dead district.

Digger was smashing a wooden pallet against a wall and feeding the pieces into a barrel fire. Another bum stood next to him. Like a dance team, they shifted their weight back and forth on frozen feet as they warmed their hands over the fire. Digger's mismatched worn clothes, long beard and two different shoes told me he was a long time on the streets.

From the darkness of an alley across the street, I learned why he was called "Digger." Every few minutes his right hand dug into his ass like he was searching for loose change.

As the fire died, the bum said something to Digger, waved, and walked into the night. Digger stood for a few seconds longer trying to catch the last of the heat from the barrel, then walked down the street in the opposite direction. I put on amber sunglasses, pulled down my ski mask, and followed. Digger shuffled along slowly, his head down. I quietly sprinted past him down the opposite side of the street, keeping to the shadows. When far enough ahead, I crossed the street and hid in an alley. With my head turned so the vapor from my breath wouldn't show, I watched and waited.

When he crossed the mouth of the alley, I leaped out. Grabbing him by his jacket, I spun him around and slammed him into the brick wall. I jammed my forearm against his throat, and he exhaled a sour wine and bad food smell.

"Tell me about the dead naked woman in the park."

His eyes were too stunned to show fear. "Hey, man. What –"

I leaned in. "Tell me about the dead naked woman in the park."

"I don't know –"

I held up my knife, making sure he saw the blade glitter in the moonlight. "Tell me about the dead naked woman in the park. Don't say you don't know nothing."

He stared at the knife a moment, then looked at me. "Hey look, man –"

I slid the knife point into his nostril. "Tell me!"

Fear flooded his eyes. "They'll kill me, man!"

I pushed the knife in until blood ran out of his nose. "I'll kill you right now."

"No man!   No!"   He held up his hands.   "It was them gangbangers."

"Which?"

"The Eastside Dragons."

"Tell me more!"

"I – I saw two of them pull her out of the trunk of a car and dump her."

"What kind of car?"

"It was a light-blue chromed-up oldie. I've seen it around town. The car was quiet when they pulled up – that's why I watched them. Usually the music is blasting."

"What else?"

"Nothing, man! Nothing. They dumped her and pulled away!"

I removed the knife from his nostril, wiped it on his shabby jacket, and stepped back. I pulled out two twenties from my top pocket, jammed them into his hand, then turned and sped into the darkness.

Chapter 17

After a few phone calls and a fruitless hour of surfing the net, I had learned little about the Eastside Dragons. The gang had evidently risen to power as the town's economy declined. Unemployment had given way to despair, and drugs filled the void. Their leaders and organization weren't easily found – no one wanted to talk about them.

I did find a website for a halfway house that helped kids get out of gangs and it mentioned the Dragons in particular. The "Soaring Free" halfway house was on the edge of the Dragons' turf and my only lead. Despite the pretentious name, I dug out my cell and called the number.

"Yo," said the person on the other end of the line.

"Is this Soaring Free?" I asked, wishing the first things taught to ex-gangbangers were docility and phone manners.

"Yeah, man. What up?"

"I'm looking for the Director."

"Direct-who?"

"The person in charge."

"Oh. That be Monica." The phone clattered to the desk and the courtesy-challenged receptionist yelled for Monica. Make that phone manners, then docility.

After several minutes, a woman picked up the phone.

"This is Monica Brown. How may I help you?"

Ahhh. Phone etiquette at last. "Hello, Monica. My name is Phillip Morris and I was wondering if you could give me some information about the Eastside Dragons."

There was silence on the phone for a moment, then I heard a "tsk" and felt attitude burning through the phone line. "Mr. Morris, I am not in the information business. Try dialing four-one-one."

"Are you interested in an exchange? I'm looking to donate a thousand dollars to Soaring Free."

More silence. "Is this a joke?"

"Cash."

Longer silence. "Not over the phone," she said. "And in a public place."

We agreed to meet Saturday night at eight. I gave her the bar's address.

Eight o'clock found me in Becky's bar, but seated in a booth rather than my usual barstool. The bar was doing a brisk business tonight. Becky had hired a waitress for the weekend crunch and "i not a y Carli" was working the floor.

Stereotypes do come from somewhere and young Carli was the poster girl for blonde airhead waitresses. With tits bigger than her IQ, a cute face and little girl giggle, when she invariably screwed up a customer's order they didn't mind too much.

Short-skirted Carli wiggled to my booth.

"Hiya, Jack."

She placed a hand on my shoulder and rubbed. Carli was a toucher.

"Can I get you another Jack, Jack?" The giggles started and were almost infectious.

I looked down at my drink. "Not yet, Carli. And I drink Johnny Walker Black."

The giggles stopped and Carli's puzzled face said she struggled with my comment.

"Did you make up that Jack, Jack joke on your own?" I asked.

The smile came back and her head bounced up and down like a bobblehead doll. "Yeah! Good one, huh?"

"Yeah. Good one."

"Say, Jack." She ran her hand down my arm. "Dwayne said you were sitting in a booth because your bar stool was giving you hemorrhoids." The puzzled face slipped back on. "What's hemorrhoids?"

I sipped my Black. "Dwayne is."

"Is that another name for mailman?" she asked.

I smiled. "Yep. You got it."

She returned the smile and jiggled to the next booth, spreading confusion and bewilderment in her wake.

I sat facing the door and checked my watch. At 8:02, a very pretty, petite, light-skinned African-American woman entered. When she just stood in the doorway, I knew Monica Brown had arrived. She caught my wave and, clutching her purse, weaved through the tables to the booth. I stood and extended my hand.

"Hello, Ms. Brown. I'm Phil Morris. Pleased to meet you."

She accepted my hand. "You as well, Mr. Morris," she said, and sat.

As we settled into our seats, I studied her. Her high cheek bones and classic elegant features made for a very attractive face. A tasteful dark suit covered her well-built, but tense body. Light blue-gray eyes studied me just as seriously.

"I hope you're not uncomfortable in a 'cracker' box such as this," I said. "If you'd like, we can go elsewhere."

I watched those eyes narrow and a spark of anger ignite. "I'm comfortable wherever I am." She leaned forward. "I'm difficult to intimidate, Mr. Morris."

I held up a hand. "I wouldn't dream of it, Ms. Brown. May I buy you a drink?"

She sat back and some of the tension left her shoulders. "A lot of people want me to give up on Soaring Free." Her hand fisted on the table. "But I never will."

"Good. We need more people like you." I caught Carli's eye and she sauntered over.

"I don't appreciate snowjobs, either, Mr. Morris."

I smiled. "Good. We need more people like you." I turned to Carli. "Another Johnny Walker Black for me and the lady will have…"

Monica gestured with her chin to Becky. "See if the bartender can make me an Irish Car Bomb."

Carli nodded and Monica turned her attention to me. "Mr. Morris, you don't look like a reporter, and you're too slick to be a cop. Why do you want to know about the East Side Dragons?"

I spread my hands. "Let's just say I'm writing a book about the urbanization of Gary, Indiana."

"Sure. If that's what you want me to believe, fine." She leaned forward and tapped a glossy-painted fingernail on the table. "Listen, Mr. Morris, getting interested in the Dragons can get you killed." She looked around the bar. "I shouldn't even be telling you this."

I nodded, then looked up as Becky brought over a tray. She wore another of the T-shirts I had given her. This one was black with white letters that said, "*I see drunk people.*" Her eyes saw only green fire though, and her shoulders were tight.

"Your Irish Car Bomb, *Miss*," Becky said, and placed the drink in front of Monica. "And your drink, Sir." She plopped a drink in front of me, then dumped a bowl of pretzels onto my crotch. "The pretzels are on the house."

Becky whipped the tray under her arm and stormed back behind the bar.

"What was that all about?" asked Monica.

I looked back at Becky and smiled. "Just something I'll deal with later."

"She should be reported to the manager," said Monica.

"Don't worry." I brushed the pretzels off my lap. "I promise you I'll come down hard on the manager later."

Monica sipped from her glass. "She makes a good drink, though."

I raised mine and the smell stopped me. It was Jack Daniels Whiskey. I smiled and downed the shot anyway.

"Getting back to the Dragons, Ms. Brown. I don't want to get you into any trouble."

"Humph. The Dragons tolerate me. In fact, I've heard that they are glad I've taken boys away from their gang. They say that I'm doing them a favor by shaking out the weak ones." She looked into her drink and that hand clenched again. "But I *am* making a difference."

Oh, man. Where had I heard that before? I sighed and made up my mind. I didn't want Monica Brown-who-wanted-to-make-a-difference to get hurt.

"Ms. Brown, I don't want to put you in a difficult position." I reached into my jacket, withdrew an envelope, and slid it across the table. "I promised a donation. Here it is. No strings attached."

She stared at the envelope for a moment, then her eyes sought mine. "I don't understand. But –"

I placed my hand on hers. "Some things you don't need to understand, just accept."

She looked back down at the envelope and chewed her lovely bottom lip. I saw the wheels turning in her head, and when they stopped on a decision. She reached into her handbag and withdrew a thick envelope.

"I don't know why you want this information, and don't want to know." She picked up my donation and dropped it into her bag. "But be careful." She looked down at her purse again then met my eyes. "And thanks. You don't know how much this donation can help." She slid out of the booth.

I slipped her envelope into my jacket and stood, pretzels crunching under my feet. "Let me walk you out."

"There's no need, Mr. Morris."

"Yes. Yes, there is." I held her elbow until we were out of the bar. I called a cab on my cell phone and we waited in silence until it arrived. After the cab pulled away, I waited outside for a few more minutes just to let the jealousy pot boil over, then sauntered back in to my usual barstool.

I held up my finger, but Becky ignored me.

Ralph took a long pull on his Coors, then looked at me. "Looks like you fucked up big time, Jack."

"Naaah, it's just a misunderstanding."

He shook his head. "That miss won't be understanding. She'll just kick your balls off."

I grinned and signaled Becky again. She slowly made her way down the bar, wiping as she came, her face stone. She wouldn't meet my eyes. "Yes, Mr. Daniels. Can I get you something?"

"Yes. A Johnny Walker Black. Please be sure it's JWB. My last drink tasted a little funny."

"That's probably because I spit in it." She turned and hefted the bottle of JWB.

"I thought it tasted too sweet."

Becky slapped a glass on the counter and poured about a quarter-inch of whiskey. "That will be twelve dollars, please." She finally met my eyes. "In advance. You don't have a tab here anymore."

She started to walk away, but I snagged her arm. "Becky. That was just business."

She tore her arm free. "Business? What? Paying off your hooker? I saw you playing patty-fingers with her."

I sighed. "Put that green-eyed monster back in its cage and think about it. You know I'm not a stupid man. Would I cheat on you in your own bar? In front of you? That makes no sense!" I had her attention now. I leaned over the bar, placed my hands on her arms, and pulled her gently toward me. I hauled out my trump card. "We've talked about trust, and how we would respect that trust. Was that just talk?"

When she sighed, and her head fell to her chest, I knew it was over.

I squeezed her shoulders. "I'll tell you all about it after closing. OK?"

She took a deep breath and let it out. "OK." She raised her head. "Sorry, Jack. I warned you I was a green-eyed rotten bitch."

"Oh, you're not so rotten." I grinned. "Now give us a kiss."

She smacked me in the face with the bar rag.

Chapter 18

Ralph was the last to leave as usual, and after I ushered him out, I locked the door and turned off the "Open" sign. Arms crossed, Becky stood in front of the bar, foot tapping a rapid tattoo.

"Can't let it go, can you?" I said as I walked to her.

She dropped her arms. "I let it go for a moment, then I get pulled back into it."

I could almost see the little demon that sat on her shoulder, grinning as he shoveled in the lies. The battle between what she knew was right and what the demon was cramming into her head was evident in her eyes. "Ego and attachment are soul destroyers," I said.

Her arms crossed again and she stamped her foot. "Spare me the Hindu horseshit, Jack. What's this 'business' you had with her?"

I placed my hands on her shoulders. "It's about Angel."

That wasn't what she expected, and confusion clouded her eyes. "What about her?" She stared at me a moment, then those eyes narrowed and filled with understanding. "You're going after her killer, aren't you?"

I dipped my head once.

Becky raised her arms and brushed my hands off her shoulders. She covered her mouth and stared off to the side. After a moment, her hand lowered then curled into a fist. The stone-hard countenance I'd seen when Tedesco's goons had first walked into her bar was back.

"I'm in." She reached up and grasped my arm. "But – I'm all the way in this time." She shook a finger in my face. "Promise you won't sandbag me like you did with Teddy!"

I stared into her fire-backed blue eyes. Before me stood a strong-willed woman with a vise-grip on my arm and a finger in my face. The true goddess of the hunt radiating her power. Diana reborn.

How could a mere mortal refuse her bidding?

"OK," I said.

She released my arm and stepped back. "OK? No bullshit?"

"No bullshit, Counselor."

She nodded as she absorbed my words.

I walked to the nearest table and started putting up the chairs. "Let's clean up, then go upstairs and talk about it, all right, Counselor?"

"Forget the cleanup. We'll get to it tomorrow."

I pointed to the booth I'd occupied earlier and felt a grin start. "But there's a pile of pretzels on the floor over there for some reason. I should sweep them up."

Her head lowered. "Sorry about that." When she raised her head, a small smile played across her lips. "Come upstairs. There's something I want to show you that might make amends for the pretzels." She held out her hand.

"Whatever you say, Counselor." I slipped my hand into hers and she led me up the stairs.

"Why do you keep calling me Counselor?" she asked.

"Your last name. Quinn. It's Irish for counselor. It's perfect. From now on, you are my advisor, confidante, comrade, friend." When we reached the top of the stairs, I pulled her toward me and held her tight. I felt the beat of her heart against mine and it felt good. "And my lover." I brushed my lips over hers, then kissed her lightly.

With eyes closed she whispered, "*A ghrá mo chroí.*"

"What does that mean?"

Her eyes opened and she smiled, but hesitated before saying, "Ummm… It's Irish for 'Come in. And welcome.'"

She unlocked the door and we went into the kitchen.

"What did you want to show me?" I asked.

"I'll get it," she said. "And since we're in this Irish mood, get down the bottle of Jameson and two glasses."

She walked into the bedroom, leaving me to search for the whiskey. After fumbling through mountains of Tupperware and recipe books, I found the bottle, then went on the hunt for glasses. "Business at the bar is sure booming," I said, as I peered into the broom closet. "I bet Carli did well on tips tonight."

"She won't really know how well until she shakes out her underpants," replied Becky from the bedroom.

I chuckled at the image, then noticed the partially open oven door. There they were, God knows why. They were stacked on a tray in neat little rows – but in the oven. I poured two shots and sat at the table. I had just raised my glass when Becky appeared in the bedroom doorway.

With both hands on the doorjamb, she leaned into the room. She wore a lacy-black transparent teddy, matching shimmering stockings, garter belt, and stiletto-heeled "fuck me" pumps. Her hair was down and a slash of ruby-red lipstick adorned her lips.

The drink stopped halfway to my lips and my brain went numb.

"I bought this with you in mind. What do you think?"

I put down the drink and stood. "You've made it very hard to think."

She smiled and nodded. "Hard is good."

"I hope you didn't pay too much for that lust launcher."

She put a fingernail between her teeth and sauntered toward the table, sly smile on her lips. "Why?"

"'Cause I'm gonna rip that off you in about three seconds."

Becky stopped short, eyes popping wide. With a squeal, she turned and ran into the bedroom.

I rounded the table and chased after her. She avoided my grasp by lunging forward and scrambling over the bed. I stopped and spread my arms wide.

She turned and held up her hands, a big grin on her face. "Jack, this is too nice an outfit to have it ripped off."

"Too late. You should have thought of that before." I feinted right, then tackled her as she tried to leap back over the bed. She squirmed, but I got on top and pinned her hands over her head.

"Jaaack!" She giggled. "Don't rip it!"

She wanted me to do just that, but I had different thoughts. I rolled off her, but cuffed her wrists over her head with one hand. "I have a better idea."

I slowly traced a finger down from her neck to her groin, then back up. I gently circled a hard nipple. "Your intent, Counselor, was to drive me crazy, was it not?"

She moaned, and her breaths came in quick gasps.

"Was it not?" I asked again as my hand traveled downward.

Her "yes" came out like a hiss between clenched teeth.

"Then I guess it's my turn to drive you crazy."

I slid my hand under the lace and proceeded to do so.

Chapter 19

The morning sun streamed in through the window and the coffee pot did its slow drip. While Becky cooked breakfast, I described my visit to the police station, Detective Rinaldo's notes, and my interview with Digger.

"Why would the Eastside Dragons kill Angel?" she asked over the sizzle of bacon. "It doesn't make sense."

"That only means we don't have all the pieces to this puzzle yet." I sipped my orange juice and thought about it. "After breakfast, we'll go over the information Ms. Brown gave me and maybe that will add in some of those missing pieces."

Becky turned the eggs and drained the bacon. "Angel would never have anything to do with gangs." The toast popped up and she plated the toast and bacon and slid two eggs onto my plate. "You only met her twice and couldn't know her well, but she was the sweetest person you'd ever know."

"She might have developed a desire to walk on the wild side."

"No. Not Angel." She plopped down our plates, filled our coffee cups, and sat across the table from me. "She was a truly gentle soul." Her hand drifted to her throat, and her eyes focused on the past. "Angel had this unique heart-shaped locket. It looked solid, but if you pushed on the base, it popped opened. Inside, she kept a tiny bluebell flower. I asked about the significance of the flower and Angel just shrugged. Well, I hounded her until she cracked." Becky's gaze came back to me. "You know how I can be."

"Umm... Implacable? Unyielding? Relentless? Dogged?"

She flipped me the bird, then continued. "Angel said that when she first saw that flower she felt a deep connection with it. She felt like it represented her life as it would bloom, yet still be connected to the world and everything beautiful in it."

"Wow."

"Yeah. That was Angel."

Becky leaned forward to grab a napkin and her robe gaped open. I found myself staring, hoping to get a glimpse of her breast. I forced my attention on buttering my toast. "There's some

connection with the Eastside Dragons. We just need to dig deeper."
I cut into my eggs.

Becky smiled and raised her coffee cup. "I like that 'we' part."

"About that…"

Her back stiffened and the coffee cup clattered down on her saucer. "Oh, no you don't, Jack Daniels. You promised."

I nodded. "I won't go back on my word, but I don't want to see you in a shootout with a bunch of gangbangers."

"Me neither." Her shoulders eased back down. "We'll just have to work together to meld our respective strengths and bolster our weaknesses."

I grinned. "I love it when you talk like that. Let's get naked and meld some more."

"Put your glands on hold, stud muffin. We have work to do after breakfast."

"Yeah, you're right." I nodded, then stared across at her. "Wait. Did you just call me stud muffin?"

She giggled and covered her mouth. "I hoped you hadn't heard that. It was a slip of the tongue. Pretend it didn't happen."

"Hmm…"

"Besides, I should call you 'steel muffin.' You taste good and seemed to have buffed up a lot lately." She bit into her toast. "Have you been working out?"

"Yeah. I always toughen up before a mission."

She pursed her lips. "I should do that as well."

"You can come over to my house and work out. You never did see the master bedroom."

"That's not the kind of workout I meant, Jack."

"OK. We'll do the other kind."

"Good."

"After." I grinned.

"I should call you 'Jack Rabbit.'" She sighed. "Trouble is, I like it just as much as you do." She reached across the table and placed her hand over mine, her eyes softening a bit. "Will we still be going at it like this in forty years?"

"Humping like rabbits?" I thought about that while I chewed some bacon. "I don't see why not. Tomorrow can be a duplicate of today. Like pearls on a string, tomorrows stretch out into the distance of forever."

Becky propped her chin on a hand. "I'd like to meet your Hindu cellmate someday… maybe thank him… maybe kick him in the nuts."

I shook my head. "Can't. He didn't make it past the barbed wire during our escape."

"Sorry."

"It's just life." I turned over my hand and curled my fingers into hers. "And death is a part of life. The trick is to live as if you were going to die tomorrow, and learn as if you were going to live forever."

"Another one of his?"

I nodded. "Shakkar was a good guy, but not very lucky."

She rose and cleared the table. "I hope we will be."

"Count on it."

Becky smiled. "I like your attitude, Jack Daniels."

"I like your… everything, Becky Quinn."

She pulled her chair next to mine. "Let's get to work."

Chapter 20

Monica Brown's info was remarkable, complete with an Eastside Dragons' top-level organizational chart, the rackets they were into, a map marking their territory, and a synopsis of their inroads into politics.

"How much did you pay for this?" asked Becky.

"Not enough." I scanned the papers again. "There is more here than I ever got on a government assignment."

"She's monitored the gang very closely," said Becky.

"Yeah. I get the idea that she uses this data to get close to boys she wants to talk into leaving the gang."

Becky tapped a finger on the top of the organization chart. "Juan Johnson Cruz. Everyone's heard of him. He's managed to get Hispanic and Black gang members to work for him. I've heard he's a community organizer. And I've heard he's a vicious monster."

I grunted. "I'd go with the vicious monster part. That's probably how he unites different street factions. The rest is probably just good PR."

Becky's hands curled into fists. "I hate people like him. Always looking to intimidate and hurt people."

I put my finger on a line in Ms. Brown's notes. "Look. The night Angel was killed, Cruz was attending a five-hundred-dollar-a-plate fund raising dinner for Councilman Douglas."

Becky's fist slammed onto the table. "Just because Cruz wasn't there doesn't mean he didn't order Angel's death."

I placed my hand over her one of her fists. "True. Or maybe he had nothing to do with it." I gave the fist a little shake. "We have to be sure."

She sighed and her fist relaxed. "Yes. We have to be sure." She pointed to the org chart. "There must be twenty names here. We can't just kill them all."

I picked up the map and studied the drug distribution areas. "Sure we can. It will just take a bit of planning."

I didn't realize Becky was staring at me until I looked up. "What?"

"Could you really do that?"

"Do what?"

Her eyes shifted to the right. "Kill them all."

"Morally or physically?" When she didn't answer, I continued. "Physically, yes. Morally, the same answer – yes." I pulled my chair closer, gathered her hands in mine and stared into her eyes. "Because someone wears a human body, that doesn't make them human. It just means they have the potential to be human. To me, being human means treating every other person with kindness and as an equal." I shrugged. "Unless you're in combat."

Becky looked away. "But they're still human and have the ability to change."

I gave that remark five seconds of thought before answering. "Someone that preys and spews violence on other humans is the same as a crazed animal. Look, suppose a rabid dog was biting and ripping at a child. Would it be OK to put a bullet in the dog's brain?"

She gave me the "duh" look. "Of course."

"Now what if I told you that there was a long involved series of drugs that would eventually cure that dog of rabies."

"All right."

I rose, retrieved a Sig, opened Becky's right hand and slapped the weapon into it.

"The dog is still biting that kid and won't let go. He will eventually kill the child." I sat across from her. "You have the gun. The dog is still ripping and tearing but has the potential to be cured."

She stared at the gun.

I cupped her chin and lifted her face, forcing her to look at me. I dropped my hand. "Do you pull the trigger on that rabid animal even though it could be cured?"

She lowered her eyes to the gun again, and hefted its weight. Her hand tightened around the butt. "Yes." Her voice was almost a whisper, but the look on her face was thunderous. "Yes, I could," she said louder. She stared into my eyes, face filled with fierce determination. "Teach me how to use this."

"I will." I took back the Sig. "Well, not this gun. That's tooled to my hand." I put on my best "Arnold" accent. "We'll get you something that's more suited to the Beckynator."

She snorted.

I leaned back and just looked at her. This Becky Quinn person who had come into my life was quite a package. In finding her, I hadn't just found a lover, I had found a friend.

"What," she said, wiping a napkin over her mouth. "Is there egg on my face?"

"Hopefully, we won't have any egg on our faces during this entire action."

Becky rose and refilled our coffee cups. "Okay. Keep our faces clean. What else do we need to do?"

"To start with, we need to cover our tracks. I suggest an old banger, a fully functional cut-out center, and a plausible tale."

She sat back down and nodded. "Yeah. That's just what I was thinking." Becky cupped her hand over her mouth. "*Krrrch.* Earth to Jack. *Krrrch.* Come in Jack." She dropped her hand and beamed a smile at me. "I know you speak several languages, but please press number one for English."

I held up my hands. "Sorry. Banger is just an old innocuous vehicle. A cut-out center is a headquarters area where we can plan, stage, and whatever, without it being traced back to either of us. A plausible tale? Let me give you an example."

She laughed while I told her the Brazilian gangs story I'd spun for Teddy Tedesco. I sat back and sipped my coffee.

"How do we make all of that untraceable?" she asked.

"Cash and fake I.D.'s. I have a few for myself and I'll have one made for you."

"Can I be Leia Organa?"

I put down my coffee cup – just in case. "I was thinking about 'Betty Ballbuster.'"

She straightened. "Really? I was thinking yours should be 'Tommy Dick, Twisted... Off.'"

I scrunched up an eye. "That didn't quite work, did it?"

"No. It was spur of the moment. But pick something nice for me." She leaned forward. "What do I get to do?"

I could see the excitement behind her eyes. That's something that would be squashed at our first violent encounter. For the moment, I let it go.

"Let's go over Ms. Brown's map and pick out possible headquarters locations, then check them out visually.

She nodded. We cleared the table and spread out the map. When Becky pulled a pad of paper and a pen from the pocket of her robe and placed it on the table, I smiled.

We rented a small brick warehouse for our headquarters six blocks outside the Dragons' haunts. I had a story ready about used furniture storage for this mission, but the owner didn't ask for anything but the cash. That told me a little about the gang's influence in the area.

I took a bus to Chicago. The *Sun-Times* listed several vans for sale, and I was looking for an innocuous vehicle. The third one I saw was the best – twelve-year-old Econo-van, faded dark blue, rusty, with a cracked windshield. Perfect as a stealth vehicle. The van cost me three hundred dollars, and the tune up and parts another seven-fifty. Costly perhaps, but I had learned that a ride has to be reliable. The heap might not be able to outrun a hollow-point, but it was better than sitting still and waiting for one to kiss the back of your head.

The sun had already set by the time I got back from Chicago several days later. I pulled into the alley leading to the warehouse's overhead door. The building across the way was abandoned, and all the windows facing the alley were boarded over. That was one of the reasons we chose the place – it gave us privacy.

I exited the van and yanked the chains that opened the overhead. With a squeaky rattle, the door rose. I pulled the van in, shut down the engine, and got out. I glanced up and down the alley before pulling down the door and locking it.

My job tonight was to install an electric door opener, grease the door rails and re-route the electric so the warehouse lights went out when the overhead's remote-control button was pushed.

Becky and I had already installed cameras in the building, both inside and out. They weren't the "Hey, look, I'm a camera" cameras. These were state of the art, wireless, infrared jobs, that are nearly invisible to the casual eye.

While I spent time in Chicago I asked Becky to take a stab at setting up a control center in the small empty office on the second floor. I headed up the rusting metal stairs to see how she had made out. I flipped on the office lights and stared. A semi-circular desk held four monitors, split by a laptop. Each monitor was sectioned into four screens, displaying our sixteen camera angles. But what drew my attention as I plopped into the swivel chair were the daisies spilling over the rim of a blue vase behind the laptop. I smiled. Working with Becky was going to be different from my other assignments, that was for certain.

I leaned back in the chair, glancing at the steel ladder that led to the roof. The hatchway was barred from the inside and camouflaged on the outside as a vent. I always have a second or third escape route planned and this time was no different. Once on the roof, I had two exits planned from there.

My men once labeled me Paranoid Prick, but that stopped after a job went all to hell and the only thing between us and perdition was my well-planned escape route. I didn't think I'd need these precautions from a bunch of gangbangers, but it never hurt to have a backup plan in place.

It said something about Becky that she never once questioned the reason for a redundant backup plan. It spoke of trust.

I rose, sniffed the flowers, then went downstairs to start work.

Chapter 21

When I had finished the job, I stopped by the bar. Waving to Sam, Bernie, and a few other regulars, I perched on my usual barstool and crunched on a pretzel. Becky came my way toting a bottle of JWB. "Nice job setting up the office and monitors," I said. "Have any problems?"

"No. Unlike most men, I can read an instruction manual."

"Real men don't need instructions."

"Ha!" She poured two fingers, then leaned on the bar. "Did you like the flowers?"

"Brightened my whole day."

"I was thinking of you when I bought them, but–" Her eyes shifted as she polished the bar. "–they were out of pansies."

I smiled and shook my head. "You're one hard momma."

Her head jerked up, face filled with misgivings. "Sorry, Jack. I didn't mean…"

I rose up, cupped her chin and kissed her. "You have a beautiful mouth. But it gets you in trouble sometimes." I patted her cheek and sat back down. "Thank you for the flowers."

The anxiety vanished and Becky smiled. "Thanks. What's up for tonight?"

"Well, our lair is prepared for guests, invited or un." I ran my finger around the rim of the glass. "It's time to cruise the Dragons' territory for the car that Digger mentioned."

She slapped a glass on the counter, poured another JWB, and lifted the shot. "So it begins."

I raised my glass and clinked hers. "It began when Angel died."

She nodded. "What are you going to do if you find them?"

"Tonight, I'll just observe. But if I have the opportunity… I'll take them."

"Be careful." She touched my cheek, then dropped her hand. "Should I say 'luck' or do you have another phrase like 'break a leg?'"

"Crash and burn."

"Interesting euphemism," she said. "Well, break a leg, crash and burn, choke and die, whatever, but take care." She squeezed my hand. "I'll stop by the warehouse after I close up."

"See you then."

She walked back down the bar, polishing as usual, but I could see the tension that I'd just put in her shoulders.

I'd better make sure everything went well.

Chapter 22

I found the '66 blue Chevy Nova after less than fifteen minutes of cruising. It was parked in front of the "Plummeting Cage," a bar/community center/brothel/drug den. The name was an obvious slam at Monica Brown's "Soaring Free" halfway house and it told me that Juan Johnson Cruz wasn't just a vicious gangbanger. He was a clever, vicious gangbanger.

From the outskirts of the Dragons' territory, I trained my binoculars on the Nova. While I waited, thoughts of Becky snuck into my mind as they often did these days.

A wise man once said that love is the triumph of imagination over logic. I'd never been in love, so I didn't really know what that meant or how I was supposed to feel. I only knew that being with Becky made me feel complete, like losing a hand then getting it back again. We meshed very well, like a team that has worked together for a long time. Yet, she still managed to surprise me with her quick wit, a funny outlook, or a see-through teddy.

If she hadn't been a civilian and I was putting together a surveillance or strike team, she'd be high on my list. Her thinking patterns were different from mine and opened avenues that didn't naturally occur to me. That widened our scope, and her appeal.

Becky fled from my mind as two thugs left the club a little before midnight and headed for the Nova. They were dressed the same: crooked ball caps; flashing bling; oversized team jerseys; and baggy pants with the crotch hanging down to their knees. If I had to run these boys down, it would be easy when their pants hit their ankles.

They started the Nova and I could hear the bone rattling "thumps" from their stereo five blocks away. The rumble of their loud muffler lent an underscore to the music. The car rolled down the dark streets, a bright, loud, jacked-up punk-mobile with a dull, rusty shadow far in its wake.

I tailed them to a brownstone on the edge of their territory. They backed the Nova into an adjacent alley, exited, and strolled up the brownstone's steps like they owned the world. It would be fun to show them how wrong they were.

A skinny Latina woman in a halter-top and cutoffs came out onto the porch and greeted one of them with a kiss and a hug. He returned the greeting by grabbing her ass.

I rolled on by and parked on a side street a quarter-mile away. I walked back to the Nova through alleys and side streets, keeping to the shadows as much as possible. I approached the car from the rear and waited several minutes to make sure it was clear. Keeping below the window level, I crab-walked to the passenger-side and tugged on the door handle. It was unlocked.

Arrogant bastards.

I quickly got in and pulled the door shut so that the interior light went out. I pinched the plastic dome cover, removed the bulb, and replaced the cover. I slid out of the car and quietly closed the door. I hurried to the rear of the vehicle and squatted.

All thoughts were banished as I tuned my senses to the surroundings. The night was crystal clear with no moon. A rat scuttled down the gutter. Water dripped from a pipe and ran into a sewer. The Nova's engine clicked as it cooled. I felt one with the night and did what a good hunter does best.

I waited.

At 1:15, footsteps and laughter echoed down the alley. Crouched behind the car, I watched as two pairs of hi-tops shuffled toward the vehicle. I tensed and readied my stun baton. When one guy opened the passenger door, I leaped out and tagged him on the back of his neck. As he collapsed, I yanked him out of the way, and jumped into the passenger seat. The driver didn't even notice the switch and fumbled putting the keys into the ignition.

"Nice night, isn't it?"

The driver looked up. "What the fu–"

I stunned him on the temple and the crackle of the electric-blue light lit up the interior. The keys slid from his hand and I snagged them before they hit the floor. It took me only a moment to drag him across the seat and out of the car. A quick glance told me I was still in the clear and I snugged plastic zip strips on their hands and feet.

As I pulled out my trusty duct tape, I thought of Becky and had to smile. I ran a strip over their mouths, then patted them down. One carried a .357 Smith & Wesson down the front of his pants, the other had a Mac-10 stashed in his back and the magazine in a pocket. I tossed the guns and I.D.'s onto the backseat.

Making sure they were well secured, I dragged them to the back of the car and dumped them in the '66 Chevy's spacious trunk. Ah, they just don't make 'em like that anymore. There was enough room there for one or two more assholes.

With the slamming of the lid, I thought how apropos it was to transport them the same way they had transported Angel's body. I got in the car, put in earplugs, and started the engine. I wasn't worried about anyone seeing me through the heavily-tinted windows, but I pulled my hat low just to be sure. The heavy thumps from the beefed up stereo made me glad for the ear protection.

I rode down the street, and slowly lowered the stereo until it was off. When questioned about the disappearance of these two gangbangers, witnesses could only say that they drove off into the night, and vanished.

I drove around awhile, keeping to the side roads. When I was certain I didn't have a tail, I made my way to the warehouse. With headlights doused, I pulled down the alley, hit the remote door opener, and pulled inside the darkened space.

When the overhead door shut, the warehouse lights automatically came on. I stepped out of the car, anticipation flowing.

Time for an in-depth interview. Pictures of Angel's tortured body flashed through my brain and put me in the right mood. I leveled a Sig, opened the trunk and stepped back. Neither thug moved. Their hands were still cuffed, so I holstered my gun.

"Welcome to the audition, chuckleheads," I said.

Still, neither of them moved. I leaned into the trunk and the smell of exhaust fumes shot alarm bells through my brain.

"Shit, shit, shit!" I yanked the gangbangers onto the concrete floor, and checked for a pulse on each.

Nothing.

Fury poured red fire into my eyes. "You dumb fucking bastard!" I shouted to the dead driver and kicked him in the ribs. "You fix up the outside of this heap to look pretty but skip a bad muffler and holes in the trunk!"

I kicked him again. "You're like your car! Bling on the outside and shit on the inside!" I laid my boot into his side several more times until exertion overrode frustration, then sat on the edge of the trunk with my head in my hands.

My only lead to Angel's killer was as dead as the gangbangers.

Chapter 23

My cellphone vibrated and I checked the screen. Becky.

"Hey," I answered.

"I'm five blocks out. How did it go?"

I blew out a long breath. "Not as well as I'd hoped."

"Something's wrong. I can tell from your voice. Are you all right?"

"Yeah. I'm fine. Karma just kicked me in the balls, that's all. I'll tell you about it when you get here."

"Rogerwilco-over-and-out."

I made a mental note to teach Becky proper radio procedures, then stared down at the bodies. After a few more curses, I dumped them back into the trunk, closed the lid, and sat on the bumper.

The warehouse lights doused and as the overhead door rattled open, I rose. Becky drove the bar van in and parked over to the side. When the door closed, the lights came on again. I was glad to see she had remembered to stick the magnetic sign on the van door that read "Willard's Used Furniture."

She stepped out and we walked toward each other, stopping a foot apart. Becky's leather jacket was open and she slipped her hands into the back pockets of her tight jeans. Her white T-shirt proclaimed in black letters, "Alcohol and Calculus Don't Mix. Never Drink and Derive."

Becky studied my face. "You look like shit, Jack."

"Not surprising. I feel like shit."

She twined an arm around mine and we walked back to the Nova. "Sit rep."

I stopped. "Sit–"

"Situation report. I heard that on TV." She tugged on my arm and we continued walking. "What happened?"

"I took them easy. Dumped them in the trunk and drove here." I kicked the side of the Nova. "I didn't know the muffler was filling the trunk with carbon monoxide." I kicked the car again, denting the door. "Now I've got nothing but two bodies. We're at a dead end."

Becky chewed on a thumbnail for awhile, then turned and gripped her hands on my shoulders hard. "No! We're not at a dead end. We can't be, this is for Angel!" She dropped her hands, shook her head, blew out a breath and clenched her fists. "We'll find another clue and pick up the trail. We have to." She looked at the Nova. "Your past occupation has taught you that there is one goal. Get in. Destroy. Get out." She looked back at me. "This isn't like that. There will be another trail to pick up. If these punks didn't kill Angel, we'll find out who did another way. There must be someone else who knows what happened."

I let that sink in.

Becky stared at the vehicle. "Are they in the trunk?"

"Yeah."

"I want to see them." She held out her hand for the keys.

"Listen –"

She jerked her head toward me, eyes narrowing. Her voice filled with ice. "I want to see them."

I dropped the keys into her hand and she walked to the trunk. She popped it open and stared down. I watched her eyes for a sign of sorrow, regret, sadness – anything. She just pursed her lips for a moment, then her face became cold.

"They don't look so tough now," she said.

"The dead never do."

She closed the lid and looked up. "Who were they?"

I shrugged. "I.D.'s are in the back seat."

She opened the door, then turned and looked at me. "Come on, Jack. Let's see where they sit on the organization chart. We'll see how close they are to Cruz." She stared at me a moment longer. "This may sound funny coming from me, but… Get your head in the game."

Ego raised my hackles and I took a step forward before I realized she was right. This was just the start of the mission. I'd had clusterfucks happen right out of the gate and had to improvise. This was no different.

"Wow," I said. "I think I just kicked my own ass."

"That's OK," she said with a laugh. "I'll kiss it later and make it all better." She gestured to the car. "Let's go up to the office and check them out."

Ramon "Diesel" Williams, and Akim "not-yet-badassed-enough-to-acquire-a-street-name" Jackson were listed on the org chart.

Diesel was the number three man in the Dragons. Akim was way down the list.

"A trusted lieutenant and his worker bee." I tapped the paper. "Their disappearance will get the rest of the gang wondering but not worried."

Becky scowled. "I want them worried. Worried and afraid. As Angel must have been."

"No. That's for later when you have them in your pocket. Now, I just want them to stay loose."

"You're right." Becky perched on the desk and crossed her long legs. Damn, the woman looked good in boots, T-shirt and jeans or with nothing on but the light.

"What do we do with the bodies?" she asked.

"I have an idea about that. I'll ditch them and the car tomorrow. First I need to make a few exterior improvements to it."

"I've been thinking about what to do next." She stood and paced the small office. "I think we should check things out from Angel's viewpoint. See what her life was like in those last days." She stopped and whirled around. "Maybe she scratched their car and they went after her."

"Smart. After I take care of the bodies, I think it's time for 'Daniel Ruse' to check out her home life."

"Who's Daniel Ruse?"

I stood, jammed my fists on my hips and raised my head. "It is I! Daniel Ruse. Stalwart reporter for the Post."

She grinned. "OK, Danny. What do we do tonight?"

I jerked a thumb at the Nova. "Make that pretty car look like a piece of shit, then pick up the old van."

She nodded. "The toolbox is downstairs. Let's get to work."

Chapter 24

"Look, I know it's not your usual procedure, but I need your help." I put on my friendly but helpless smile.

"We got rules," said the fat man behind the desk. The name "Ted" was stitched under the "Arty's Car Crushing Service" logo on his stained blue jumpsuit.

I nodded. "I understand, but my nephew wants to use his college money to fix up that old heap." I gestured to the Nova hooked to a tow bar behind my van. We had removed the fenders, smashed the doors and painted the whole thing in primer and fake rust spots. It didn't look anything like the pimped-up ride it was yesterday. The dead gangbangers were in body-bags loaded with kitty litter.

"If it's crushed, he can't do that." I placed a palm on his desk. "We've already drained all the fluids and removed the battery. I know it's a lot of trouble for you, but maybe you can help me out." I moved my hand, revealing the folded one-hundred-dollar bill.

Ted glanced down and put a clipboard over the hundred. "Sure. I'll fit it in." He smiled. "After all, it's for education. There's room between that Toyota and the Jeep. Just leave it there and I'll get right to it."

I gripped his hand hard. "Thanks, Ted. This means a lot."

With the van, I backed the Nova into the right slot, unhooked the tow-bar and left the auto yard. I drove down the street, parked, and trained binoculars on the junkyard. A dirty yellow forklift soon picked up the Nova and dropped it into a yawning pit. The hydraulics whined and metal screamed as it turned the Nova into a rectangular cube.

After a forklift loaded the car onto a flatbed, I headed for the warehouse. Time to switch to a rented car and my new identity as Daniel Ruse, dedicated Post reporter.

Chapter 25

Armed with glasses, fake business cards and a rumpled old suit, I drove to Angel's apartment building. The well-kept six-story brownstone was close to the center of town, so she had probably walked to her job at the Department of Environmental Protection. I made a mental note to check out her route.

I jogged up the wide stone steps and entered a small vestibule. One wall held a dozen mail boxes with buttons underneath. I punched the one labeled "Superintendent Halper," and the door clicked open. As I stepped into the hallway, a door past the elevator and stairs opened and a tissue-thin old man stepped out of the super's office. Baggy brown pants, a sleeveless t-shirt and grey hair sticking up at odd angles completed the picture. I brought my hand up and waved as I approached the wary super.

"Hello, Mr. Halper? I'm Daniel Ruse from the Post." I pulled out a business card and handed it to him. "I wonder if I could interview you for the paper about Angel Anderson."

His suspicious attitude fell away as he stared at the card. He glowed like a movie star with a hard-on.

"Of course, Mr. Ruse. I've been a subscriber to your fine newspaper for twenty years. Please come in." He opened the door wide and I followed him into an apartment decorated sometime back in the nineteen-forties. "Please, have a seat. I was just about to make some coffee. Would you like some?"

"I'd love some. Thanks."

I settled into a worn purple velvet wing-back chair and tried not to wince as he fixed Sanka for both of us.

"Tell me Mr. Halper, what was Angel Anderson like?" I asked.

"Nice," he said from the kitchen. He carried in the cups and sat on the couch across from me. "A real nice girl. Damn shame what happened to her."

I reached into my jacket pocket and pulled out a pad and pen. "A lot of men friends? A lot of parties?"

He frowned and shook his head. "Not Angel. She was a real nice girl." He sipped his coffee and smiled down at it like it was a treat. "She had a boy she was seeing about six months ago, but he stopped coming around."

"Was she upset by that?"

"No." He stared at the floor for a moment. "She always had a cheery 'Hello' or a smile and a wave. Was always happy." He set his coffee down and leaned forward. "One day, when I was sweeping the front steps, she stops to talk. 'How are you, Mr. Halper? You're looking nice today.' I had on my new jumpsuit, the light blue one with my name on it." He stroked his jaw as he remembered. "I asked her, 'How come Ben never comes around to take a pretty girl like you out anymore?' and she says, 'He's a good friend, but that just wasn't the right path for me.'"

Halper's hands flew wide and his shoulders rose. "I say, 'What do you mean?' and she says, 'I felt that just wasn't the direction my life should go.' I say, 'Don't feel sad' and she says, 'How could I feel sad when life is so beautiful?'

Halper smiled. "Then I say, 'But it's better with a boyfriend' and she smiles at me – she had this really great smile – and says, 'Maybe I'm holding out for you.'" The old man grinned and shook his head. "Holding out for me. Can you imagine?"

I could. It just confirmed my image that Angel Anderson really was an angel. Was that a front? Or was that my cynicism creeping in? I remembered how I felt about her when we met in the bar, and kicked my cynicism to the curb.

I focused on the super and decided I could get into Angel's apartment with a little stroking. "Running a six-story apartment building like this must be quite a chore." I picked up my pad and pen and leaned forward to take notes. "What's the toughest thing you've had to do?"

For the next half-hour Mr. Halper rolled out his litany of hard tasks and I felt my eyes glaze over. He spent fifteen minutes on how to get a refrigerator up four flights of stairs to apartment 4A and another on the plumbing problem in 2D.

More out of boredom than as part of my role, I made squiggle marks on the pad. At one point he looked at the pad and pointed.

"You're not writing words."

"Yes I am." I held up the pad. "This is journalistic shorthand. That's to insure that I don't miss a thing."

He leaned back. His impressed look said it was time to ask for a favor. "Say, Mr. Halper. Do you think I could take a look at Angel's apartment?"

Worry creased his already lined face. "The police said not to let anyone into 6B." He tapped his fingers on the table, then sighed. "I'd like to, but, it's, it's the law."

"That's too bad. It could really help with my story," I fibbed.

His face brightened. "Her family is coming to move her stuff into storage Thursday. Maybe you could ask them?"

From his attitude I knew then that he couldn't be budged, so I agreed. "Excellent idea." I stood. "Thanks for all the information and the coffee. I'll be back Thursday to talk to her relatives if I can make it." I slipped the pad into my pocket and offered my hand. "Will you be available for a follow-up interview if I need one?"

He pumped my hand vigorously with both of his. "Certainly, Mr. Ruse. Certainly."

I left his apartment and walked down the hall to the building's front door. A quick push threw open the door then I turned and ran back up the stairs toward 6B before the front door slammed.

It took me a full five seconds for my latexed-gloved hands and a quick-pick gun to open the locks on Angel's door. I slid inside and softly closed the door behind me.

My first impression was that I'd died and gone to pastel heaven. Soft pinks and blues abounded, with white and pale greens for decoration on the plethora of pillows. It was like falling into a little girl's birthday cake complete with the sweet smell. I opened the window and checked out the fire escape. With safe egress assured, I searched the apartment.

My early training taught me to look for the obvious, then double check it. I moved couches, chairs, looked for secret hiding places in lamps and table legs, and kept an eye out for anything odd or out of place. Except for a Tic-Tac that had rolled behind a stuffed chair and twenty-six cents in change under the couch cushions, I found nothing.

Angel's bedroom offered more of the same. Fluffy duvets and stuffed animals seemed to be the theme around her four-poster canopied bed. The dresser and closet held nothing out of the ordinary, the bathroom the same.

The top drawer of the night table held a variety of hair bands, lotions, and a box of tissues. The second drawer held a book clip-on reading lamp, several pink, fine-point pens, and a black book with "Holy Bible" embossed on the front in large gold lettering. I started to close the drawer, then stopped and stared.

Pens.

No paper.

It didn't click. I picked up the Bible and flipped it open. Pretty cursive handwriting covered dated pages.

A diary.

Using the Bible cover overlay showed she obviously didn't trust someone, or possibly it was just a girl's secret desire to hide something very personal.

I slipped the diary into my pocket and headed for the safety of the fire-escape and the serenity of the bar.

Chapter 26

It was still early afternoon when I pulled up to the bar. Becky stood on the curb, eyes trained on the bar's big plate-glass window, face shining with excitement. Two workers were pulling off the masking tape around gold lettering outlined in black. The large word "BAR" was painted in the center with "Hope's Province" in smaller letters curved above it. A small "Quinn, Proprietor" rested at the bottom. What caught my eye were the three-inch-high letters under the giant "BAR" characters that read "– No Grill."

I got out of the car and walked to Becky.

She gave me a brief hug, and then turned back to the window, keeping an arm around my waist. "Doesn't it look terrific?"

"Looks super," I said. "No Grill?"

A grin popped on her face. "That's an homage to Dad. I went with that rather than the 'booze – no bread' line he used to quip." She looked up at the old "Tavern" sign. "That gets replaced on Monday." Her face became wistful. "I'll almost miss it."

She gave me a squeeze. "How was your day?"

I squeezed back, enjoying the way we fit together, either face to face, or side by side. "Successful. I accomplished more than I'd hoped for."

She turned and looked into my eyes, her shoulders tense. "Any trouble dumping those two... bags of garbage?"

I saw the look of unease cross her face and chose to ignore it. "None. Everything went as planned. We'll discuss it inside."

"Good." The tension left her body and she gestured to the window. "This calls for a drink."

"Sounds great," I said.

"Sounds wonderful," said the older, stick-thin worker. "We'll be right in."

Becky stepped away from me, propped her fists on her hips and leaned forward. "And why do you think you deserve a drink, Mr. Hennessy?"

He tilted a palm toward the window. "Spelled everything right didn't we? And a difficult chore it was."

"Pure luck, no doubt." Becky grinned. "But luck deserves saluting. When you're finished, come on in." She looked down at the younger man who was kneeling and putting the lids on the paint cans. "Jimmy. You old enough to have a beer yet?"

The freckled-face boy looked up. "Certainly, Ms. Quinn."

Hennessy glared down. "You're drinking Coke and will be glad you're getting it, Jimmy O'Brien." He smiled at Becky. "Jimmy's just shy of legal, but that doesn't stop him from pretending." He looked up at the window. "Your Da's looking down and smiling, lass. You've done him proud."

"Thanks, Mr. Hennessy. See you inside." Becky took my arm and we entered the empty, snug sanctuary of Coors and camaraderie.

She walked behind the bar and started pouring a Guinness.

"How do you know Mr. Hennessy will want a Guinness?"

Becky shot me a "duh" look. "First of all, he's Irish."

I perched on a barstool. "And second?"

She smiled as Hennessy and Jimmy entered. "There is no second."

A chuckle escaped my lips and I turned at Mr. Hennessy's sigh.

He pulled off his newsboy tweed hat, closed his eyes and inhaled deeply. "Ah... There's nothing like a quiet pub to soothe a troubled soul."

"You're a man after my own heart, Mr. Hennessy," I said.

He sat next to me, eyes on the Guinness. "It's not your heart I'm after, lad, but this beer." He raised the glass. "Sláinte!"

Becky slid a coke and a bowl of pretzels down to Jimmy, and poured a Johnny Walker Black for me.

Hennessy took a deep drink and sighed with pleasure. "T'was many the time I'd sit here and discuss life with Becky's dad, Connor. A deep thinking, philosophical man was Connor."

"Really?" I asked and sipped my JWB.

Hennessy nodded. "Yes. But always saw the practical side of everything as well." He looked at Becky. "Remember when that German fellow came in?"

Becky's smiled widened. "We never did know why he wandered in."

Hennessy turned to me. "This German fellow comes in, strides to the bar, raps twice with his cane and says something in German. Connor, now, he doesn't take kindly to raps on his mahogany and takes his time strolling over. 'What can I get you?' he asks. Well, this man lets out a string of German and points to the door. Connor just shrugs and says, 'Sorry. I don't speak German.'"

Hennessy turned, leaned back, propped his elbow against the bar, and sipped his beer, the enjoyment of tale-telling evident on his face. "The man then rattles off something in Spanish. Connor shrugs again in that way he had, and says, 'Sorry. I don't speak Spanish.' The German is getting frustrated. He switches to French and asks another question. Well Connor does it again. 'Sorry,' he says. 'I don't speak French.'" Hennessy chuckled. "The German's face goes red and he storms out of the bar."

Hennessy gestured to Becky with his beer. "This young lass is sitting in a corner booth, doing her homework and pipes up, 'Say, Dad. Maybe we should learn another language.'

"Connor gives another one of his elegant shrugs and says, 'What for? That German knows three and none of them did him any good.'"

I laughed and watched Becky's face glow with the memory of her father. "Thanks for sharing that story, Mr. Hennessy. Let me buy you another and you can tell me more about Connor Quinn."

He finished off his drink and plopped the empty glass on the bar. "I'd love to, but we've got another job we should be doing." He slid off the barstool and nodded to Becky. "Thank you for standing me the 'round, lass." He put on his hat and stared at Jimmy, who was stuffing pretzels into his mouth. "Lad?"

Jimmy mumbled something that sounded like "thanks" and headed to the door with Mr. Hennessy.

"I think I would have liked your dad," I said.

Becky nodded. "He would have liked you, once he got over the fact that you were sleeping with his daughter."

I snorted. "Would I have had to face the shotgun?"

"No. Worse. You would have had to face the stare. His stare looked as though it could call down the lightening. It was more powerful than any shotgun."

"I bet you saw it many times."

She tilted her head. "A few. It only took a few before I learned not to let him find out about whatever I'd done."

She came around the bar and kissed me on the cheek. "You said you had a successful day. What happened?"

I pulled Angel's diary from my pocket and held it up.

Becky took a quick step back. "Oh, God. You've found religion."

"What?" I glanced at golden letters on the cover. "Oh. Sorry." I flipped the book open. "No. It's Angel's diary, hidden in a Bible cover."

Becky stared at the book for a second, then reached for it with a shaking hand. "This is probably the last thing she wrote." She held the book and slowly stroked a hand over the cover. "It feels wrong to be reading something so personal of hers."

"Like violating her privacy?"

"Kind of." Becky opened the diary and turned a few pages. "It's Angel's handwriting alright. She always put little hearts over the i's." She looked down at the book and pursed her lips. "I'm torn between reading Angel's personal thoughts and wanting to read it right now to see if she's named her killer."

I glanced at my watch. "The bar opens in fifteen minutes. Perhaps it would be better to wait 'til we get home and can read it in private.

She nodded and held out the book. "You're right. I'm just…"

I placed the book in my pocket.

She looked up at me and sighed. "But, you're right. We'll wait." Becky blew out a breath and walked back behind the bar. "How about getting me a keg of draft from the storeroom?"

"If you promise to get naked."

Her eyes twinkled a moment, then she whipped off her T-shirt and reached for the button on her jeans.

"I don't mean now!" I shot a quick glance at the front door. "I meant later!"

Laughing, she slipped the shirt back on. "Jeez, Jack, you're so easy."

Chapter 27

After closing time, we decided to retire to my place, dig into Angel's diary, and sleep in. At two in the morning, Route 65 was empty and the chugging bar van made it to my house in good time.

I unlocked my front door, pushed it open and stepped back. "*A ghrá mo chroí*," I said.

A cross between pleasure and surprise lit Becky's face. She placed a hand on my shoulder and stared into my eyes. "What did you say?"

"*A ghrá mo chroí*," I repeated. "You said it meant, 'Come in. And welcome.'"

A small smile replaced the surprise and she stroked my cheek. "Right. I'd forgotten."

She entered the house and I followed, making a mental note to Google that bit of Irish.

"Let's work in the kitchen," I said. "The table is big enough and I can whip us up some food if you're hungry."

"You can cook? You're a man of many talents, Jack."

"True." I opened the refrigerator and took out a container. "But my culinary talents consist of reheating takeout." I plopped the contents of the container in a pot and fired up the burner.

"What is that? It looks good."

I nodded. "Best Irish stew in town." I gave the stew a stir. "I get it from the Kosher Irishman over on Belleview. Best Philly cheese steaks in the area, too."

"Irish stew and Philly cheese steaks? Sounds like a diversity delight."

I nodded. "You should try their blintzes sometime. Your mouth will be praising Allah in Yiddish."

Becky raised an eyebrow. "Somehow I doubt that."

I pointed to the stew. "Give that a stir every once in a while and get down some bowls. I'll get some paper and pencils."

In the den, I grabbed a couple of empty notebooks and some pens. As an afterthought, I took the large calendar off the wall and searched through my desk for colored markers I knew I had somewhere.

Becky spooned the stew into two bowls when I returned. The table was set with silverware and folded linen napkins I didn't remember I had. I sat down and spread my hands. "What, no beautiful centerpiece?"

She brought the bowls to the table, sat, then reached across with her spoon. The spoon dove into my bowl, extracted a carrot hunk, then dumped it in the center of the table. "There. Stare at that and pretend it's a beautiful centerpiece."

"I'd rather stare at you," I said.

She smiled around a mouthful of stew. "You can show me the master bedroom–"

I started to stand.

"–later."

She tucked into the stew with gusto as did I. After scraping down to the bottom of the bowl, Becky sat back and sighed. "Ahhh. That *was* good." She gestured at the calendar. "What's that for?"

"I thought we could timeline Angel's activities."

Becky nodded. "If you have a city map we can coordinate her movements as well."

"Good idea." I rose and retrieved one from my desk. When I returned, Becky had cleared the table and had her nose buried in Angel's diary. I tossed the map on the table and sat.

"Angel started a new diary every year," said Becky, "so there are only a few months of notes."

"It might be enough."

"Listen to this. Her first page is a poem." Becky cleared her throat and read.

"Another year, another day.
Brush aside what thoughts may say,
Follow your heart you must to cope,
And minute by minute build a mountain of hope."

"It's hard to imagine someone being so positive about life. Or was she just naïve?" I asked.

"No. Not naïve. Just sweet."

She lowered the book and stared at me, her eyes going cold. "Now let's find her killer."

Chapter 28

We stared at the calendar and map pinned to the wall in my kitchen. We had plotted all of Angel's movements and her work schedule. The overlaid colored lines were thick from her city hall office at the DEP to her home, with a few lines scattered elsewhere.

"Angel must have shopped on her way home," I said. "I'll match her route and ask questions of store owners along the way."

Frustrated, I blew out a stream of air. I'd hoped that Angel's diary would give me a name that I could track down, but she only wrote an initial when mentioning people. It felt odd reading a dead woman's intimate wishes and dreams, but as I read, I got a better handle on Angel Anderson.

Her diary painted a picture of a woman with aspirations, hopes – and worries. But her glowing optimism always made the worries seem small and unimportant when compared to the beauty of life. Her concern for the welfare of others permeated all the entries.

Angel, it seemed, was indeed aptly named.

Becky grunted as she stared at her notes. "I never knew she worked at the soup kitchen twice a week. She was never one to blow her own horn." She shook her head and tapped the pad. "The only thing suspicious is these two entries. *'D asked me out again. He was insistent, but it still doesn't feel right. I said no.'* Two weeks later she writes, *'D asked me out yet again. He stood close to me this time, almost intimidating.'"*

"D," I said. "It could be a first or last name." I glanced at the diary. "The first entry is on a Tuesday, the next on a Saturday. We can't narrow it down to someone at her work. 'Who' is going to be tough to track down."

Becky nodded and pushed aside her notepad. "Yeah... but I feel..."

I touched her arm. "What?"

She shrugged. "Oh. I don't know."

"Intuition is a valuable resource. If you feel something, give."

She looked up. "If Angel thought this guy didn't feel 'right,' he must have been a scumbag. Not feeling right would be her harshest criticism of someone."

I scratched a big "D" at the top of the map in red magic marker. "All right. We'll make this 'D' a primary target and gather more intel." I tapped the pen on the map. "We can't forget the Dragons either. I think I'll touch base with Monica Brown again and ask about the two buttheads we tagged and bagged."

"Might be risky."

"I doubt it. The ex-gangbangers surrounding her are all tame."

Becky put her hands on her hips. "I meant risky for her. I don't like the way she looks at you."

I leaned forward and peered into her eyes. "Huh! The color of your eyes changed from blue to green."

She shut those affected orbs. "Sorry, Jack." She shook her head. "The green monster just grabs me by the throat sometimes and I react."

I placed a hand on her arm and leaned forward. "Ah. The blue is back. I like that much better than green." I slid my hand down to hers and squeezed. "Listen. You're for me. If that ever changes, I swear I'll let you know up front."

Becky let out a big breath and nodded.

"Of course, I'll be letting you know by phone while I'm incognito and living in another country."

"I'll just track you down." She squeezed my hand back. "Never fear."

"But that would make me fear, so it negates your 'Never fear.'"

Her eyes scrunched. "What?"

"Never mind." I waved a hand and folded the map. "Since the diary didn't give us the killer, I guess it's time for private detective Joe Hawkshaw to interview everyone in Angel's world."

Becky tilted her head. "Joe Hawkshaw? Would he be a friend of Daniel Ruse?"

"Yep. Could pass for twins, but Joe dresses better."

"Think people will open up to a gumshoe, no matter how well dressed?"

"I think so. I'll let them know that I'm working for her family and they would like closure on Angel's death."

"Should work." Becky stretched and yawned. "I'm tired. Let's go to bed."

"Ahhh. Super suggestion." I rose.

Becky held up a hand. "I mean to *just* sleep."

"Just sleep with a woman." I stroked my chin. "Novel idea. Might give it a try."

Becky smiled. "There's always the morning."

I grabbed her hand and led her to the bedroom. "Then let's sleep fast."

Chapter 29

Early Monday morning, I hit the streets. My first stop was Cameron's Coffee Shoppe, the closest store to Angel's apartment. As I opened the door, the wonderful smells of coffee and sweet baked goods flooded my olfactory nerves. I stopped in the doorway of the almost-empty store, closed my eyes and just inhaled the marvelous aroma.

"Smells just like momma used to make, eh?" said a gray-haired man behind the counter.

"My mother never made anything that smelled that good." I walked to the counter and handed my "Joe Hawkshaw – Private Investigator" card to the man dressed as all bakers should be – white shirt, pants, and full white apron.

The man read the card, frowned and handed it back. "I can't help you." He crossed his arms, and gave me a 'get out stare.'

I nodded. "I get that, but let me tell you why I'm here." I slipped the card back into my pocket. "I've been retained by the family of Angel Anderson."

The man's demeanor changed in an instant. His hard stare turned to one of grief for a moment, then back to hard. He pointed to a table against the wall. "Go. Sit. I'll bring you a cup of coffee."

I did as he asked and within moments he headed my way, cup of coffee in his hand. He stopped at the entrance to the back and shouted. "Ginny, come take the counter."

A small, pretty, twenty-something woman emerged from the back, wiping the flour from her hands on her apron. Her long red hair was colored with blue at the tips. My gaze slid to the row of studded earrings marching down her ear, amazed that such a delicate ear could hold so many piercings. My observation stopped as the baker sat down across from me.

"What does Angel's family want?" he asked.

I lifted my cup. "The same thing we all want. Her killer."

He reached a hand across the table. "Gabe Cameron." We shook hands. "How can I help?"

I gave him the answer I had rehearsed in the car. "Angel's family is dismayed at the lack of progress the police have made in the hunt for her murderer. They've asked me to see if I can help expedite their investigation."

"Expedite hell!" He banged his hand on the table, causing the cups to jump. "I want you to squeeze the life out of that bastard."

"It may come to that, but first I have to find out who did it."

Gabe relaxed and nodded. "Yeah. Sorry for the outburst, but Angel was something special." He shook his head. "She's like my Ginny. When she came in the door, she brought sunshine in with her."

"Can you tell me anything about her? If she came in with anyone, if anyone seemed to be bothering or following her?"

Gabe pursed his lips, then shook his head. "No. She came in here most every morning, ordered a caramel macchiato to go. Occasionally, she'd sit with Ginny if we were slow and Angel was early." He shook his head again. "She was a beautiful person. Sorry. I can't tell you more." He glanced over to Ginny, who was bagging a loaf of Italian bread for a heavyset woman. "Hey, Ginny. When you're done, come sit with Mr. Hawkshaw, here. I'll take the counter."

Ginny rang up the sale, turned, slid a bagel through the cutter, and headed my way. Gabe left. Ginny plunked a plated sesame seed bagel and a small plastic tub of cream cheese down in front of me, then sat. She did seem to bring sunshine with her.

"You look like you missed breakfast this morning."

"You must be a mind reader," I said, and slattered my bagel with the cream cheese."

Her bright smile and lively eyes erased my opinion of anyone who would wear that many earrings. She became a very easy-to-look-at woman with great green eyes, and sparkling personality. She reminded me a lot of Angel.

"I overheard you talking to my dad about Angel."

"Yeah. I'm trying to get a handle on her life, who was in it, and who might want to harm her." I took a bite of my bagel and my taste-buds thanked me.

Ginny's eyes narrowed and her teeth clenched. "Angel was a sweet person. Never a bad word for anyone, never a cross look."

"Were you two close?"

She shook her head. "Not so much. We had lunch together whenever I brought lunches over to her building. We'd talk about girl stuff, mostly."

"Girl stuff?"

"You know, guys, jobs, the classes we took – girl stuff."

"Can you tell me about these guys? Anyone special?"

"No. Not since she broke up with Ben. There might have been a group date with friends, but nothing serious." Her face grew thoughtful and she tapped a purple-swirled fingernail on the table. "Listen. Angel was a good woman. A friend. The nicest person I ever knew. Don't think that she might be the victim of her wild ways. Or any crap like that."

I nodded. "Thanks. I'll keep that in mind." I finished my coffee. "Can you tell me anything else that might help track down the monster that killed her?"

Ginny thought for a moment, then shook her head. "No. Sorry."

I stood. "Thanks." I waved to Gabe on my way out.

Continuing to masquerade as private detective Joe Hawkshaw, I canvassed the route Angel walked to work. At diners, boutiques, bodegas, and the soup kitchen, I flashed her photo and asked questions. I didn't even have to use the "family closure" bit much. Everyone wanted to see her killer behind bars. People always smiled when they talked about Angel. Their smiles always turned to outrage that her sweet nature and sunny attitude had been taken from them.

Though people were willing to talk, no one knew a damn thing.

I flopped into my rented car and loosened my tie. So far, it had been a frustrating day with nothing to show for my efforts but a pair of sore feet in wing-tipped shoes. Now I knew why the P.I.s wore gumshoes, and thought seriously about switching. It wouldn't look as classy, but certainly would be more comfortable.

I started the car and cruised for a parking spot near the cluster of official city buildings. The idea that Angel's death might be somehow connected to a DEP investigation crossed my mind. There was a ton of money in toxic cleanup and more in keeping a hazardous dump site hushed. The brutality of her murder didn't fit a DEP cover-up, but maybe the brutality was a red herring. If that were true, how were the Eastside Dragons connected? The questions circled in my mind as I circled the block.

After ten minutes, I gave up looking for a free spot and pulled into a parking garage near Angel's office. My smile and "thank you" wasn't returned by Kia, the oblivious, sour-faced little female Napoleon manning the booth.

I parked and headed to the walkway that connected with the Spencer Building, the twenty-story high-rise that held Angel's office. I passed a score of hurrying people along the way, any of whom could be Angel's killer. How do you find a single drop of water in a rushing river?

Negative feelings crowded my head, and I shook them off and scanned the marquee in the busy lobby. The building held dozens of city departments, councilmen's offices, and of course, the law firms that go hand-in-hand with government. The DEP had offices on the eighth floor.

I crammed into the elevator with a herd of folks dressed in everything from construction garb to five-hundred-dollar suits. Typically, no one spoke and everyone stared at the changing floor numbers.

The eighth-floor doors opened directly into the office of the DEP and I stepped out into a small reception area. A hard-faced, nail-chewing blonde receptionist manned the desk. The smile that curved her lips didn't extend to her cold, dead eyes. Knowing that this might be a hard sell, I put on my best grin.

"Good afternoon–" I glanced down at the "Barbara Poell" placard centered prominently on her desk like a barrier. "Hi Barbara," I said and fished out a fake card. "I would like to speak to Angel Anderson's supervisor."

At Angel's name, her demeanor hardened even more. "I'm sorry, it's appointment only." She ignored the card and raised her head in dismissal. I was surprised that the stick up her ass allowed her that much flexibility.

"I'm here on behalf of her grieving family," I said in my most sympathetic tones.

"Sorry, Sir." She said "Sir," but pronounced it "cur." "But as I said, it's appointment only." She glanced down at her desk. "The next opening is in five weeks."

My muscles bunched, torn between retreating or choking the living hell out of her. While the latter would certainly be satisfying, it would be counter-productive.

I looked into her eyes and tried another smile. "Is there any way to shorten the wait?"

"No." She sniffed, turned, and busied herself at her keyboard.

Those few seconds I had looked into her eyes revealed her ugly attitude and uglier soul. To her, the world held her back. The pressure against her self-imagined glass ceiling had ruptured her spleen and spread bile through her heart and mind. There was nothing I could say that would make her life any worse than the hell she had created for herself, so I bit my tongue.

"Thank you so much for your time," I said, trying not to let sarcasm seep into my words.

A blue-suited older man opened the door to the inner sanctum and headed for the elevator.

"Have a nice lunch, Mr. Barrett," chirped the receptionist. She sent him a fake smile but he ignored her.

The doors opened and I joined the man in the elevator.

"Lobby?" asked the thin, grey-haired guy as the doors closed.

"Might as well," I sighed

He snorted and shook his head. "Did the Sentinel give you a hard time?"

"No harder than she gives herself."

The man tilted his head and stared at me. "Very perceptive."

"Have to be in my line of work."

"Which is?"

I handed him my card and his eyebrows rose as he read it. "Private detective, eh?" He handed me back the card and sly grin touched his lips. "Someone cheating on his wife?"

"Always." I pocketed my card. "But I'm not interested it that today. I've been retained by the family of Angel Anderson."

"Angel?" His smile dropped and his brows crashed together as anger filled his face. "Damn shame about her. Can't imagine anyone wanting to hurt her." The anger faded away and he shook his head and sighed. "I didn't know her well, but her presence always lit up the office."

The elevator doors opened and we stepped out. As we avoided the onrush of people, he grabbed my arm. "Say, did you tell Barbara you were there inquiring about Angel?"

"Yes."

"That bitch. She disliked Angel, probably 'cause everyone liked Angel and no one likes Barbara." He held up his hand. "Hold on a second," he said, and pulled out a cell phone. After a single push of a button, it was against his ear.

"Say, Don. It's Larry – Yeah, sure. No, I'm down here in the lobby with a private detective named Joe Hawkshaw. He's been sent by Angel Anderson's family. Barbara gave him the boot." Larry was silent for a moment. "Doesn't matter. I'd like you to talk with him." More silence. "No. Today. Good. Thanks." He pocketed his cell. "Don was Angel's supervisor. He'll clear you through the door dragon."

I reached out my hand. "Thanks, Larry. I really appreciate it."

"Sorry about Barbara," he said as we shook. "She's a real piece of work. If she wasn't related to someone, she wouldn't be here."

"Nepotism in government?" I said. "I'm shocked."

He laughed and nodded. "Yeah. Just don't mention it to Don when you see him – he's her uncle."

"Will do," I said and headed back to the elevator, glad I didn't have to find a back door to Angel's offices, though my mind had already envisioned doing a Spider Man number eight stories up.

After the short ride, the doors opened and it was déjà vu all over again with one difference. An older, pudgy man with tie askew and sleeves rolled up to his elbows stood in the inner office's doorway. "Joe?" he asked.

"Yes. Joe Hawkshaw." I extended my hand. A firm grip belied his flab.

"Don Kramer. Come on in."

I didn't look at Barbara Poell, but felt the waves of hatred and anger pulsing from her like an exposed angry heart beating black blood. I shook off the bad vibes, but was glad when Don led me into his office.

"Have a seat." Loose glass rattled as he closed the ancient door. "I understand you are investigating the death of Angel Anderson." He plopped into an old swivel chair behind his desk.

"Yes, I am."

He sat forward, and leaned on the desk. His hands found a paperclip and proceeded to twist its practical form into modern art. "Don't you think that's something for the police to handle?"

"Her family is frustrated at the lack of progress on the case, and has asked me to look into the matter."

Though it wasn't that hot in the office, a bead of sweat formed on his upper lip. "I've told the police all I know." He tossed the wire mess into the trash and reached for another. "I'm sorry, but I can't divulge any of her ongoing cases to you."

My bullshit meter was veering into the red zone. I spread my hands and sent him a placating smile. "I totally understand, Mr. Kramer. This was a crime of passion. I'm sure it had nothing to do with her work."

His hands stopped.

"I'm just looking into her background, her friends, who she was dating, documenting the nice things that people say about her for her family."

He sat back and the tension left his shoulders. "Well, Angel was a nice gal, and a fine worker. Always had top marks on her evaluations, was rarely late, and her paperwork was very neat." He leaned forward again, propping his arms on the desk. "We're going to miss her around here. We're understaffed as it is."

Chapter 30

After a few more questions, I left Don Kramer's office with permission to talk to Angel's peers and the admonishment: *"But keep it brief. We're very busy around here."*

The handful of people in Angel's department chatted up a storm, but no one told me anything I didn't know. I did notice that nobody seemed to care about how much of their time I took, and no one looked "very busy." They all worked with bureaucratic glacier speed. I glanced at Don Kramer's office as I left. Something was wrong there.

I thought about sending Barbara Poell my "I'll be back to cut your throat" look, but decided ignoring her would bother her more. I whistled as I waited for the elevator and could feel her laser eyes burning into my back. The elevator door opened and I grinned and entered.

An older lady stood next to the button panel. "Floor?" she asked.

The ground floor button was lit. "Ground's good," I said.

She looked me over as I did her. Carefully coifed hair, inexpensive beige suit, and fake pearls. I pegged her as having many years as a secretary under her belt.

"You must have had a good meeting at the DEP," she said.

I tilted my head. "Good call. How did you know?"

She flicked a hand at the door. "Very few people come out of there smiling. The DEP can be a costly place."

"Very observant," I said.

She jerked her head down once. "Pays to be. Not many people are, these days."

"True. Tell me, how long have you been a secretary?"

She straightened. "Humph. I see you can be observant as well." She punched the "G" button again several times, as if it would make the elevator go faster, then turned back to me. "I'm an administrative assistant for the city planning board."

I smiled and just looked at her.

Her ramrod demeanor softened and she smiled back. "But I did spend twenty years as a secretary right here in this building."

"And now you've moved up to administrative assistant. Good for you."

"Well, after my kids were grown I needed to do something useful with my time." Her eyes squinted. "Tell me, young man. Does the elevator sound funny or is that your stomach?"

I looked down as my stomach growled louder. "It's me." I patted the culprit. "Sorry about that."

"No need to be sorry. It's a natural bodily function. If people would stop worrying about being politically correct, there'd be fewer communication failures, I say." She jerked her head down once again. "You should fill your stomach. The Spencer Building boasts the Rose and Crown restaurant on the ground floor. Good, honest food at a good price." The head jerk happened again. "That's where I'm headed."

My mind spun with possibilities. Twenty years in the building. Twenty years of gossip. "That sounds terrific." I glanced at the lighted buttons across the top of the elevator, then back to her. "Do you mind if I join you?"

Her hand touched her chest and a delighted smile flashed over her face. "With me?" The delight faded and her eyes hardened again. "Are you selling something?"

"No, Ma'am." I pulled a card from the breast pocket of my suit and handed it to her. "Joe Hawkshaw, private detective."

She studied the card then studied me through narrowed eyes. "Prying into people's private lives is a disagreeable business."

"Yes, but it also can do some good." She stared at me for a moment and I knew the instant I passed her test.

"You can try to convince me of that over my tuna melt." My card disappeared into her purse.

The doors opened and I held her elbow and gestured outward. "Please, lead the way."

After the short wait to be seated, we were escorted to a booth. The waitress arrived as we settled. She gave me the once over and smiled, then nodded to my lunch date. "Hi, Marilyn. Coffee and a tuna melt?"

Marilyn nodded once. "Why change a good thing?"

"I'll have the same," I said, though I hated tuna.

The waitress scribbled on her pad, and gave another sly smile to Marilyn. "Be right up," she said as she left.

"I'm sure you observed the waitress's attitude toward us," I said. "She thinks we're an item."

Marilyn jerked in her seat. "That's ridiculous. Why I'm old enough to be your mo – older sister." Her eyes strayed to the departing waitress and her hand flew to the faux pearls hanging from her neck. "You really think so?"

"Absolutely."

"Good! My reputation needs a little gloss." Her smile said she was pleased on many levels. "We should be properly introduced then, since we're an item." She reached a hand across the table. "My name is Marilyn Colmbes."

Her grip was stronger than I expected. "Joe Hawkshaw."

"Now, Mr. Hawkshaw." She unfolded a paper napkin and placed it on her lap. "You can explain to me how your business can be anything but unpleasant."

"Please. Call me Joe."

For the next half-hour and halfway through our tuna melts, I related a few "Magnum P.I." reruns I'd seen while on a stakeout in Bulgaria. With the Magnum theme music playing in my head, I made myself the hero of the story. Marilyn nodded through the tales, listening to every word.

"And now I'm working for the family of a murdered woman. The police seem stymied. The family wants closure for their much-loved child."

Marilyn's eyes changed from listening mode to bright sparks. "The woman who worked at the DEP. Angel Anderson."

I nodded.

"I didn't know her, but any murder is a deed most foul." She reached across the table and patted my hand. "I know you'll find her killer."

"Why, thank you for your confidence."

"You're observant. That alone will fill in the pieces." She sipped the last of her coffee. "That and the little grey cells."

"Grey cells?" My mind pictured octogenarian terrorist groups.

At my blank look her brow furrowed. "Agatha Christie? Hercule Poirot? The fictional Belgian detective who used the little gray cells in his brain to find criminals instead of fists and guns?" She sighed. "What do schools teach these days?"

"Ah. " Understanding filtered through my concepts. "I don't believe I've ever read Dame Christie's work."

"You should. It might help expand your deductive horizons." She leaned back. "I wish the police had used some of Poirot's cleverness to find Betty Pepperdyne." She waggled a finger in my direction. "I never met your Angel Anderson, but I knew Betty."

"Betty Pepperdyne?"

"Yes. Almost two years ago now. Betty disappeared on her way home from here. Some said she ran off with a man her family disapproved of, but I knew Betty. She would never do that."

That blast of information filled my head like a bright light. "Tell me more about Betty."

Through the rest of lunch Marilyn spoke about Betty, shifting between happy memories and anger at her disappearance.

I reached for the check as did Marilyn. "Please," I said. "Allow me."

"No." Her tone spoke of her independence. She opened her pocketbook, withdrew a smaller clasp bag, and then some bills. "Thank you for your offer, but I must decline." She laid down the bills, added some coins, and we stood.

I did some quick math. She had paid her half of the bill plus exactly fifteen percent. I matched the amount. "Thank you, Marilyn, for a most enjoyable lunch."

"You're quite welcome, Joe." She smiled a knowing smile. "And you're much more handsome than that Tom Seleck fellow."

I lowered my head and grinned. As the waitress came to collect the bill, I leaned in and kissed Marilyn on the cheek. "Thanks. I hope to see you again."

As I left the cafeteria, Marilyn was still standing there, hand raised to her cheek.

Chapter 31

As I headed to the library, I thought about what I'd learned from Marilyn.

Betty Pepperdyne.

Another clue or a side track? I took the steps two at a time and flashed on the library of my youth. I remembered spending many hours as a kid immersed in musty books, wondering if I'd ever visit the fabulous lands described. Now I wish I had never seen those places. Action novels describe the blue sky and the hearty adventure, but not the blood, filth and fear. The term "adventure" means reading about someone else, far away, in deep shit.

I hit the free internet computers first and searched for Betty Pepperdyne. There was little about her disappearance that made the web. My next stop was the microfiche department.

I retrieved back issues of the *Post* and started my search. After two hours and a growing headache, a picture of Betty Pepperdyne stared out at me. There wasn't much coverage of the story. A missing girl doesn't draw readership the way a dead body does. Eighteen months earlier, Betty Pepperdyne left her job at the Commerce Commission on a Friday night and was never seen again.

The article described Betty as a vibrant person, well liked by everyone. The police had no leads and her family had offered a reward. Betty's picture burned into my eyeballs as I flicked off the machine and stood. There was nothing to connect her to Angel at all.

Nothing, except that she and Angel Anderson could pass as twins.

Chapter 32

As it was still early, I drove to Monica Brown's "Soaring Free Halfway House."

On the way over, thoughts of Betty Pepperdyne swirled in my mind and I wondered how much I should tell Becky. She should be kept in the loop, but I couldn't decide if it would help or muck up her thinking. Her perspective was needed and I decided to withhold this until the proper time. Then the visualization of her thanking me for holding back was quickly erased with the visualization of her kneeing me in the groin. I'd better tell her.

The halfway house was a small brick two-story building in a rundown neighborhood on the edge of the gang's turf. I parked in front of the building and got out of the car. A logo hung in the window, the white outline of a flying bird on an azure blue background, the words "Soaring Free" at the bottom.

Another fool trying to make a difference. I stopped and shook my head. That was my usual pessimistic thinking and Becky would slap me for being such a cynical bastard. If Monica Brown was making a contribution in fixing society's ills she certainly was going about it differently than I had.

Cigarette hanging from his lip, a thirteen-year-old wanabee tough guy in jeans and ragged shirt leaned up against the chipped brick front and eyed the car.

"Nice ride, playa." He blew smoke toward me. "Think it be here when you come out?"

"It's a rental, but if it's here when I come out, you get a Jackson." With a shrug I glanced back at the car. "If it's not –" I let my jacket swing open and watched his eyes drift to the Sig in my shoulder holster. "– I'll be angry."

He tossed the cigarette down. "Shiiit. You a cop?"

"Nope. Which means I don't follow rules." I grabbed the building's worn door handle. "All the more reason to earn your Jackson."

Rap music assaulted my ears as I entered a twenty by twenty room. A few male and female youths sat on a worn couch against the wall smoking and drinking Cokes from an ice chest. Several others kids were scattered around the room. The sound of pool balls clacking and the bouncing of a basketball jumped out as the music cut off. A second later, even those sounds stopped.

All eyes were on me as I walked to the center of the room. The largest hulk of male rose from the couch and swaggered toward me. "Hey. You got no bidness here."

With a crooked "Bulls" ball cap, sleeveless Gold's Gym tee and his pants hanging six-inches below his blue plaid boxer shorts, he looked the part of a tough gangbanger, but the ridiculous image just made me grin. "I'm here to see Monica Brown."

His face tightened and he flexed his free-weight buffed arms. "Nobody messes wid Ms. Brown." He jabbed a finger into my chest. "You hear?"

I grabbed his hand, twisted, and pushed him down on his knees in a wrist lock. "Your willingness to protect Ms. Brown is laudable, but misplaced." I leaned closed and whispered in his ear. "First find out who your real enemy is, then make a plan. Don't let bravado push you too soon." I released his wrist, then held out a hand to help him up. "I'm not your enemy." My words of wisdom and attitude struck home, or maybe it was the pain in his wrist. Either way, he accepted my hand and rose.

"DeShawn!" Monica stood halfway down the second floor steps, a frown on her lovely face. "What do you think you're doing?" Her frown deepened. "Haven't we talked about this before? Apologize at once!"

DeShawn's shoulders slumped and he looked at the ground.

"It's alright, Ms. Brown," I said. "Deshawn only wanted to protect. That's a worthy goal." I nodded to DeShawn. "While commendable, he simply went about it without the correct information and a firm plan."

He looked up at me, his face contorted with puzzlement. "Who you be, man?"

"It's Mr. Phil Morris," said Monica. Her lips favored me with a slight smile, but her eyes were suspicious. "Are you here to make another donation, Mr. Morris?"

I tilted my head. "I am indeed."

Monica's face softened. "Then come up to my office." She turned and walked up the stairs. I followed.

Several file cabinets, stacks of paper, and two old folding chairs filled the small drab office. A laptop sat in the center of a worn metal desk.

"Please, Mr. Morris. Have a seat."

"Thank you." I glanced at the map on the wall for a second and studied the layout of red, yellow and green pins marking the Dragons territory, then took a seat.

Monica sat in the power position behind her desk and tented her fingers. "Are you really here to give another donation, or is the money just to prime me for more information?"

I opened my hands. "I don't see why they have to be mutually exclusive."

"Agreed."

I slipped a hand into my coat and withdrew a thick envelope. I rose and placed it on her desk then sat back down. "Same deal as before. The money is yours whether you decide to help me or not."

She stared down at the envelope. "Is it another thousand dollars?"

"No." I paused for effect. "It's two thousand."

She looked up and her eyes widened.

"Cash," I added.

"Humph. You must need some prime information."

"Not really. I'm just interested in two individuals. Ramon Williams and Akim Jackson."

"Ah. Diesel and Akim. I know those two." She glanced down at the envelope. "But I'm afraid I would be taking your money for nothing, Mr. Morris. It seems that Diesel and Akim have disappeared."

"Disappeared? Do you have any idea where they went?" I would have liked to tell her they went into a car crusher and were smooched to paste, but I didn't think she'd take that too well.

Monica tapped a finger on her desk. "Your interest in the Eastside Dragons is beginning to make sense now. It has gotten back to me that Diesel and Akim did illegal errands for anyone with money. No job was too dirty for those two. Procuring drugs for high rollers, breaking legs if that's what someone wanted and had the cash. I'm sure murder and blackmail were just..." She stopped and sat back in her chair. "Are you being blackmailed, Mr. Morris?"

The question was so absurd I threw back my head and laughed. "Blackmailed? Me? I'm not a candidate for blackmail." I grabbed at the line she tossed me and fabricated a tale. "It's possible others are, though."

"I see... Well, you – and those others – don't have to worry about those two, I believe."

"Why?"

"This is only a theory, but I think they decided to branch out on their own and cheated Juan Cruz Johnson out of his cut. Totally stupid. No one cheats Johnson. They knew that. Thinking they could hide their new wealth from him wasn't a smart idea."

Monica's face twisted in either hatred or pain when she spoke Johnson's name. He had hurt her or someone close to her. It explained her motivation. Since she wasn't the type to weaken his gang by violence, she'd do it by draining his resources. I had to admire her tactic.

Monica pursed her lips and shook her head. "I'm sure Diesel, Akim, and their fancy vehicle are at the bottom of Lake Michigan."

"So they were just errand boys for the highest bidder?"

"Yes, and not very smart ones, at that."

Errand boys. They could have been working for anyone when they dumped Angel's body. Damn. That widened the search.

"You don't seem very upset at society's loss," I said.

She snorted. "They were bottom feeders, Mr. Morris. Being food for Lake Michigan's aquatic bottom feeders can only be poetic justice."

I stood. "Thank you for the information, Ms. Brown. I appreciate it."

She rose as well. "I hope whoever you're working for will be satisfied with the information."

"Me? Working for someone? No. I'm just an interested civic bystander."

"Well thank you for your interest, Mr. Morris." She touched the envelope. "It's very needed."

"And well deserved." I held out a hand and we shook. "Goodbye, Ms. Brown."

I walked down the stairs and gave DeShawn a two finger salute as I left.

My thirteen-year-old street thug blocked the doorway. "Hey, man. You car OK." He held out a hand.

With my hand on his hip, I nudged him out of the way and walked to the car. "I already paid you."

Outrage blistered his face. "You lying sack of shit! I knowed you wasn't gonna pay me."

I turned and smiled. "Look in your right pocket."

His hand dove into his pocket and came out with a folded twenty dollar bill. His eyes widened and he looked up at me. "Damn, man. You good!"

"I know." I got in the car and drove away.

Chapter 33

It was after six by the time I finished up at 'Soaring Free' and returned to Becky's. Happy hour was in full swing. Becky worked the bar with that speed and efficiency I so much admired. A half-eaten pastrami-and-rye sandwich sat on a shelf behind the bar. I grinned at her white T-shirt with "Save the Ales" written in blue.

I plopped my paper bag on the bar and my butt on my bar stool. Becky glanced over and her smile said she was glad to see me. She mimed drinking and I nodded.

On her way over, she poured a draft beer for one customer and opened a bottle of Heineken for another. As she reached for the bottle of JWB, she spied the bag.

"Bring me a present?"

"Yep. Idaho pearls." I reached into the paper sack and laid a bag of potato chips on the bar. "Should go well with your pastrami."

"Thanks." The twinkle in her eye said the thought pleased her. The twinkle in her eye also pleased me. I never seemed to get used to the way her smile made me feel and was beginning to think I never would.

Becky finished pouring my JWB and grabbed the bag. "What else have you got in here?" She pulled out two paperbacks, stared at them, then stared at me with furrowed brows. "Hercule Poirot?"

I held up my hands. "Don't ask."

"I must. I must."

"Tell you about it on the way to my house after work. I also stopped to see Monica Brown and got some more info."

Becky frowned. "I'm beginning to hate her." She quick grinned then patted my arm. "Only kidding – this time."

A new customer sat at the bar and waved. She held up a finger and turned to me. "We working out again tonight?"

"You bet," I said.

"Great." Becky reached down behind the counter and slapped a tray loaded with bowls of pretzels onto the bar. "Feel like being pretzel-man?" she asked.

"It's what I live for."

Chapter 34

"Bastard!" shouted Becky. She grunted and squirmed under me. She freed a fist and launched it at my face. I knew it was coming and blocked it with my elbow.

"Great passion without forethought leads to disastrous results."

"Screw you and your annoying adages, Jack," she spat.

I kissed the tip of her nose, then got to my feet. I held out a hand to help her off the mat. "There were a couple things wrong with your attack," I said as I pulled her up. "You started your strike like this – face to face." I bent down, turned her hips and repositioned her feet. "You should try to get at a ninety-degree angle before launching that particular move." I rose and stood in front of her. "Let's try it in slow-mo, and you will feel the difference." I gave her a slow-motion shove.

Becky was a quick study. Her spin and elbow would have connected nicely to my neck or temple.

"Good! Let's try it at speed." This time, instead of pushing her and letting her practice the move, I grabbed her sweatshirt and yanked her toward me to see how quickly she could adapt. She jammed her head into my chest and sharply delivered two light taps above my groin.

I staggered back and held up my hands. "Whoa! I'm glad those punches were pulled – and that they were higher than they could have been."

Becky grinned. "I was only thinking of my own pleasure. Splattering your balls like stomped-on grapes wouldn't do either of us any good."

My lips curved at her attitude even as my sphincter tightened at her remark.

Before work for the last week, we had been practicing the Israeli martial art Krav Maga in my exercise room. Becky was a natural. She hated the stretching and warm-up Yoga exercises I insisted we start with, but the rough-and-tumble nature of the art suited her like cold on beer.

I pulled off my gloves and removed my headgear.

Becky danced around me like a TV sitcom boxer, weaving and throwing air punches. "Giving up, Jack?" She threw a vicious air uppercut. "Scared of the Blonde Bomber?" Left-right air jabs followed. "Terrified of the Vicious Vixen?" She bobbed. "Petrified of –"

With a quick leg sweep, I dumped Becky on her butt. "Startling the Supercilious Simp?"

Storm clouds rolled in her eyes. "Damn!"

"What? Didn't you expect me to retaliate?"

"Yes, I did." She punched the mat. "But I thought I was ready to handle it." She fisted her hands behind her and leaned back. "Am I any good or are you just taking it easy on me?"

"Both." I squatted and cupped her chin. "You're quick, and you think and react fast. If you wanted to study Krav Maga professionally, you could be a champ."

Her face beamed. "Help me up then and let's do some more." She held out a hand.

I pulled her to her feet and helped her remove her head-gear and gloves. "We need to move on to weapons training."

"Guns?"

"Guns, and knives, and truncheons, oh my!" I led her to the closet, opened the door, hung up the gear then turned and looked at Becky. I was about to reveal one of my secrets and checked how I felt about that.

Acceptance.

Trust.

Not bothered at all. A grin popped out on my face.

"What?" asked Becky.

I grabbed a handful of her sweatshirt, pulled her toward me and kissed her hard. "Nothing." With my arm around her shoulders we turned and faced the rear of the closet. "Watch carefully." I yanked up on the farthest left hook and twisted the farthest right hook. "Now for the fun part." I pushed the back of the closet and the wall swung away.

"Whooooaa," said Becky. "The freakin' Bat Cave!"

I flipped on the lights and led her down the stairs. "Just a safe room away from prying eyes."

At the bottom of the stairs Becky's head swiveled, taking in the beige concrete block walls, the shooting area, and the gun safes. She glanced downrange at the three hanging bull's-eye targets. "Wow. Was this room always here or did you have it built?"

"When they put in the pool, I had them do some extra digging and had this installed."

"Did you bury the construction crew under the floor to keep this a secret, as the ancient Egyptians did?"

I pointed to her feet. "Yeah. The foreman's head is under your big toe."

She hurriedly stepped aside and stared at the floor for a moment, then she looked up at me and her eyes tightened.

"Got you for a second on that one," I said with a laugh.

Becky planted her fists on her waist. "Smartass."

"But it wasn't necessary to entomb the workers as Cheops did, just parcel the job out to different contractors. The range I set up myself." I walked to a table where I had laid out a dozen handguns. "Come."

Becky followed, then glanced down at the table. "Jeez, you got a lot of guns."

I shrugged. "Tools of the trade. My old trade, anyway." I patted the table. "Pick up each one. Let it sit in your hand. Raise and lower each a few times."

Becky nodded and reached for the first one. "What am I looking for?"

"One that feels comfortable in your hand. Your body will tell you what fits."

Becky went from left to right, picking up and getting a feel for each weapon. Some she dawdled over and some she rejected immediately, but her hand kept coming back to one. She lifted her choice and weighed it. "This one. This one fits."

I couldn't help the smirk that surprised my lips. "That's the Para Ordnance .45 cal. Super Hawg. Six-inch barrel, holds fourteen rounds in the magazine, and one in the pipe. The Hawg is a heftier version of the classic Colt 1911. That's a BFG for a little girl like you."

Becky squinted and sighted downrange with the Hawg. "I don't know what BFG means, but you said to pick the one that fits."

I nodded. "So I did. Let's try it out, then."

We grabbed some ear and eye protection and stepped to the firing line. I had Becky load a clip with dummy rounds, jam the clip into the weapon and jack a round into the chamber. After a few practice runs, and an aiming, stance and grip lesson, I had her load three live rounds and I set the target at twenty feet.

"OK. Now bring the weapon up and aim at the target."

Becky did as I asked. "How come you always refer to it as a weapon rather than a gun?"

"Training. Guns refer to something too big to hold in your hands. Leave it on safe and lower the weapon." I adjusted her stance by placing my hands on her hips and twisting slightly.

"You're not getting handsy, are you, Jack?"

"When you're holding a loaded forty-five? I'm not crazy."

Satisfied with her posture, I stepped back. "Bring the weapon up, snap off the safety, aim like we practiced and fire three rounds when ready."

The first shot echoed loudly. Even though the room was baffled and sound-proofed, the noise and concussion were palpable.

After a few seconds, Becky cranked out the second shot, then the third. She placed the .45 on the shooter's table and removed her ear protection. When she turned, the smile on her face was huge. Excitement poured out of her like draft from a tap.

"Wow! I didn't know it would be such a violent explosion. Such power!"

"We could step down to a smaller caliber," I said.

"Uh-uh, no way! I like this gun, weapon... hawg, gat-rod-heater-blaster, whatever you want to call it." Excitement had her bubbling.

"OK. Let's check the target and see how you did." I pushed a button and the target advanced toward us on its steel chain. Her three shots were high and to the right and a hand's-width apart.

"Not a bad shot grouping for a first time," I said. "You handled the recoil better than I expected." I held her hand and kissed her knuckles. "You have strong hands."

She raised an eyebrow. "Of course they're strong. I've been lifting beer cases and kegs since I was ten. What? Did you think I was a pussy?"

My brows furrowed. "Is that a trick question?"

She placed her hands on her hips and was about to answer when I cut her off.

"Load up a full clip and we'll do it again."

Becky fired and adjusted. Fired and adjusted. Fired and learned. As she blazed through a clip, I pulled a Para Ordnance Warthog from the weapons locker. "Try this one. It's the same gun but with a three-inch barrel."

Becky hefted the pistol. "Doesn't seem as balanced."

"You're right. It's not. With the Hawg, the longer barrel gives better stability, but it's harder to hide in your garter belt. The Warthog gives a smaller outline." I hung a new target and sent it twenty feet downrange. "Load up three rounds and give it a try."

Becky did as I asked and cracked off three rounds down range. She lowered the weapon and brought the target toward us. The shots were scattered on the target.

"The shots are all over the place," she said.

"Shorter barrel – less control. I'd like you to get used to it. Use five-round bursts and shorten the time between shots."

She nodded and loaded the magazine.

Fifty rounds later, she put down the gun and turned to me. "Shot grouping's improving, but I'm not as good with it as the other gun. I suck."

I pushed the target button and the bulls-eye clanked toward me. I switched it out with a man-sized silhouette target, and sent it twenty feet downrange.

"Try a full magazine on this target. Rapid fire. Don't worry about shot groupings. Shoot for the center mass."

Becky loaded up, took a shooter's stance, and quickly emptied the magazine at the target. The ventilator shifted into high as the last brass cartridge clinked on the floor.

Becky slipped off her ear protection and I did the same. "Scattered grouping. I still suck."

I brought the target to us and studied her shots. "Scattered? Perhaps." Her shots might have been scattered, but they were all within a fourteen-inch circle. I unhooked the target and held it against my chest. "But any of these hits would put an enemy on his ass and in a world of hurt. A forty-five-caliber slug punching through your lungs is God's way of telling you it's time to go home." I lowered the target and grinned. "Damn, Beck. You did super."

She returned the grin. "Really? Or are you just shining me on?"

"Really. We'll keep both guns, but I'd like you to get used to that shorter barrel. It'll fit nicely in the small of your back and can be drawn fairly quickly."

She nodded and looked down at the Warthog. "Are we really expecting this kind of trouble?"

I tilted my head. "No. If I was expecting trouble I'd bring a sawn-off Saiga shotgun." I walked to the weapons locker. "Speaking of which…"

Chapter 35

Becky and I sat in Migliano's. Heaping portions, homemade sauce, and good wine made for an outstanding lunch. As I leaned back and sipped my cappuccino, Becky chased the last of her spaghetti sauce around her plate with a hunk of bread. Watching her eat like a starving wolf always gave me pleasure for some reason. Becky sat back, sighed, and looked up at me.

"What? Do I have sauce on my face? " She quickly wiped her mouth with a napkin. "What are you smiling at?"

I shrugged. "Just watching you eat."

"Bullshit. That's the same look you have on your face when I come out of the shower."

My smile widened to a grin. "That's not the same thing." But maybe it was. I felt at ease and happy when we were together.

I'd heard a lot of men say that they don't know what love is, and I'm one of them. If just watching someone eat made my insides smile, then that was good enough for me. Maybe it wasn't the rockets and shooting stars love as the romance novels portray, but it filled the bill.

What to do about it was another matter.

"Ja-ack. What's on your mind?"

I chased away my thoughts and gazed at Becky. "The case. Stuff. You."

She reached across the table and took my hand. "Let's hear about me."

"No, you egotist."

"Yes, you sadist."

I laughed and squeezed her hand. "Thanks for being in my life, Becky Quinn."

She squeezed back. "Right back at 'cha, Jack Daniels." She released my hand and gestured at my clothes. "You don't have your P.I. suit on today."

I nodded. "Yeah. I think Joe Hawkshaw has covered all the ground he can. I've been to every business, shop, and government office in the area. People are getting tired of my face. Now, it's time for a stealth operation."

Becky sipped her coffee. "Don Kramer?"

I nodded. "Yeah. Of all the people I interviewed, he has something to hide."

"Is there a Betty Pepperdyne connection with him?"

I had filled Becky in on my findings in the library about the missing Betty Pepperdyne.

I blew out a breath. "Slim. Betty worked three flights up in the Spencer Building, but that's all I could discover." I leaned forward and tapped the table. "We can't forget about the East Side Dragons. They still might be connected to this somehow."

"If those two gangbangers were just evil handymen, maybe Kramer paid them to ditch Angel's body."

She had said it casually, but her hand was white-knuckled around the edge of the table. A layer of rage still boiled beneath the calm. I leaned over and placed my hand on hers until she relaxed and her hand turned and cupped mine.

"That would be giving a heavy blackmail hammer to a gangbanger. I can't see him doing that. But it is a possibility."

"Maybe he's secretly running the gang."

I thought about pudgy Don Kramer as a secret gang leader and had to smile. "No. Not possible." I leaned forward and lowered my voice. "We'll check out Kramer first, then focus back on the Dragons."

Her head nodded, her eyes drifting off to the side. "What exactly do you consider a stealth operation?"

"Just a late-night check of his home and office files."

Becky's eye darted back to me. "You're talking about breaking and entering into someone's home and then a city building."

"I won't break too much."

She crossed her arms and shook her head. "You mean *we* won't break too much."

I sat back and gazed at her. Becky's determination, obstinacy, and sheer will power had me caving to any protests. Besides, I had promised. "You'll look real sexy in stealth gear."

Chapter 36

I had already planned how to infiltrate the Spencer Building, but it took me two days to collect Kramer's personal information and tap his phone.

Kramer drove to work every day, leaving home at precisely 7:30 AM and returning at 6:00 PM sharp. I learned a lot about his private life from just the public records. Kramer's three bedroom ranch sat on a quarter acre in a suburb ten miles from his office. He had gone through a costly divorce two years ago. Most of the battle was over custody of "Pippy," Don and Shirley's three-year-old Lhasa Apso. Shirley won the dog and their savings, and Don won the house and its second mortgage. Shirley was now a blackjack dealer in Vegas, and Don had a girlfriend named Doris. I hoped Pippy wasn't in therapy from the breakup.

In my upstairs bedroom, Becky stared into the mirror, tied her hair into a ponytail, then jammed it under a black watch cap. I couldn't talk her out of the long-sleeved black shirt, black jeans and boots. I didn't think it mattered – if all went according to plan, we wouldn't be seen anyway. I had on a dark blue shirt and charcoal pants. I wore my black boots, but I hadn't tucked in my trousers as Becky had. I looked like a civilian but she didn't. I packed a big bright silver necklace to throw on Becky if we had to pass as a couple. With the necklace on, she could be accepted as a style maven.

Becky slipped on black gloves, then turned. "How do I look?"

"Like a 'Mission Impossible' wannabe."

She frowned.

"But you look sensational in black." That brought back her smile. "You sure you want to go all in black?"

"You said I look sensational. Don't knock it." She adjusted her cap. "Guns?"

I shook my head. "Not necessary. I'm bringing mine as a matter of course, but you don't need one on this outing."

Her open mouth and sharp inhale said she was about to protest, but she nodded instead.

Part of my agreement in letting her come along was that she heeded my every word. We had talked about the need for single-minded action and instant response. She agreed to follow my lead and I trusted she would. For me, this operation was nothing to break a sweat over, but it would give me an opportunity to observe Becky in a high-pressure situation.

I glanced out the window at the setting sun and checked my watch. "It's seven-thirty. Time to move out. Kramer should be leaving his house now for his dinner date at Chez Sky with Doris."

"Chez Sky?" said Becky. "Expensive. And how do you know this?"

"I tapped his phone a couple of days ago." I picked up my black nylon bag of supplies. "Remind me to pick up the tap box when we leave his house."

"Tap box?" she asked.

I headed down to the garage with Becky close behind. "Yeah. It records the call, then sends the conversation to my computer."

"Neat. And very high-tech."

"Naah, that's three-year-old stuff. I have one box that can forward the call to anywhere in the world in real time."

Becky was silent for a moment. "Were there any other calls?"

"Just orders for takeout and phone sex with Doris."

Her eyes slid over to mine. "Did you enjoy listening to the phone sex?"

"Nah. They lacked imagination and zeal."

"Think you can do better sometime?" she asked, with that playful little smile on her lips.

Keeping my back to her so she wouldn't see, I grabbed my phone off my belt and hit her number on my speed dial. Her brows furrowed as she looked at her phone and lifted it to her ear. "Hello?"

I brought the phone to my mouth. "What color panties are you wearing?"

With a frump, she hung up. "You are pathetic, Daniels. Pathetic."

I grinned and opened the door of the van, making sure the magnetic DEP logo was adhered well to the side. Becky got in the passenger side. We slammed the doors and I tossed my bag onto the space between us. I pushed the remote and the garage door swung open. "Buckle up," I said and started the engine. I reached over and squeezed Becky's hand. "How you doing? Excited?"

Her gaze narrowed and she looked down at the bag. "No. Just nervous,"

I smiled, put the van in gear, and pulled out. "Good. Me too."

"Really?" Her pretty blue eyes studied me. "I should think this would be old hat to you by now."

"Yeah. But I don't let that happen. Old hat can get you killed."

"Nobody dies tonight," she said. "This is for Angel."

"Good perspective."

Becky lifted the bag onto her lap and unzipped the opening. "Let's see what Jack Daniels considers essential for burglary." She pawed through the items. "Rope. Wire. A wand thingie. Camera. What looks to be a small grappling hook." She stopped and stared into the bag. "A hand grenade?"

"It's just a small flash-bang. Not lethal."

She inhaled deeply, then puffed it out. "Good." She rooted around in the bag more carefully and lifted out a plastic bag filled with a brown substance. "What is this? It looks like a turd."

"Dog turd, actually. A very smelly, sticky dog turd."

She gingerly put it back. "That should stop the guards in their tracks."

I laughed. "It's a present."

Her face crinkled. "Remind me never to tell you my birth date."

"It's not for you, but I can get more if you want it."

"Pass." She grimaced and tossed the turd back into the bag.

The thought of the dog shit made me smile the rest of the way to Kramer's house.

Kramer's neighborhood was a typical suburban setting, small lots, trim lawns, and boring sameness. We pulled down the street and slowed. Lights glowed in most of the houses but no one was out and about. I backed into Kramer's driveway and gestured to the bag. "Pull out the frequency hunter-activator."

"English, Jack."

"The wand thingie."

Becky pawed through and lifted out a box with a short attached antenna. "This?"

I watched the side-view mirror. "Yeah. Point it at the garage door and hold down the button. It pumps out short range frequencies that will eventually match the door's remote."

Becky did as I asked and within a few moments, the garage door opened. I backed in, surprised that the garage light didn't come on. "Hit the red button again." The garage door closed and I shut off the van's lights, plunging us into darkness.

Becky inhaled sharply. "It's dark."

"Yeah. Goes with your outfit."

From out of the blackness her fist pounded my arm.

"Gloves and flashlights from here on out," I said. "Don't slam the door, just click it." We exited the van and walked to the door leading into the house.

"Kramer has an alarm system, but it's probably not too sophisticated. House alarms usually aren't."

I ran the light around the doorframe, stopping at the top. The magnetic contact was on the outside of the door instead of inside. "Either very sloppy or a trap." I glanced at Becky's face. Focused, aware, and stone cold. She was doing fine.

I offset the activator and picked the door lock. The whole process took twenty seconds.

"Geez, Jack. You sure know what you're doing."

With a grin, I grabbed the doorknob. "Well, now we'll see if you're right." I opened the door and scanned the alarm system mounted on the wall. All systems blinked green. "We're good to go."

Kramer had graciously left a few lights on and we walked through the house.

"Early American CC decor," I said.

"CC?"

"Cheap crap. Wifey probably got all the good furniture."

We found his office in a spare bedroom, if a computer on a desk and a file cabinet in a corner could be called an office. His PC was already booted and I pulled a box out of my bag.

"What's that?" asked Becky.

"A super-fast ghost mechanism that will copy the files on his hard drive. If any files are encrypted files we can break them at our leisure." I plugged the device into his USB slot and started it up.

"What do I do?"

I flipped the window curtains closed and turned on the desk light. "Look through his desk and file cabinet for checkbooks, statements, anything financial." I handed her the camera. "If it looks at all important, shoot it."

Becky nodded and went to work.

"It will take a few minutes to download his drive. Meanwhile, I'll check the other rooms."

I did a quick search through the rest of the house. Their were no hidden safes, weapons or drugs. The only detail I learned was that Kramer wore boxers, not briefs. Hardly the kind of information that would bring a killer to justice.

I stared at the picture of his dog on the bureau and shook my head. Kramer seemed less and less likely to be Angel's killer, but whatever he was into, I wanted to know. I walked back to the office. The green light on the ghost device blinked. It had finished. Becky was closing the bottom drawer of the file cabinet.

"Anything interesting?"

She shook her head. "No. Most of the drawers contain warranties and manuals for garden equipment and a few tools. The top drawer held all the good stuff." She held up the camera. "Got all the bank statements, personal mail, and his divorce papers."

"Great. We're done here. Let's hit our next stop."

I flipped off the desk lamp and Becky carefully slid the curtains back to the way they were. Yeah. She would do, all right. I went out the side door of the garage and collected my tap box, then we hit the road. I checked the time. "Twenty-eight minutes." I squeezed Becky's leg. "Good work."

"I hope we got something."

She sounded down and I glanced over to her. "You ok?"

"Yeah. I guess." She shrugged. "I'm disappointed that nothing jumped out for us, and I think I'm a little nervous about this next part."

"Not to worry, it should be a cake walk."

Chapter 37

The drive to the Spencer Building downtown was uneventful. I parked behind the building a half a block away from the loading dock. Becky's hands were clenched on her thighs.

"Relax. We'll get through this as planned. All right?"

She nodded. "Yeah, but this hiding in the shadows and timing and stuff makes me sweat."

I rubbed her leg. "Save it. After this is over and we're in bed, I'll make you sweat up a storm."

She smiled and some of the tension left her. "I'll take you up on that – pervert."

We exited the van and hugged the shadows on the side of the building. I peeked around the corner. A short three-step concrete staircase with a metal pole railing led to the receiving door, the stairs leading down to the other side of the building. A lone light above the door shown down over the area. I glanced at my watch and flashed Becky a five minute hand-sign.

Becky leaned close. "What if someone comes this way?" she whispered.

"You grab me and we start making out. Toss your legs around me for effect."

She snorted. "You'd like that, wouldn't you?"

"Who wouldn't?"

The creak of the door had Becky flattening against the building and me peeking around the corner again. A man wearing a security jacket bent down and let the door close on a small wedge against the door jam. Then he walked down the stairs and rounded the opposite corner.

"There goes, Bill. Punctual as usual. We have as long as it takes him to smoke a cigarette to get inside."

We quietly moved to the back of the staircase and climbed over the rail. I dripped some WD-40 on the hinges, waited a moment, and opened the door. Becky dashed in. I entered and eased the door back onto the wedge. Becky's eyes were bright and her breath came in shallow pants.

"Second hallway on the left," I whispered. "Go!"

We ran past the vacant guard's desk, down the hallway and turned left. I stopped, squatted, and glanced around the corner back at the door. Bill hadn't returned nor seen us. As long as he didn't smell the WD-40 and wonder about it, we were gold.

We walked down the short hall to the stairway. "Eight flights up. I'll race ya," I said, and ran.

The sprint up the empty eight flights of stairs got my blood pumping and my lungs burning. Becky was close behind me and never faltered. When we reached the landing I turned and studied her. She was red-faced and breathing hard, but ready for more. "You're doing great," I said, and opened the staircase door. The hallway opened on the rear entrances of the eighth floor offices and I led the way to the DEP office. "Glove up." Becky nodded and we pulled on latex gloves.

When I had talked to Angel's office mates, I had examined the door from the inside, and it hadn't looked alarmed. I stooped to give it the once over from this side. Nothing. I reached up and turned the knob. It was locked, but my quick-pick gun unlocked it in a second. The door opened and I checked the frame for contacts. Nothing.

In a guarded building, I didn't think they would alarm all the doors, but it never hurts to check. There's nothing more embarrassing than breaking into someplace and relaxing into thinking you're safe while a silent alarm blinks at the security desk.

Becky slipped through and I closed the door behind us. I pointed out Angel's cube in the office warren. "Check Angel's desk. Get any info about what she was working on in the camera. I'll be in Kramer's office."

The door was locked, but it only took a moment to get inside. I sat at his desk. He'd left nothing on the surface but a few twisted paperclips. The drawers were locked. "A bit paranoid, aren't we, Don?"

I picked up two paperclips and straightened them out. It seemed apropos to use them to pick the desk lock. Five seconds later I was going through the paperwork in the drawers.

This would be the hard part. It's one thing to look for the proverbial needle in the haystack, but if you don't even know what a needle is, it'll take longer.

Becky walked in as I was going through his middle drawer. "Angel's desk is empty," she said. "It's like she never existed."

The pain in her voice, and the anger in her eyes touched me. I'd lost teammates before but they didn't affect me. It was a life (and death) we had chosen. Angel's horrible death was forced and it had deeply affected Becky. "Angel lives in the people who loved her. And in you. Keep her there with love."

The anger vanished from Becky's face, but not the pain. She sighed and nodded with pursed lips. "What else should I do?"

I tossed her the quick-pick gun. "Open the file cabinet and look for any folders with worn edges or tabs. Something that has seen a lot of use."

"On it."

Nothing in Kramer's middle drawer was of interest. I opened his right top-drawer and lifted out his Rolodex. Turning the knob slowly, I let the cards fall where they might. The most used cards fell open first. I ignored the numbers to any other DEP agencies, the local deli and dry cleaners, but Carver Auto and Weller-Brice Petroleum slid open on each of three turns. I quick-scanned the numbers, locking them into my memory.

I returned the Rolodex to the drawer and opened the second. It held a pharmacy of various headache pills, allergy medicines and antacid remedies. It must suck to be Don Kramer. I searched through the other drawers, but found nothing of interest. "Find anything, Beck?"

She finished snapping a picture of a file. "No. Just inspection reports, letters, and personnel files."

"Is Angel's still there?"

Becky bent and focused the camera on another file. "Yep. Already in the camera."

"Good." I thought a moment. "How about Weller-Brice Petroleum?"

She put away the folder. "I'm on the V's now. I'll let you know in a moment."

Her long gloved fingers flipped through the V's. She returned the folder and reached for the W's. "Weller has its own folder. A thick one, too."

I joined her at the cabinet. "I'll check the rest. Sit at the desk and shoot all Weller's info."

She sat and began clicking away.

It didn't take long to finish going through the files, and I finished shortly before Becky. She shot the last paper in the folder and turned to me. "What else?"

"Put everything back the way it was. I have one more stop to make." I reached into my bag, pulled out the dog turd and left.

In the receptionist area, I tried to open the second drawer down, but the desk was locked. "Trusting bitch, aren't you." I picked the lock and slid open my target drawer. I pushed the latches on the rails and lifted the drawer out of the desk. As I unzipped the sealed baggie, the smell of ripe dog shit permeated the area.

"What on earth are you doing?" asked Becky from the doorway.

"Just returning like for like," I said.

With the bag turned inside out, I smashed and smeared the dog shit on the back the drawer, then re-sealed the ziplock and stuck it in my bag. I carefully returned the drawer to its proper place, and locked the desk.

"She must have really pissed you off," said Becky.

I stepped back and sniffed. The strong scent of Barbara Poell's perfume was overlaid by the more pungent odor of poo. "Yeah. She gave me shit and I'm just returning the favor." I turned to Becky. "Let's get out of here."

We closed up behind us, leaving everything the way we found it. We made our way slowly down the stairwell and sat on the last step.

"How much time?" asked Becky.

"It took us less than an hour, so…" I glanced at my watch. "Six minutes, give or take."

"He always goes for a smoke break on the hour?"

"Pretty much. But we'll observe and be sure."

We sidled into the side hallway and I pulled a small mirror on a flexible wand out of my pocket. I slid the mirror around the corner near the floor and watched Bill. He sat, slumped in his chair, reading a paperback novel. He glanced at the clock on the wall, put down the book, and stood, hand reaching for his cigarettes.

I gave Becky the "get ready" signal, as Bill headed for the door. He set the wedge and walked out, leaving the door to swing shut behind him.

"Now?" asked Becky.

"Wait." I held her arm and could feel Becky's excitement building as we neared the end of this gambit.

I visualized walking down the stairs with Bill, strolling around the corner, reaching into his pocket and lighting up. I imagined his first satisfied puff and exhale.

Time to move.

We had just turned the corner when the outer door was thrust open. I pushed Becky back and dove after her. Footsteps hammered down the hall. I pulled out the mirror and snuck a peek. Bill was back at his desk. He tossed a disposable lighter in the trash, rooted through the drawers and came up with another. Bill slammed the drawer and headed back out. I let out the breath I was holding.

I gave him the same amount of time again, then grabbed Becky's hand and ran for the exit. I opened it a crack and looked out. Smoke drifted from around the corner. "Go," I whispered and pushed the door open. Becky dashed around me and vaulted over the railing. I eased the door closed and followed. I was a second behind her as we reached the van.

We entered, closed the doors, and drove away.

Becky pulled off her watch cap. "Wow. That was nerve wracking and that last bit sure had my heart pumping." She took the band off her ponytail and shook out her hair and sighed. "And you used to do this kind of stuff for a living?" Becky ran her fingers through her blonde locks.

"Not quite." She should know how it was. "Me or a member of my team would most likely have killed the guard, then entered the building."

Becky's hands stopped fiddling with her hair, then lowered to her lap. "That changes the complexion of whole thing, doesn't it?"

"Yeah. It was a dangerous game with staying alive the only real prize."

We drove in silence for a while, then she reached over and placed a hand on my leg. "I'm ok with what you've done in the past, if it matters."

It did. It mattered a great deal. I squeezed her hand. "Thanks."

She rolled her shoulders and sighed. "Tell me about the sweaty sex."

I grinned. Becky was not only my lover, but my first close friend.

Life was good.

Chapter 38

The champagne fizzed as I filled the crystal flutes sitting on the edge of the Jacuzzi. Becky had her hair pinned up and had slid into the water up to her chin. Soap bubbles made islands on the surface that drifted occasionally to show the wonders in the depths below.

I jammed the bottle of Dom Perignon '96 into the ice bucket and slid a foot into the water. "Shove over a little."

She had her eyes closed as she sipped her champagne. "Can't. Bones have melted."

I lowered myself across from her into the hot water, wincing at the heat. The champagne looked to be a good cooling agent and I downed half the glass. "Ah... God bless that blind monk."

Becky sipped more champagne. "Yes. You can truly 'drink the stars.'"

"Ah, you know Dom Perignon's eureka utterance."

She shifted over to give me more room. "Of course. I'm a barkeeper's daughter. I know all about the cellar master of Hautvillers Abbey."

I flipped water onto my shoulders. "I bow to your rarefied knowledge of wine."

She opened her eyes and placed warm toes with pink-painted nails on my chest. "I also know that Andre the Giant drank one-hundred and nineteen twelve ounce bottles of beers in a six hour stretch."

I saluted her with my glass. "Your knowledge of spirits is unmatched."

"And I also know about your personal best."

"Drinking beer?"

She slowly trailed her toe down my chest to my groin. "No." She sat up, soap bubbles slowly sliding down her breasts. "Wanna try for a new record?"

Her skin glowed a rosy red from the hot water and her nipples peeked through a striptease of bubbles.

I was pretty sure she wasn't talking about beer at this point, but at that moment, I didn't care. "I'm in."

She leaned over and replaced her foot with her hand. "Not yet. But we can fix that."

Chapter 39

I sat at my kitchen table behind fat piles of paperwork. As the clock on the stove slid to 3 AM, I sighed and leaned back. Sorting through Kramer's printouts had given me a headache. As the key turned in the front door, I rubbed my tired eyes.

"Jack?" Becky called from the foyer.

"In the kitchen," I yelled.

I heard her keys dump on the table, the rustle of her removing her jacket, and the soft woof as it landed over the newel post. I rose and waited for her, glad that she felt at ease enough in my home to use the key I'd given her.

She walked to the doorway and leaned on the jam. She wore her usual jeans and a T-shirt that stated "Mary – Queen of Scotch."

"Honey, I'm home."

She came into my arms. I held her tightly, feeling her heart beat in time with mine. I kissed her and looked down into her face. "Missed you."

She leaned backwards against my arms and I got a nice crack out of her back.

"Ahhh… thanks," she said, and straightened. "We missed you at the bar as well."

"We?"

Her eyes became impish, then she looked off to the side. "Yeah. Everyone who ran out of pretzels wanted to know where Pretzel Boy was."

"Pretzel Boy, is it?"

"Yeah. I told them I had you handcuffed to my bed as my love slave."

"Humph. That's a nice way to be treated."

Her eyes came back to mine coated with a little misgiving.

"No," I said. "Really. That's a nice way to be treated."

Her smile returned.

"I've dinner ready if you're hungry," I said.

"Good. I'm starving."

"Gee, I'm surprised."

She gave me a little elbow jab, then turned and gestured at the heaps of paper. "There's no room to eat. You've been role-playing an accountant's version of Sir Edmund Hillary."

"We'll eat in the dining room."

"That would be novel." Her hand slid down into mine. "Any luck with all of this?"

"Possibly. Get out some plates and I'll tell you over dinner."

"What are we having?" she asked as she stepped to the cabinet.

I rattled off the dish names in Mandarin.

"Oh," she said. "Either we're having Chinese, or you're having a stroke."

I slid the food from the warming oven. "Pot stickers, egg rolls, fried rice, Won Ton soup, sweet and sour pork, Ma Po bean curd, Kung Pao chicken, and tea."

She grabbed two forks and a bunch of serving spoons from the silverware drawer. "What? You're not eating?"

I set the tray down on the dining room table. "Hand me one of those forks for a moment, will you?"

She snatched them behind her back. "What? So you can stab me in the butt, again?"

"Training. It's called training."

"Training my ass," she said.

"Exactly."

She dumped the silverware on the table and handed me a plate. "How about giving me a penalizing proverb instead. That should be punishment enough."

I sat, spooned rice onto my plate, and thought for a moment. "OK. 'It's better to do a good deed near home than go far away to burn incense.'"

Becky sighed. "Awww, it's too long to fit on a T-shirt." She sat and piled food on her plate. "And it's so meaningful, too."

I grabbed her plate and slid it toward me.

"OK. OK. Sorry!"

"Really?" I asked.

"Naw…" she grinned. "Just hungry."

I pushed her plate back and she dove in. "Tell me what you've found in Kramer's files."

I lifted an egg roll with my chopsticks. "I'm not sure yet. But I'm narrowing it down to the Weller-Brice Petroleum investigation."

Becky poured soy sauce over the mound on her plate. "Any way we can connect Angel to it?"

I swallowed a mouthful of Kung Pao. "She was the first person to work on Weller, then it seems Kramer took the case away from her."

Becky's eyes' brightened. "Got him!"

I shook my head. "Not necessarily. It looks like he took the bigger accounts away from all his subordinates and left them with the Dogpatch oil tank leaks and little Johnny's chemistry set spills."

Becky put down her fork and frowned. After a moment, she picked it up and began eating again. "I want it to be him."

"What you want is Angel's killer caught, but I don't think it's Kramer. There's something wrong about him, for sure, but..." I thought about the picture of his dog on his bureau. "He's not the type."

Becky looked down into her plate; her hand was white-knuckled on her fork. "I serve people everyday. Talk, joke, commiserate, but underneath it all, I think of Angel."

"We'll get him. Count on it."

She blew out a deep breath. "I do." She reached over and gripped my hand. "I count on you, too."

"I'm there to be counted on." I squeezed her hand. "After we eat, we'll concentrate on the Weller files and see what turns up."

The talk turned to bar gossip, what we did during our day, and an exchange of thoughts on the current local political scene.

Becky pushed away her empty plate. "Ahh... That was good." She leaned back. "Any pot-stickers left?"

"Several, but you can't still be hungry."

"No. I'm planning breakfast." She reached for a fortune cookie. "I do have room for one of these, though." She snapped it open and read aloud: *"He who throws dirt is losing ground."* She smiled. "Open yours."

I grabbed a cookie and opened it. "My lucky numbers are six, ten, twenty-three, eleven, and forty." I looked up. "Boy, they got that right. How did they know?"

Becky rolled her eyes. "Read the other side, Jack."

I turned the slip of paper over. *"Woman who seeks to be equal with men lack ambition."*

"Wow," she said. "They got that right, too."

"Let's clean up, and get to the Weller files," I said.

"Cleaning up sounds like Pretzel Boy work."

"I'm gonna get you for sticking me with that moniker, ya know."

Becky smiled and stacked the plates. "Counting on that, too."

Chapter 40

"This is interesting." Becky laid the printout she was reading on the table and highlighted a section. "Angel's reports say Weller-Brice Petroleum is dumping waste products into Lake Michigan. But Kramer's report doesn't mention it." She fished through the reports until she found the one she was looking for, then flipped it open. "Yeah, wait a minute. He does in his earlier reports."

I yanked out Kramer's financials. "When was the last time he mentioning the dumping?"

She ran her finger down a page. "August eighteenth."

"Interesting. Kramer shows a cash deposit of twenty-five hundred dollars on August twenty-first."

Our eyes met.

"Payoffs!" we said in unison and slid our chairs together.

I put Kramer's bank statement between us. "Look. Every month since, there is a cash deposit of a thousand bucks in his account." I shook my head. "Dumb bastard. Does he think the IRS won't notice?" I glanced at the rest of his statement. "That's a piker amount of money. He must have more hidden somewhere."

Becky ignored my statement and grabbed my hand. "Maybe Angel found out about his scheme and he killed her. He's the 'D' she mentioned in her diary."

"Maybe... maybe." Don Kramer still didn't fit as a killer, but it was a lead to follow.

"I think it's time I paid Mr. Kramer a nighttime visit."

Becky placed her hands flat on the table, her face somber and serious. "Think you can get him to confess?"

I slid my eyes over to hers and smiled. "I can get him to confess to Abe Lincoln's assassination, but what we want is the truth."

Becky sighed. "Ok. Stupid question." She drummed her fingers on the table. "How about threatening to turn over the payoff info to the IRS? Rather than threatening death that is. You might get more honest answers."

"I'll know when he's lying. I spent a whole month in Langley learning the techniques." I turned my chair to face Becky, then turned hers so that our knees were touching. I placed my hands on her thighs and leaned close. "I have a question for you, though. If he is Angel's killer, what do we do with him?"

The question slapped her hard and she straightened in her chair. "What do you mean?"

The look on her face said she knew what I meant, but her denial was expected. It was one thing to talk theory, but another to know you were deciding a man's fate. This might be a bitter pill for Becky to swallow, but I had to know where she stood.

"There are three alternatives, the way I see it." I raised my index finger. "First, we find evidence, then turn him in to the authorities. He will go to prison and have three hots and a cot for twenty or thirty years until parole."

I held up the next finger. "Second, he leaves proof, writes a confession, and commits suicide by eating his gun."

I extended my ring finger. "Lastly, he can disappear from the face of the earth, never to be heard from again."

When the choices hit home, she turned her head away. "Are those the only options?"

I leaned back. "Can you think of any others?"

She slowly shook her head. "No. But let me think about this for a bit." She looked back into my eyes and forced a smile. "Ok?"

"Sure. No hurry." I turned my chair back to face the table. "But we can't move on him until we decide which course to take."

The strain of the decision showed on her tight face. "Let me sleep on it."

"As long as I can sleep on you."

"Sounds like something I need." She reached for my hand. "Let's get started now."

Chapter 41

The coffee dripped too slowly into the pot for me this morning. I strolled over to the window and watched a chickadee peck at the feeder Becky had hung in the backyard. At least the bird knew what he was doing.

The sun was bright but the chill was back in the air. It was a normal morning, but I sensed things had changed.

I had left Becky sleeping upstairs in case she needed some time alone. Last night when we made love, she had held tightly to me like a drowning person. Was I flotsam that had drifted into her life to help support her, or was I a toxic raft, leading down a dark path from which she might never return.

The slap of bare-feet on hardwood floors had me turning to watch Becky stagger into the kitchen. Sleepy-eyed, she reached for the still-filling coffee pot, poured herself a cup, and sat at the table.

"Good morning, mo chroí," I said.

She just grunted and stared into her cup.

"Would you like some banana-nut pancakes this morning?"

"Option number two." She took a big swallow of the hot coffee. It had to burn all the way down.

I sighed. "If you need more time –"

"No!" She lowered the cup. "Sorry, Jack." It was her turn to sigh. "I want him to be punished. I don't want him to live even if he's in prison. He has no right to be alive. Not after what he did." Becky wrapped her hands around the hot cup as if draining its warmth. "I want Angel's family to know who murdered her, and that he can never hurt anyone again."

"Will you be all right with that?"

She shook her head. "I never will be all right with Angel's death. But I will be all right with his."

The hard lines that had etched her face this morning faded slowly. I saw that with the decision made, she began to live with the choice.

"So… Good morning, Jack." She picked up her cup and sipped. "Do you know what 'mo chroí' means?"

"I do."

Becky nodded and brightened my life with her first smile of the day. "Good. Now where's my banana-nut pancakes?"

Chapter 42

After closing the bar, we changed clothes in Becky's apartment.

"Wearing all black tonight, Jack?" she asked as I pulled a black T-shirt over my head.

"Yes. As should you. We'll stick to the shadows and should be unseen."

I finished dressing and glanced at Becky as she laced her black boots. I slipped my K-Bar into its sheath on my left side and picked up my pack. Becky stood and I checked her over. Boots, long sleeved T and jeans. Damn she looked good.

"If we are taking the bar van we need to go back to town," she said.

"No. We'll take the stealth van."

"You call that rolling piece of junk a 'stealth' vehicle?"

"Sure. It's so crappy no one's eyes want to linger on it. If no one sees it – stealth."

"We can't park in his garage this time. What if someone notices the clunker in his driveway?" Her eyes narrowed in thought for a moment. "Or are we parking someplace safe and walking?"

I grinned at her thinking through the problems. She'd be one hell of a mercenary. "Two strangers walking around that neighborhood at night would draw suspicion. We'll park in his driveway. I have a City Pizza delivery sign for the top of the van."

"Who delivers pizza at three in the morning?"

"City Pizza does. Delivers twenty-four hours a day." I shrugged. "At least that's what I put on the fake sign."

We walked down to the delivery door.

"Too bad the sign's a fake," said Becky. "I could use a pizza after tonight's work."

"I have a couple frozen pizzas at home."

Becky thrust a finger near her open mouth. "Gaack. Frozen pizza."

I unlocked the van doors, turned and faced Becky. She might fool someone else with her casual attitude, but not me. I knew her too well. Not for the first time I thought about what this might do to her. I studied Becky's face. "How you doing?"

Her mouth hardened. She pulled her glove on tighter and flexed her fingers. "Let's do this."

Chapter 43

I cut Don Kramer's phone line and we entered the house through the garage side door. Once inside, we donned ski-masks over pale yellow sunglasses. They allowed us to see, but kept our anonymity. I had found that being all dressed in black with bug eyes helped loosen tongues.

Becky held the small red-lens penlight for me as I by-passed the alarm and opened the door. I listened, getting used to the general house noises. We crept down the hallway and stopped at Kramer's bedroom. Soft snores greeted us as I swung open the door. I tapped Becky's arm twice, our signal that plan "A" was in effect. She remained at the door while I slipped inside.

Kramer was sleeping on his back, one arm tossed over his eyes. His snores hadn't changed since I had entered. The smell of cheap scotch wafted in the air when Kramer exhaled. If he was still a little drunk this would make restraining him easier. I searched in my front pouch for the wrist ties, guided by a pale light shining from the bathroom. I did a quick peek at the light, then did a double take. What the hell? A Mickey Mouse nightlight? The more I learned about Kramer, the more it felt that he couldn't be Angel's killer. I shook off the feeling and got down to work.

I lifted the arm that covered his eyes, slid a velcro restraint onto his wrist and secured it to the bed post, then repeated it with his other arm.

I gently tightened them until his arms were spread wide. I motioned Becky into the room. "So far, so good," I whispered. I picked up Kramer's cell phone from his night table and handed it to her. "Take care of this and get a glass of water from the bathroom. I have a way to dispel any lingering drunk stupor. Turn on the fan in there, too, it might help cover any sounds."

I pulled his covers off. Don Kramer slept in his boxer shorts and socks. That would make my next job easier. I heard a splash as Kramer's phone plopped into the toilet and felt Becky come up behind me. "Mickey Mouse?" she said.

"Yeah. What can I say." I gestured to Kramer. "Do the tape."

Becky slammed a strip of duct tape hard over his mouth and his eyes popped open. A muffled scream came through the tape and he yanked at the restraints. With K-Bar in hand, I quick cut his underwear off him. I took the glass from Becky and tossed the water on his naked balls.

"Mmuph!" Kramer jerked and his body arched. I knelt on the right side of the bed and backhanded him hard, slapping him again with my return swing. His eyes cleared and panic flooded in. The adrenalin rush cleared away the rest of his cobwebs. His body bowed and he yanked at the bindings. His screams were muffled by the duct tape. Kramer kicked at me so I held the K-Bar to his throat. "Stop!" His thrashings ceased, and he began sobbing.

Sweat and fear poured out from him and I was afraid he might go into shock. I backhanded him again across the face. I lowered the register on my voice and made it raspy. "We want you to talk."

Kramer's body trembled.

I glanced at Becky. She was staring down at Kramer, her body rigid, her hands clenched. I couldn't tell if she was upset now that we were actually doing it, or if she wanted to kill Kramer with her own hands. I held my splayed fingers into the air then curled them into a fist.

Becky replied with splayed fingers. I nodded. We wouldn't take a direct route to his questioning. If she had made a fist we would get right to questions about Angel, and not be gentle about it. Her answer told me she was having serious doubts about Kramer being Angel's killer.

I backhanded him again and gripped his throat. "I'm going to take off the tape," I said in my raspy voice. "Scream or call for help and I'll cover your mouth while Billy here cuts off your balls." I squeezed harder. "Understand?"

He nodded and I ripped off the tape.

"What do you want?" he gasped. "You have the wrong man!"

"Oh, so you're not the man who's allowing Weller-Brice Petroleum to dump their filth into our beautiful lake?"

"What? I – "

"You're not the man who's taking money to poison our children's drinking water?"

"No! Listen, I was just – "

"You take away the important cases from your office underlings so you can blackmail the companies."

"I only –"

I held my knife at his throat. "And you killed Angel Anderson when she threatened to expose you."

His body stilled for a moment and confusion coated his face. "What? Are you crazy? I needed money, but I would never hurt anyone."

I had interviewed enough people at the end of my knife to know he was telling the truth, but Becky needed to believe it as well. I stood and continued the play. "The PPLM – People for the Protection of Lake Michigan – need to punish you." I looked at Becky. "Let's cut off his balls. It will serve as an example of how we will emasculate any attempts to poison our children."

"No! No!" Kramer's body went ridged as I slapped the tape back over his mouth. His bowels let loose and he pissed himself, but the stench of fear was worse. Becky took a step back and I looked at her. She shook her head, then gestured with her thumb to the door. I nodded.

I ripped one velcro cuff from Kramer's wrist. "Stop the dumping or the PPLM will be back to seek retribution."

I pulled off my ski-mask and glasses as we drove away. Becky sat in the passenger seat unmoving. "Take off your mask."

She did as I asked and ran her hands over her face. "He had nothing to do with Angel's murder."

"No. He didn't."

I placed a hand on her leg and she covered my hand with both of hers. "How're you doing?" I asked.

She stared out the side window. "In the beginning I was angry. I wanted him to pay." She squeezed my hand. "But… As it went on…" She puffed out a breath. "I could tell he wasn't the one. It just didn't feel right." She turned and looked at me. "We frightened him badly." She looked back out the windshield. "Were we wrong to do this to him?"

"We had to know for sure. And remember, he's an extortionist scumbag." I reached up and rubbed the back of Becky's neck. "We didn't hurt him, only scared him. It might turn him honest. He'll get over it. The fear will fade. Cutting off his balls would be harder to get over." I turned onto the entrance ramp and got on Route 75.

"Would you really cut off his balls?" she asked.

"Not me!" I shook my head. "But that Billy character is one mean mother. There's no telling what he'd do."

Becky snorted. "You think Kramer will buy that PPLM baloney?"

"Sure. There are enough nut-jobs out there to make it seem more than plausible."

Becky nodded and we rode in silence for awhile. "What do we do now?"

"I drop a note to the IRS. They'll take care of the rest." I glanced over at her. The earlier tension was gone and had been replaced by slumped shoulders, a look of heavy fatigue, and a touch of disappointment. "But I sense that's not what you mean."

I drummed my fingers on the steering wheel. "Maybe we should have stuck to the biggest lead we had – finding out how those gangbangers were involved."

"We needed to check him out. Now we cross this one off our list and move on." She shifted her body to me. "Besides, we have saved the children from terrible toxic poisoning."

I glanced at Becky. A small smile graced her tired face.

She would be all right.

Chapter 44

The late morning sun streamed in through the kitchen window. I stared at the light glinting off a dewy spider web in the grass while I lingered over my morning coffee. Becky was still asleep upstairs and that gave me time to consider our next move. I smiled as I thought about the word "our." She had become more than a lover and a friend – she had become essential in my life. The realization didn't cause the confusion and stress it used to. It was rather soothing.

What I was going to do about it I still hadn't figured out – or even if I needed to.

The woman in question staggered into the kitchen, bleary eyed, hair askew. Even in her ragged condition, she still lightened my heart.

"How you doing this morning, Beck?"

"Coffee," she mumbled, and shuffled to the pot. Becky poured a cup and sat down.

"I was going to make stuffed french toast."

Head bent over her cup, she slurped her coffee. "Your cooking sucks."

"Yeah. That's why I'm just going to heat up the takeout I bought yesterday from the diner."

Becky looked up. "Yesterday's takeout?" Her lip curled into an Elvis sneer.

"Pour enough syrup on anything and it will work." I walked over, lifted her chin, and looked into her eyes. "Or you can cook breakfast."

Becky gave me a sleepy smile. "OK. I'll cook. Put the french toast in the microwave, and I'll push the start button."

While breakfast heated, I got out plates and poured some OJ. I watched Becky out of the corner of my eye. "How are you handling last night?"

Her back and shoulders straightened, and she plopped her cup on the table. "The more I think about it, the more upset I am."

"He'll be alright."

Becky swung around and placed her arm on the back of the chair. "No. Fuck him. You were right. We only scared him." She turned back, lifted her coffee and stared into the cup. "I saw the fear in him. Angel had to go through that fear. Add horrible pain, humiliation, suffering and..." Her fist clenched and she spun toward to me. "I want the man who hurt her, Jack. I want him to die for what he did. I have no doubts."

"Then we'll find him and end it." The strength of her determination impressed me. I just hoped it wouldn't lead to any rash action. Then again, it was my job to make sure that didn't happen.

The microwave dinged. I served breakfast, sat, and picked up the jug of maple syrup. "I'm not sure what our next move should be."

"Well..." Becky snatched the jug out of my hand drowned her french toast in syrup. "Now our only lead is the Eastside Dragons." She handed me back the jug.

"Yeah. Should've stuck with that from the beginning."

"No. We had to be sure about him." Becky snowplowed a piece of french toast through her syrup. "After last night, I realized we have to be very sure of our final action." She raised a dripping bite with her fork. "We have to have the right man next time."

I nodded. "Yeah. We'll need to interrogate some gangbangers. I don't see how else to get any information."

"Same ploy as before?"

"No. Not yet at any rate. I think I need to bug the Dragons kingpin's crib."

Becky raised an eyebrow. "That's a stupid idea. Juan Johnson Cruz isn't someone to play around with."

"And if he's the killer?"

She puffed out a breath. "He does have an alibi for that night. But..." Becky reached across the table and grasped my hand. "He's a nasty customer. He might not have killed Angel, but I'm sure he's killed before."

"He'll never know I've been there."

Becky's gaze narrowed. "You mean, he'll never know *we've* been there."

I ran my hand over the stubble on my chin. "Well, this really is a one-man job."

Storm clouds roiled in Becky's eyes. "Oh really?"

"Really." Her deep inhale was the beginning of a verbal blast so I cut her off. "But I could really use a good backup man – or woman in this case."

Chapter 45

Most of the buildings around the "Plummeting Cage" were rundown tenements and abandoned warehouses. The only building in prime condition was Cruz's. Monica Brown's info said he lived on the top floor of the six-story building.

No one pays much attention to roof tops, and I decided that a high approach would give us our best chance to enter Cruz's living quarters. Though the abandoned tenement across from his building was twenty feet away, it was the same height and would make entry easier.

We drove the crap van to our warehouse and changed into our black "stealth" clothing. There was no need to pretend we weren't anything but what we were – thieves. In Cruz's neighborhood there would be no convincing someone that we were just two white people dressed in black out for a stroll.

I lifted my small "modular lightweight load-carrying equipment" backpack out of the back of the van and slipped it on. Wearing the Molle gear gave me a burst of adrenalin. It was like old times.

"How are your nerves?" I asked.

She finished tucking her hair under the rolled-up ski mask and gave me a thumbs-up. "Steady."

I handed her a small, black, single-sling Molle packed with food, water and medical supplies, then reached into the van for our weapons. I handed Becky her Para-Ordinance .45 cal. Super Hawg and watched her check the magazine, jack a round, and put the weapon on safe. She spun her pack around and placed the gun in the concealed pouch. Her sure hands moved with confidence and practice. I didn't let her see my smile as I clipped a Taser X26C onto my belt and slipped a suppressed Sig 9 into my shoulder holster.

I tugged on Becky's pack and looked down to check that her boots were double knotted. "What's the plan?" We had rehearsed the steps many times, but she knew not to ignore my question.

"One, use the shadows and alleys to approach the abandoned building next to the target. Two, gain access to the roof." She reached out and tugged on my gear, making sure nothing was loose.

"Three, we set up the grapple-slide. Four, you take stupid risks without me."

I sighed. Becky hadn't been able to get past this part of the scenario. "Beck, you know that a single entry is our best chance to bug and peek without being discovered."

She reached out and stroked my cheek with her fingers. "I know. I just don't like it."

"Ah, come on. It'll be fun." We walked together to the warehouse's side door entrance. "Besides, you're afraid of heights, as I vividly remember from the Ferris wheel incident."

"No fair! We were stuck at the top and it was swinging in the wind!"

I turned off the lights, opened the door and looked out. The alley was empty. "I always wondered why you chose my shoes to puke on."

"Simple. I didn't want to puke on any unfortunate below us." She followed me out the door. "And my shoes were new."

We lowered our ski masks over our safety glasses, and sprinted down the alleys and unlit side streets. Within a few minutes, we were at our target building.

I crouched next to an old dumpster and did a quick look around the side. The alley was empty and I motioned Becky to join me. Passing car headlights shone from the street and party noises spewed from the next building down. Though it was 3 A.M., the Eastside Dragons' Saturday night bash was still in high gear.

Good. Drunk, stoned and coked-up people's reaction times would be slow to nonexistent.

"This is as close as we can get," I said, and glanced back down the alley. Two boarded up windows, about six feet off the ground, were our best choice of entry. "Keep watch, I'll check the windows."

Becky nodded and I scooted to the first set of windows. The boards were still tightly nailed in place and I moved to the next set. The bottom board was loose and I used my cat's paw to remove the board and started on the next. When there was sufficient space to get inside, I gave a low whistle and Becky joined me. I gestured to the opening and clasped my hands. Becky put a boot in my hands and I hoisted her up. She slithered through the window and I jumped up and pulled myself through.

"Anything?" I asked as her flashlight finished scanning the room.

"No. Just scurrying rats."

"The only rats we need worry about are next door. Let's get to the stairs."

The stairs were across a large open area that looked like it might have been a cubicle farm in the past. We crept through the dust and fallen ceiling tiles and made our way to the stairs. I played my flashlight around the area. It was clear. I nodded to Becky and we started to climb. We were up two flights when something nagged at my brain. I signaled a stop and crouched low. Becky reached me and whispered in my ear. "What?"

"I don't know. Something doesn't feel right."

Becky stepped back, turned, and kept watch down the stairs. God she was good. I squelched the pride that threatened to overpower the feeling of caution and shone the light up the stairs and on the sides, looking for alarms or booby-traps. There were none. I thought I might be losing my touch when I realized what was wrong. I gave a low hiss and Becky again joined me.

"No dust on these steps. They've been used lately and frequently. Someone might be up top, so stay sharp."

Becky nodded and we resumed our climb. When we reached the top, the door to the roof was ajar. Tazer in hand, I slowly eased the door open. The smell of marijuana wafted in the air. Across the roof, thirty feet away, a skinny, black gangbanger stood with his foot atop the two-foot side wall. A joint hung out of his mouth and he gazed down at the street. My attention was on the AK-47 across his back. I stepped lightly on the roof's gravel until I was close enough to guarantee a solid hit and aimed. With a small snap, the barbs hit the guard in the back of the neck. A sizzle of electricity filled the air and with a choking sound he twitched and collapsed.

The sound of a scuffle behind me had me whirling and drawing my silenced Sig. Becky and another guard were wrapped together, his hands on her neck. Becky punched him with a groin strike, then drove her elbow into his face. He fell to the ground, pulling her ski-mask off as he went down. By the time I got to her, she had him sitting up in an arm lock and was kneeling next to him.

"Thanks," I said.

Becky nodded and tightened her grip as the gangbanger continued to struggle.

"I'm gonna kill your ass, you stupid bitch!"

I grabbed his jaw and jammed the Sig under his chin. "Shut up. How many more guards are on the roofs?"

"Hey, fuck you man. I ain't gotta tell you nothing." He looked at me, then at Becky. "Hey... You ain't no cops." He turned again to stare at Becky's face, only inches from his own. "Hey... I seen you at the fair! You that bitch that runs that bar." He grinned. "It's gonna be fun busting you place and you ass." He looked at his tasered buddy who was starting to move. "Hey Jamal, guess who here. It's – "

I pulled the trigger.

His head exploded, spewing blood onto Becky's face and clothes. She stared a moment at the body in her arms then dropped it and jumped up. Eyes wide, she looked down at the blood and pieces of skull and brain on her chest.

"Had to be done," I said. I ran to the Tazer, jolted the other guard again and placed the Tazer into my holster. He had been too far away to have heard what his buddy said, so I decided not to kill him. I raced back to Becky. "Abort! We have to leave."

Shock had slammed into Becky and she stood with eyes seeing nothing. She tentatively reached up and pulled a brain fragment off her face, then looked at her shaking hand.

I grasped her arm. "Get downstairs." Becky didn't move, just stared at her hand. I grabbed her shoulder and shook her hard. "Move!" I pushed her toward the doorway and she staggered away and started down. I grabbed the dead gangbanger and dragged him to a spot over the dumpster. I tossed him over the edge and watched the plummeting body bury itself in week-old trash bags. I picked up Becky's ski-mask and kicked aside some skull fragments on the way to the stairs. There was nothing I could do about the blood.

Damn. I had missions go to hell in a hurry, but this one really burned. I knew there was more than just one casualty. From Becky's expression, I knew this was going to be bad.

Becky stood at the bottom of the stairs scraping her hands at the blood on her face. I handed her the ski-mask. "Put this on." There was no reaction. I shook the mask in front of her face. "Put this on! We don't want you to be seen again."

Her head jerked toward me. The recognition in her eyes said she knew why I killed the gangbanger. And her look said she blamed herself.

"Not now, Becky. We gotta get out of here."

She pulled on the mask and we headed for the window.

Chapter 46

The trip back was a lot faster than the trip from the warehouse. Becky ran most of the way not really caring about stealth. I dogged her heels, letting her run it out, hoping the exercise would purge the emotions running through her. I knew it wouldn't, but it might help.

When we got to the warehouse, I unlocked the side door and Becky rushed toward the bathroom. I locked up, gave her a minute, then joined her.

Bent over the large industrial sink, Becky washed her face and hands. Her ski-mask and shirt lay on the floor by the door. Steam billowing from the hot water floated up and fogged the mirror. She splashed water on her face and scrubbed it hard, again and again.

I stood in the doorway and said nothing. After several minutes, she turned off the water, placed her hands on either side of the sink, and hung her head. A minute passed and she looked into the mirror. Slowly, she wiped away the fog and stared at herself.

"You're not any different than yesterday," I said.

Her head hung down again. "Yes, I am. I killed him."

I stepped close behind her. "No. I killed him."

Becky's head lowered. "It's my fault. If my mask hadn't come off, he'd still be alive."

"You don't know that." I gently placed my hands on her shoulders, but she shrugged them off. I raised my hands again then dropped them to my sides. "He wasn't an innocent. He chose his death with every action he took. We all do."

Becky shook her head. "I never... I didn't think..." Her hands flew up, the heel of her palms pressed into her eyes. "There was so much... his head..."

I turned her around and held her tightly. Her breath came in ragged gasps. I hoped she would cry, but she didn't.

She pushed away from me with a forearm and broke the hug. I fought the urge to reason with her, shake, yell, or simply hold her. I knew she had to deal with this on her own. "Come on. Let's go home," I said.

Becky nodded then looked at me with hard, flat eyes. I knew then she no longer blamed herself.

She blamed me.

Chapter 47

The next few days were tough. Though we resumed our routine of Becky running the bar and me sitting on the bar stool, things had changed.

Changed?

They'd taken a high dive into the crapper.

Becky went through the motions, but her attitude to life remained cold. Her attitude toward me was Siberian-meat-locker cold. Lame excuses of being tired and perfunctory goodnight cheek kisses followed a hasty retreat to her apartment after the bar closed. I was never invited, nor did I force the issue.

I sat on my barstool and perused the newspaper, looking for any item that mentioned a shooting death. Nothing came up in any media. The gang probably had a very good body disposal system at their beck-and-call.

I pushed aside the paper and sipped my drink. As I watched Becky polish the already sparkling clean mahogany I wondered how to handle her. I didn't think gentleness would work, and she knew too much Krav Maga to give her a dose of tough love.

The only way I knew to get over the shock of a killing was heated anger and more killing. That certainly wasn't the way I wanted to go with Becky.

Ralph looked up from his bottle of beer and leaned toward me. "Fucked up again, eh, Jack."

I grunted. "Always."

"It's a simple fix." Ralph peeled a strip of label off the bottle. "It's a lesson I learned too late with my ex."

My ears sharpened and I stared at him. With Becky, I was grasping at straws, and any hair-brain idea caught my attention. "Ralph, if you can suggest anything that would work your next dozen beers are on me."

"One word, Jack."

I leaned forward, knowing a joke on me was probably coming next, but couldn't afford to not take the chance.

"Jewelry," he said.

"What?"

"Jewelry. Works every time with a woman." He drained his beer.

I pondered the idea, then rejected it. "Think a shiny bauble would work on her?"

Ralph glanced over at Becky as she muscled a case of Bud into the cooler, then shook his head. "Nah. Probably not." He grinned over at me. "It would shock the shit out of her, though."

My brain tweaked on an idea. Jewelry wouldn't shock her, but I knew what would. It might totally end our bond, but our relationship was pretty much loitering on Titanic's lido deck anyway.

I pulled two twenty's from my wallet and dropped them on the bar. "Ralph, the next dozen beers are on me."

Ralph grabbed my arm as I stood to leave. "No rings, no tiaras. One raises too many questions, the other is just ridiculous."

"Thanks. I'll keep that in mind."

I walked to the door and headed to my house.

The bar's closed sign was lit when I returned. I used the key Becky had given me for when I opened up occasionally.

Becky was sweeping the floor and looked up as I closed and locked the door. A cloak of sadness covered her, and she seemed small and very vulnerable, but a patina of anger overlaid all.

"I thought you'd left," she said. "Maybe for good." She had mumbled that last under her breath but I caught it anyway.

I couldn't decide whether her words were a wish or held disappointment. It didn't matter. I was never one to waffle. This had to be settled now. I strode over to her, reached up and held onto the broom handle. "I want to show you something."

She released the broom and walked to the bar, keeping her back to me. "Listen, Jack. We've had fun, but..."

"Bullshit!" I threw the broom across the room and it clattered against a table. I marched to the bar, gripped her shoulders and spun her around. "Getting rid of me won't get rid of the image in your mind!"

She jerked away and turned back to the bar. I pulled a brown 9x12 envelope from inside my coat and slapped it on the bar.

Becky glanced down, but didn't touch the envelope. "What's this?"

"Something to put what you're feeling into perspective."

"Jack, I don't think – "

I opened the envelope and slid photos onto the bar then spread them out.

Angel's autopsy pictures stared back at us.

One of Becky's hands gripped the bar and the other covered her mouth.

"You're feeling sorry for yourself and what you were a part of." I slid the close up of the burn marks on Angel's breast under Becky's face. "Angel is who you should be sorry for. This and all she had to endure before death claimed her!"

She picked up the picture and brought it closer, her eyes wide with shock.

"There is no place here for emotional sentiment," I said, barely containing the anger in my chest. "We are trying to stop the evil animal that did this to her! The bastard I killed was part of that. And I killed him, not you!"

Becky lowered the picture and grabbed the bar, catching herself as she sagged. Her knuckles were white and tremors shook her body.

I raised my hands hold her, then halted, unsure of what to do. The sob that wrenched from her made up my mind and I placed my hands on her shoulders. With another sob, she turned and launched herself into my arms. She clung tight to me, like someone avoiding being sucked into a twisting tornado.

I held onto her and said nothing.

After awhile, her sobs ceased but the hitches in her breath continued. The force of her grip lessened, but mine didn't.

She lowered her head onto my chest. "I'm sorry, Jack."

"Nothing to be sorry about." I dropped a kiss onto the top of her head. "It's just something we can work out."

Becky looked up at me with red puffy eyes. "Thank you."

I released my hug and she stepped back. Becky gestured to the bar. "I don't want to look at that again."

"Got it." I gathered up the pictures and jammed them back into the envelope, then turned to look at her. An easy-to-read "*what now*" sign was plastered on my head in red neon.

It was her move.

Becky reached out a hand. "Let's go upstairs."

I clasped her hand and she never let go of mine until we were in her apartment. Becky got out two glasses and the bottle of Jameson. She poured, then placed the bottle on the table. Her lowered eyes wouldn't meet mine. "Don't hate me, Jack." She sounded unsure, her voice shaky.

"I could never hate you, Beck." I drummed my fingers on the table. "Maybe sucker punch you, but I could never hate you." That brought her eyes to mine and I picked up my glass. "Sláinte."

She raised hers as well. "Sláinte." This time her voice was firm.

We downed the shot and clinked our glasses on the table at the same time. Becky gave me a little smile and again reached out her hand. "Make love with me, Jack."

The words reached in, touched my heart, and flooded me with gladness.

I had Becky back.

Chapter 48

I glanced at my watch as the last patrons left the bar unasked. 2 AM on the dot. A drunk can be more punctual than the US postal service.

As Becky wiped the bar down she moved in my direction.

"Since tomorrow's Sunday, let's go out to dinner," I said.

She gave the bar a few more unnecessary swipes and looked up. "We eat out most nights." Her raised eyebrow and puzzled look said it all.

"I thought we'd try Chez Sky."

Both of her eyebrows flew upward. "The Sky?" She quick-rubbed the mahogany again before looking at me. "Can we afford – " Becky held up a hand. "Never mind. Forgot who I was talking to."

That she didn't remember at first that I had tons of money brought a smile to my lips, as well as the "we" in her question.

"We'll get dressed up and be elegant. I'll drag on a suit and you can pick out a clean t-shirt."

"T-shirt, huh?"

"Yeah." I smiled. "The yellow one that says 'Do not disturb I'm disturbed enough already.'"

Becky didn't rise to the bait, but instead leaned on the bar. "How about I wear that black see-through teddy number instead?"

That vision punted away all coherent thoughts as my blood rushed south. "Uhh..."

She beamed a smile as she buffed the bar. "Or maybe I'll wear something else."

"Uhh... Maybe you can wear that teddy thing tonight and something else tomorrow."

Her eyes gleamed a mischievous glint. "I can do that."

"Let's spend the night at my house. I'll finish cleaning up and you go pack."

Becky nodded. "Be right back," she said and headed for the stairs.

I picked up the broom and started sweeping. "And don't forget the teddy!"

The rhythmic swoosh of the broom became automatic as thoughts about Becky rattled around in my head. The memory of the gangbanger's violent death still shadowed her slightly, but she had accepted it, and that acceptance would eventually dispel the visions. I was sure it would work for her – it had worked for me for many years. Lucky for me she hadn't come into it hard and brittle as some I'd seen. I raised the broom in the air in a salute to her father. "Connor Quinn. You've done a fine job with your daughter. She's righted herself and reaffirmed herself as the positive person I've come to love." I lowered the broom and continued sweeping.

Wait a minute. Did I just say "love"? I played with those thoughts and feelings while I made little piles of trash on the floor. Love was a four letter word that held no meaning for me. I wanted to be close to Becky, felt affection for her – even need. Was that love? And did it matter what I called it? A rose is a rose...

"I'm ready," said Becky as she came down the stairs. She had a small suitcase in one hand and a garment bag draped over the other arm.

I stared at her face. A rose is a rose, and Becky was indeed my rose.

That was good enough for me. No labels needed.

I walked to her and stroked the side of her face. "A rose indeed."

She stared, puzzled for a moment. "What?"

"Nothing." I stepped back and gestured to the garment bag. "You don't need a garment bag for that teddy. It would fit in your pocket."

She lifted the bag. "This is for my T-shirt. I didn't want to get it wrinkled. It's one of the long ones." She gave me a sideways look. "I plan not to wear panties under it to keep your appetite up."

I laughed. "Beck, you're killing me."

"I won't kill you completely dead," she said, as she headed to the storage room door. "Just completely tired."

"Not completely dead, eh?" I leaned the broom in the corner and followed her. "I can live with that."

Chapter 49

Sunday evening I paced my foyer, waiting for Becky. Once again I shot a nervous glance at the velvet box on the side table and made another circuit of the floor. As I adjusted the shirt cuff in my suit for the fourth time, she came down the stairs.

"Final–" The word choked off as my throat closed when I saw her.

Dressed in an electric blue, ankle-long, off the shoulder silk dress, she looked absolutely stunning. Her hair was up in a french twist that gave her a regal look I hadn't realize she could pull off. A small fake diamond broach held the coif together on the side of the twist. A diamond broach. Perfect. I felt myself relax.

"You are... Stunning... Incredible..." I shook my head. "I'm out of words."

Her smile broadened as she reached the bottom tread. "That's what I was going for. Making you speechless is always a worthy goal."

I glanced down at her neck. "You need something around your neck."

She grimaced. "I know. I put on my cross, but it was too small. It looked lost."

I stepped to the side table and picked up the velvet box. "Let's try this and see if it looks lost."

Becky stared at the box for a moment then jerked her hands behind her back. "Jack... I can't..."

"Sure you can. Just pretend you're a princess." I opened the box and watched Becky's eyes pop wide. I removed the teardrop diamond pendant hung from a single strand of pearls. "Let's try this on." She tore her stare away from the necklace and looked at me, her stunned eyes filled with disbelief. I smiled, glad I could make her speechless as well. "Turn around."

She did as I asked, and I fastened the clip at the nape of her neck, then sealed it with a kiss. "There. That should make your ensemble complete." I walked her to the mirror over the side table and stepped aside.

Becky stared a moment, then her hand reached up and touched the diamond. "Holy shit! I do look like a princess."

"Sound like one as well," I said.

She spun toward me. "Jack, I can't accept something like this!" She turned back to the mirror and her hand again reached up to touch the diamond. Her eyebrows furrowed and she shot me a sideways glance. "Is this stolen?"

I shook my head. "Nope. Tiffany's." I stepped behind her and lightly traced my fingers down her shoulders. "It was made for you, and only you."

She turned and faced me. "Jack, I don't know what to say."

"Just say 'thank you,' and get your wrap – I'm hungry."

Becky leaned in and kissed my cheek. "Thank you."

The maitre d' at Chez Sky wore an ear-to-ear grin as we arrived. "Mr. Astor, please come this way. Your table is ready."

He led us to a table next to the panel of tall windows that spanned three sides of the restaurant. Situated on the top floor of the Kaiser Building, Chez Sky featured a birds-eye view of the waterfront and Lake Michigan.

The maitre d' seated us and signaled for the sommelier. "If there is anything I can do for you, Mr. Astor, please let me know." He bowed and backed away.

"Thank you, François."

Becky fluffed her napkin. "Mr. Astor?"

"Sure." I nodded. "Just as real as Benny's name is François."

"You've been here often?"

I smiled. "Naahh. I just injected a shot of monetary grease on the wheel when I dropped by to make reservations."

Becky glanced out at the view. "Well, this wheel certainly doesn't squeak." She reached over and held my hand. "This is great, Jack. And I'm loving our masquerade in high society, but..." Her fingers fondled the pendant. "I've been thinking about this necklace."

I squeezed her hand. "Don't even think about refusing it."

"I just have one question."

At that moment, a flurry of waiters arrived with champagne in a bucket, bread, and small garden salads.

I waited until after the wine tasting ritual then answered. "Go ahead, ask your question."

Becky leaned forward. "Have you ever given jewelry like this to another woman?"

It seemed like an odd question, but I answered truthfully. "No." I thought about it a moment longer. "I did leave my handcuffs with a woman, once. Does that count?"

She raised an eyebrow. "This is going to distract from my original question, but why leave your handcuffs?"

I shrugged. "She was using them at the time. Well, one cuff, anyway. The other was locked to a radiator."

With tilted head, she gestured with her fingers. "More."

"The Polizei were on their way, and it would be better if I wasn't around when they picked her up."

"Was she bad?"

"Nasty."

She flapped her hands in front of her face in what looked like an attempt to erase the vision and get back to the original question. "Then if it's true that you've never given any other woman something this wonderful, I'm keeping it."

Her statement pleased me. The rationalizations I had readied to convince her otherwise were lame in the extreme. "Why no argument?"

"'Cause you bought it for me, and you've never done anything like that for anyone before. It makes it special."

"You're special, Becky."

"And I'm planning to wear this necklace with just one other accessory when we get home."

"What's that?"

"The bedroom lamp."

The vision sent a spear of heat to my groin. "Will you leave you hair up like that?"

She placed both elbows on the table and her chin on her laced fingers. Her lips turned up in a sly smile. "At first."

I leaned back and looked down. "If you see the table levitating, it's not telekinesis."

She picked up her fork and her tongue slowly licked the tines. "I love magic tricks."

I laughed. "Eat your salad."

Becky speared a piece of endive. "Do we get menus?"

"I took the liberty of ordering in advance."

"Presumptive of you. Perhaps I'd like to see what type of cheeseburgers they serve here."

"Quite right." I gestured to our waiter. "Would you bring mademoiselle a menu?"

With a bow the waiter fled and returned moments later with a menu. He opened it for Becky and left. She scanned the items for a moment before lowering it and looking up over the edge. "It's all in French."

I nodded. *"Bien sûr. C'est la langue de l'amour."* I refilled our glasses. "I've ordered a plethora of dishes, from escargot to truffles. It should be a treat."

"I'm game." A slight frown crossed her lips. "But I hope the truffles are chocolate."

We sat, ate, and talked about the different dishes, her bar, and our perspectives on life in general. We didn't touch upon Angel or the gangbanger's death. I took that as a good sign.

Becky glanced over my shoulder. "Don't look now, but Benny just seated Councilman Douglas."

"Politics pays well." I sipped my champagne. "Who's he here with? Campaign supporter, or cronies?"

She glanced around my shoulder. "Neither. He's alone."

"Isn't he married?"

"No. Ugly divorce three years ago. He came out on top politically. He made her look like a gold-digger and him a fool in love. His PR people spun it so it actually played well with the voters."

Tempting as it was to turn around I thought it a good time to test Becky's observation skills. "What do you see?"

She shrugged. "Nothing. He's just sitting there."

I leaned forward and again asked, "What do you see?"

Becky looked nonplussed for a moment, then nodded. "Gotcha." She stared back at the table. "The table's set for two. He's checking his watch. The waiters just brought a bottle of champagne. His fingers are drumming on the table."

"Good. Now don't keep staring at him. Look at the wall behind him, the people at the nearby table, the waiters, anything, but don't stare. People can feel it if someone's staring at them. Just glance away and look with the side of your eyes."

Her baby-blues settled on me. "Do I need to know this?"

"You never know, therefore you should know."

Becky sighed. "Reality according to Jack's world vision."

"Since reality is only perceived, it is sometimes inaccurate, as is observation." I wiggled my fingers in front of her face. "Your eyes can deceive you. Don't trust them."

She smiled and looked again over my shoulder. "Well, Obi Wan, Diego Sanchez just arrived. And, unless my eyes are deceiving me, a stunning redhead is on his arm."

I had to look. A casual glance solidified everything Becky had related. The redhead was indeed stunning in a clinging, green sequined dress. I turned back to Becky. "Does she look familiar somehow?"

She looked over again. "No... Well, kinda." She stretched her neck for a better look. "Sanchez has seated her and is leaving."

"Pimping for the Councilman, perhaps?"

Becky lifted her wine glass. "Why not? He does everything else for Douglas. I'm sure if Douglas advances to state senator, they'll be painting Diego Sanchez's name on the councilman's office door within seconds."

"Politicians – can't live with them, can't usually convict 'em." I crooked my finger and our waiter stepped to the table.

"Sir?"

"We'll have the brioche perdu with lavender honey ice cream for two."

"*Oui monsieur.*" With a snap of his heels, he bowed and left.

"Lavender honey ice cream?"

I held up a finger. "Don't knock it yet. Perhaps your palette will appreciate its subtle pairing with the brioche."

"Yeah. That's me alright. Can we stop at Mickey D's on the way home? We'd be really subtle there."

My eyes followed the stunning redhead as she walked past our table and headed for the restroom. A cloud of Channel No.5 drifted behind her. "There's something..."

"Yeah. Two something's. About a thirty-eight double-dee."

"Hey. I didn't fall over my feet when Angel came into the bar, so I'm immune to redheads," I lied with a straight face. Angel's face and her innocent eloquence drifted into my mind. I looked again at the woman as she turned into the hallway. The eloquence was there, but she lacked all pretense of innocence. "Something just tickled my brain." I leaned toward Becky. "Don't you have to go to the bathroom?"

Her head pulled back and she raised an eyebrow. "No."

I reached over and touched her hand. "Yes, you do. Go now."

The wheels crunched in her head for a moment then her eyes brightened. "Douglas. Fundraiser with gangbanger Juan Cruz. Gangbangers dumped Angel's body. Redhead." She stood.

"Harriet Hawkshaw. On the case." She turned and left for the bathroom.

I sat back and watched her go – elegance with attitude. My kind of woman. Actually, my woman. I felt the grin steal over my face. Yep. It felt right. It felt good. I realized I was in love and the word "damn" didn't even follow that realization.

The brioche perdu arrived the same time Becky returned. She stared at the dessert. "Looks good."

"I'm sure it is." I lifted a spoon. "How'd it go?"

The harsh coldness I'd seen when we first met flashed back on her face for a moment. "Well, her name is Clarissa. At least that's her working name."

"Hooker?"

"I wouldn't put her in that category. Exclusive dabbler, most likely – and very expensive."

I felt mischievous and had to ask, "Could I afford her?"

Becky dug into her brioche. "No."

"No?"

"No. You couldn't afford to lose that many body parts."

I laughed. "Get any information?"

She spooned the lavender honey ice cream into her mouth and rolled it around her tongue for a moment before answering. "Seems like a nice person but a little on the hard side. Said Sanchez contacted her after meeting her at the opera. She and Douglas have been out twice." She tapped her finger on the table and glanced up at Douglas' table again. "Seems like Sanchez is, indeed, pimping for the Councilman."

The woman left the restroom and I resisted the impulse to look at her as she passed. Instead, I smiled at Becky. "Anything else?"

"I glanced at her as she put makeup on her arm to cover a bruise, and she just smiled and said, 'My friend gets a little worked up sometimes.'"

"Humm. Interesting. What did you say?"

Becky shrugged. "I said 'All men are pigs, but it's better when they're rich pigs.' She agreed."

"Oink."

Becky patted my hand. "I don't think that of you. I was just playing a role, Jack. Just playing a role." She ate the last spoonful of dessert and smiled. "Now, let's go back to your sty."

The drive back to my place was quiet. We were both engrossed in our own thoughts.

Becky's statement broke the silence. "Douglas starts with 'D'."

"And Angel worked in the same building."

We turned to each other and nodded. "This one feels like the right direction," she said.

"Yeah. It does." I reached over and patted her hand. "It does."

Chapter 50

We spent the next couple nights arguing about a plan. My idea was just to learn as much as we could about Douglas by tapping his phone and shadowing him for a few days. Becky wanted to break into his house and do a search.

"We might find evidence in his home and this will all be over," said Becky.

"Or we find nothing and spook him into hiding evidence he has elsewhere." I wrote a list on a pad then pushed it over to her. "Here's what I think is the best way to go about this."

Becky scanned my to-do list. "I don't see my name next to any item."

I grabbed the list and wrote "kiss Jack passionately," and her name next to it, then showed it to her.

She glanced at the pad and humphed. "That's a lot of hard work, but I can pull it off."

"That's work?"

"Very hard. Well it'll be hard after I finish." Becky grinned. "Seriously, I'd like to be more in on this."

"Well, you can accompany me on the stakeouts." I rubbed my chin. "We can make out while we watch."

Becky nodded. "That would allow me to cross off that last item on the list, but we'd miss seeing a lot with the windows all steamed up."

"True." I tapped my fingers on the table and sighed. "Let me do the grunt work. I promise not to sandbag you if I learn anything."

Becky stared at me for a moment as if to determine the truth, so I tilted my head and put on my most sincere smile.

"You're an asshole." She closed her eyes and sighed."But it's a deal."

Chapter 51

I spent the next two days gathering information about Councilman Aaron Douglas. He was easy to keep track of during the day as his schedule was posted on the "Councilman Aaron Douglas – The People's Choice" website. With his ever present shadow, Diego Sanchez, Douglas made the rounds of grand openings, women's clubs, Rotary clubs, and any club or group that would listen to him talk. I attended several of his speeches and was impressed at how he could speak for an hour and never say a thing.

Douglas' website had him attending a rubber chicken fund raiser tonight, so I headed for the bar. As I plopped down on my regular stool, Becky headed my way, wiping down the bar as she came over.

"Hey, Jack. Drink?"

"Yeah."

Becky poured my JWB. "Find out anything?"

"No. Not yet. It's just a boring shadowing job so far."

"Serves you right for not going with my plan to hit his place while he was out."

I sipped at my JW Black. "Gotta know your enemy. Any small bit of info can make the difference between gold or grunge."

Becky placed her elbows on the bar and cradled her face with her hands. "How about Sanchez?"

I shrugged. "Seems to be the ass-wipe you thought him to be. He schmoozes everyone at parties and gatherings with a hard handshake or an air kiss. He gets a glass of champagne and carries it around most of the night while he works the room."

Becky straightened and scrubbed an imaginary spot on the bar. "I can't figure what their scam could be. Gerrymandering, extortion, sex trade, who knows. It might be hard to find out without a direct question put to someone like you did to Tedesco's thug."

"And if that someone had nothing to do with Angel's murder we might tip our hand to the real killer."

"True." A pensive look crossed her face as she polished the bar. "What's next, then?"

"Tomorrow I'm going to the library, to hit the microfiche department and do some back checking on Douglas."

"Since you're free tonight." Becky reached under the counter, placed a tray full of pretzel bowls on the bar, and shoved them at me. She smiled.

"Pretzel boy," I said, and shook my head. "Oh, how the mighty have fallen. What a come down."

Becky patted my arm. "Deliver these and we'll have you coming later tonight."

Chapter 52

The library computers told me nothing new, but Douglas' voting record was suspiciously absent from the library records or his website. Web searches also turned up only a scattering of older voting records.

City hall records were difficult to get, though they were supposedly public knowledge. It cost me two hours and two twenties to hurry a couple clerks before I could track Douglas' voting record for the last four years. Most votes were for or against public works, but several in the last year looked like flat out gerrymandering. I overlaid the new areas onto a map. An expansion here, a cut there. It didn't look like anything more than a politician out to grab bigger voting blocks – then a street name popped out at me. Grand Rapids Road, the location of a row of new strip clubs. Three had opened since Douglas lobbied to change the city ordinances. It smacked of kickbacks, but not murder.

Even if Douglas was dirty, I couldn't see how he connected with Angel's murder. Maybe there was no connection, but I had to follow it through. Actually, "we" had to follow it through. I smiled as I thought of Becky. With no other leads it was all we had to find Angel's killer.

Two pictures of Angel always hung in the back of my mind. The first was the vibrant, innocent Angel with her sweet smile and sweet disposition. But the second, the picture of her lying cut up and cold on the coroner's slab, always overlaid the first. I knew I had to find her killer to erase that image. It wasn't revenge. It wasn't even a way to eliminate an evil and maybe a way to atone for some of my own.

It was a reckoning.

Chapter 53

The next night, as the councilman left his office, I tailed him to his home in the center of his constituency – a blue collar and no collar area, littered with folks struggling just to get by day-to-day. If Douglas could lighten their drab lives even slightly, I could see how he kept getting elected. Maybe he really helped them, maybe it was just good PR.

Parked in the stealth van a block from his home, I scanned the area with my binoculars. Rundown businesses and ramshackle apartments flanked the streets for blocks. Douglas' clean and well-kept brownstone stuck out like a single tooth in a gaping mouth. He might live amongst the drabs, but he wasn't one of them. I'd bet my Monet that the inside of the brownstone was as well appointed as any west side manor and just as secure.

As night fell, I took a bite of my ham sandwich and drifted into a hunter's mindset – relaxed but very aware. I hoped this wouldn't be one of the nights that Douglas stayed home and watched Gilligan's Island reruns.

Four hours later, a black Mercedes E-Class sedan passed the van and slowed to a stop in front of the brownstone. After a moment, Douglas hurried down the stairs and entered the back seat of the car. He had ditched his ever-present suit, and wore casual clothes with a dark blue windbreaker. They did a quick U-turn and sped past me. Diego Sanchez was behind the wheel, still wearing his business suit.

I followed.

The Mercedes slid into the parking lot of Scarlett's Gentleman's Club. A blinking neon sign advertised sophisticated women and VIP rooms. I pulled to the curb a half-block back and watched. Sanchez exited the car and entered the club. I started to wonder if this was just a drive-thru whorehouse and the boys were getting take out, when Sanchez exited the building followed by a fat greasy guy with slicked-back hair. The rear tinted window of the Mercedes slid down and grease guy tried a smile that quickly faded. Sanchez stood at the rear of the car, hands crossed in front of him. The conversation with Douglas was one way as the fat man just stood there and listened, his shoulders slumping more with each sentence he heard. After a minute, the man nodded and stuck out his hand. Douglas ignored it, and the tinted window slid closed. Fatty dropped his hand, hung his head a moment then turned and re-entered the club. The Mercedes' window slid half-way down and Sanchez walked over. He listened a moment, then nodded and reached for his cell phone. After dialing, I saw his lips move with one word, then he disconnected and got into the driver's seat. They sat for a few moments, then the car started and they drove away.

I was about to follow when a tricked-out '69 Bonneville slid into the parking lot, music blasting. It was so reminiscent of the dead gangbangers' '66 Chevy, I hesitated. The car's engine shut off, killing the music. The passenger door opened, and out stepped a dreadlocked, skinny black man carrying a small package under his arm. Something ticked in my brain as I watched him. The man strode to the club door and walked right in as if he belonged there.

My memory clicked.

Jamal. Rooftop Jamal. I wondered if the holes from the Tazer barbs I'd shot in the back of his neck had healed. With the feeling that pieces of the puzzle were falling in place, I exited the van and walked to the club's entrance. A half-dozen frat boys with IU Northwest sweatshirts bulled past me, goading each other with crude remarks and laughter. I wondered if I had ever been that young. I knew I certainly had been that stupid. My hand patted my pocket for a smoke, then remembered I had quit. Old habits never really die.

The twenty it cost me to enter Scarlett's Gentleman's Club included one drink. A quick look around said Jamal was nowhere in sight. I gave my order to the bartender and found a seat at a side table against the wall. The only lights in the room were the red-globe covered candles on the tables and the spotlights on the stage where two girls spun, hung, and made love to steel poles. The music was loud enough to block out anyone trying to converse or eavesdrop on a neighbor.

A very pretty, dark-haired, waitress sauntered over with my drink. She plopped down my JWB and leaned over, her large breasts nearly falling out of her bikini top. "Hey there, you. I'm Vega."

I sipped the drink. "Hey, back at 'cha, far-away star system."

Amusement passed over her face before her fake smile returned. "I don't have to be light-years away." She then squatted, knees far apart, one arm on the table. "We have private VIP rooms in the back." Vega ran a hand up my leg. "You look like a VIP. Wanna come check it out? I could show you something interesting."

I glanced down at her cleavage. "Looks pretty interesting from here."

The smile on her lips didn't reach her eyes. "Oh, honey. I could show you a lot more interesting things in the VIP room. Maybe make you see stars you never dreamed of."

A chuckle escaped my lips and humor and sorrow flashed through me. Soccer mom? College kid? Someone just selling sex for money? It didn't matter. Life threw curves and you either ducked or got smacked.

The door marked "office" opened and Jamal walked out and headed for the exit, the package no longer under his arm. I peeled two Benjamin's off my money clip and slipped it into the hand caressing my leg. "I'm sorry, but I've got an appointment elsewhere and can't stay. I'm sure it would be extremely memorable with a woman like you, but business comes first."

She stood and glanced at the hundreds, confusion coating her face. "But..."

I stood and placed a hand on her arm. "Vega, some consequences yet hang in the stars."

She straightened and this time the smile on her lips was real. "The fault, dear Brutus, is not in the stars, but in ourselves."

I laughed aloud and dropped another hundred on the table. "Take good care of yourself, Vega."

"Thanks," she said, as I walked to the entrance.

As I stepped outside, Jamal jumped into the Bonneville's passenger seat, and off they sped. I ran to the van and followed.

Chapter 54

The tricked-out, candy-apple red Bonneville headed for the gang's district. While we drove, I admired the car. Restoring old vehicles must be a thing with the gangbangers. I hoped Jamal had at least fixed the muffler – I wouldn't want anyone else to die from carbon monoxide poisoning.

Two blocks from the Plummeting Cage, the car slowed and slid to the curb without stopping. Jamal's arm came out the window and handed a small envelope to a boy about twelve, then the car sped away. The boy placed the envelope inside his shirt and ran to the Plummeting Cage. He dashed up the outside steps, dropped the envelope into a mail slot, then walked to another man a block away. The man slipped what looked like some cash into the boy's hand and they parted ways.

I sped up as I drove past the duo. The entire time I kept checking my rearview mirrors, as a feeling of being watched crept up my spine. No car stood out, but I turned onto some side streets and circled for a few blocks just in case. Nothing showed, but I couldn't shake the feeling. I pulled into an abandoned parking lot and just sat and watched. A half-hour later, the feeling passed.

I'd learned not to disregard those feelings and it had paid off several times. Now, I wondered if what I felt was real or I was just getting paranoid – or more paranoid, I should say. There was more on the line this time than just myself. There was Becky. Could that up my paranoid level? Sure, but something had set it off. The only thing that calmed my paranoia was to stay alert, stay well armed, and cover all bases. After a deep breath, I patted my Sigs and drove to the bar.

"How they hangin'?" asked Ralph.

"Low and to the left." I slid onto my barstool next to him and glanced around for Becky, but Carli was behind the bar. "Carli's tending bar?"

"Yep," said Ralph. "It's Chernobyl all over again." He held up a bottle of Budweiser. "See my Coors?"

I stood. My paranoia pushed a hot flash to my chest. "Where's Becky?"

"Relax," said Ralph. "She's in the back. Mary Beth came in with her new baby and they went in the back to ooh and coo." Ralph wrinkled his nose. "And hopefully change that kid's diaper."

At the other end of the bar, Becky stepped out from the back room, baby in her arms, Mary Beth right behind her.

Becky.

Baby in her arms.

Her eyes met mine. It all focused.

I wanted that.

Fear tried to overcome the feeling with thoughts of how I wasn't deserving, but my heart pushed it away.

I wanted that.

Becky grinned at me and I knew at that moment she wanted that too.

She gestured me over and I lumbered my way down the bar, hoping the tightness in my chest would loosen.

"Hey, Jack," she said. She tilted her head to the left. "This is Mary Beth." She smiled down at the bundle in her arms. "And this is Grayson." She held the baby out to me. "Wanna hold him?"

I spied the challenge in her eyes and accepted the dare. I just hoped they had changed his diaper. She slid the kid into my arms and I held him confidently as if fear wasn't running down my spine. I hefted him a few times. "He's a big healthy boy. Lot of meat here." I wanted to stick my tongue out at Becky, but refrained and instead looked at Mary Beth. "Grayson? Cool name."

"Yes," she said. "We're on the G's."

"G's?"

"Yeah. We're running though the alphabet." She counted off on her fingers. "Avalon, Brandon, Celeste, Donovan, Ethan, Fiona, and now Grayson."

I handed the baby to Mary Beth. "Well, I hope for your sake you never wind up with a Zeke."

"Heaven forbid." She smiled down at Grayson. "No. He's our last. Bobby is having a vasectomy." She looked up, determination narrowing her eyes. "Even if I have to do it myself."

I glanced at Becky. "Ouch. She's certainly a friend of yours."

"Hey," Becky said. "Us Saint Teresa graduates are tough." They high-fived and kissed each other's cheek. Mary Beth said goodbye and left.

Becky placed a hand on my arm, grinned, and didn't say anything. I hid my smile and tried to look macho.

"How did it go today?" she asked.

"Good. I think I found a link to Douglas and the gang."

Her grip on my arm tightened. "Good let's –"

A hiss and a spray of soda erupted from behind the bar. Carli stood, knife in hand, mouth open and a poleaxed look on her face. "I was just cutting lemons!" she cried.

Becky rushed to the spray, reached down and shut off the soda valve. The spray dwindled as did the laughter in the room. "That yellow hose is the club soda."

"Sorry," said Carli, elbow on one hip with the knife waving in the air. "I was just cutting lemons, the knife must have slipped."

Becky plucked the waving knife from her hand. "Yeah, could happen to anybody. Why don't you check and see if anyone needs a refill."

I went into the back room for a mop and duct tape. On my return, Becky was wiping up the mess and shaking her head. She spied the mop and tape. "My knight to the rescue."

I handed her the mop. "Naah. If I was a real hero I'd offer to mop that up for you, but I have to answer the call."

"Call?"

"Yeah. My barstool's calling my butt."

"Lazy bum. Tell me about the link."

Sam and Bernie entered the bar and sat at their usual booth.

I patted Becky's arm. "I'll tell you later. I have to talk to Sam and Bernie."

"Bum!"

I grinned, filled a pitcher with beer, grabbed two mugs and headed to Sam and Bernie's table.

Both stood as I arrived. Sam pointed to the Lake Tahoe souvenir T-shirt he wore before reaching for my hand. Bernie reached for the beer. We shook and sat. "So, you guys finally went. How was your trip to the wilds of Lake Tahoe?"

Grins spread across two old faces. "Incredible," said Bernie.

"Super," said Sam. "And we owe it all to you."

"Don't be silly," I said. "You guys deserve it."

Sam leaned forward. "Let me tell you about this one girl –"

I held up a hand. "Before you get started, I'd like to ask you guys for a favor."

"Oh, man. Anything. Anything you want Jack, you name it," said Sam.

"Yeah, Jack," piped Bernie. "Easy or hard, you got it."

I leaned close and they followed my lead. "I'd like…" I looked up and around, then put my head back close to theirs. "I'd like you guys to go to a strip club."

Bernie sat up. "You call that a favor?"

Sam joined in. "Yeah, is this a joke or something?"

"No." I waved them back and they leaned toward me. "I need someone to act as a go-between at a strip club."

"You serious, Jack?" asked Sam.

"Yep. I'm checking into some dirty dealings that may be going on."

"Ha," laughed Sam. "Sounds like fun."

I gripped his arm and squeezed. He looked down at my hand and I released his arm. His face sobered. "It's not fun. It's serious." I sat up and poured their beers. "I'm talking about gangs, drugs, murder, and all around dangerous business."

Bernie's face creased into hard lines, both hands clasped hard around his beer mug. "You're serious."

I nodded.

Both of them sat up and looked at each other, faces disconcerted. "Shit," said Sam. "I think I just peed a little."

Bernie sighed. "Yeah, but you do that most every night." He turned to me. "What's this all about, Jack?"

"It's about Angel." I laid out the story as it had happened, omitting my killing of three gangbangers. When finished, I sat back. "I don't know how any of this is connected to her murder, but it's the only lead we have." I pushed their untouched beer toward them. "Listen, it's dangerous business. You don't have to agree now, take some time to think about it."

Bernie hoisted his beer. "I'm in, Jack. You had me when you mentioned Angel."

"Same here," said Sam. "When I think about that beautiful girl…" His hands clenched into fists.

"Yeah. Bringing down her killer will help all of us." I snagged a pretzel from the bowl and crunched on it. "I've got a lot to set up first, then I'll be in touch with the details."

I walked to my bar stool wondering if I had done the right thing. I glanced back at the pair who were drinking, somber expressions on their faces. The mention of Angel's murder had put that look on their faces, not me. This wasn't a lark, as selling their weapons had been. This could be serious business and their resolute faces said they knew it.

Becky sidled over, wiping the bar as she came. "What did you do to Sam and Bernie? They look like their VA benefits just got canceled."

"I just recruited them."

"For...?" Her ever-moving rag stopped and she looked up. "Is that wise? What if there's trouble."

I shrugged. "They can handle themselves, and we need more help from people with different faces. My face has been seen around..." I glanced at the door, that feeling once again creeping up the back of my neck. I scanned the bar. There wasn't anyone I didn't know, but the feeling persisted. After a deep breath, I turned back to Becky. "We could use more help with an idea I have and I can't be in two places at once. They'll be OK, and two old guys in a bar is a great cover."

Becky frowned. "It should be. They've been practicing for twenty years."

I grinned at the comment and looked back to Sam and Bernie while my mind drifted to the best way to approach Vega.

Chapter 55

Sitting in the van, I hacked into the strip club's wireless signal. My computer skills weren't great, but this was cake. They didn't even have a security program running. I guess they thought it superfluous as the only thing they used the computer for was employee listings. Within a few minutes, I had the information I needed. Regan Richardson, aka Vega, was 26, single, lived a few miles away, worked only four nights a week, and listed one dependent on her W-2. I spent another twenty minutes sifting through the computer's files, looking for anything related to Douglas or the gang. There was nothing but the employee data and a large listing of porn sites.

A quick Google search and my DMV hack program told me a little more about Regan Richardson. She had a baby named Olivia, took online business courses at UI, and attended yoga classes twice a week.

There were several ways to meet Vega outside of work. It felt too creepy to approach her in the parking lot after work, and meeting her at her house was too stalkish. Either of those ideas would put a woman's hackles up. I decided to go with the "white knight to the rescue" plot.

Parked next to an all night diner a mile from her house, I waited in a rented white Honda Accord. Regan's shift ended at 1 A.M., and I knew her route home would take her down this street. I spotted her 1991 Ford Escort two blocks away and hit the button on the interrupter switch. The Ford slowed, drifted over to the curb, then stopped. Regan pounded the steering wheel a few times, then popped the hood and got out, tightening the belt on her overcoat.

White knight time.

I drove slowly toward her car as she stood looking down into the open hood. Window down, I stopped next to her. "Having car..." I said. "Hey! Vega." I pulled over to the curb and got out of my car.

Regan stood, hands on hips, chin jutting forward, face oozing anger.

"Car trouble?" I asked as I walked to her.

"No," she said. "And I don't need your help."

I stopped a couple feet away. "I'm good with cars. Lemme just take a look."

Regan stared at me for a moment. "I know you. The man free with his benjamins."

I tilted my head. "Hopefully, that will buy me a look at your engine."

Her eyes narrowed, and suspicion tightly coiled her body. Then after a deep breath, she relaxed a bit. "Go ahead." She stepped away from me and stood on the curb.

With my body blocking her sight, I disconnected the interrupter and palmed it. "Looks like a loose distributor wire." I stood and stepped back from the car. "Give it a try now."

Instead of walking between me and the car, she circled around the rear of the car and got in.

A smart, street-wise woman.

With a turn of her wrist, the car started.

I closed the hood and walked to her window. She rolled it halfway down.

"Does my mechanic work rate me a cup of coffee with you?" I asked.

Her lips pursed. "Listen, pal. Thanks for helping, but I don't hook on the side. I just dance and strip."

"Understood. But I'm not interested in either. I'd just like to talk to you."

"Not interested."

"It's worth another hundred if you'd have a cup of coffee with me. There's a diner down the street. Well lit, and safe. Hear what I have to say for five minutes and the hundred is yours whether you decide to help me or not."

She looked forward for a moment. "Help you with what?"

I pulled a hundred out of my top pocket. "Five minutes."

She inhaled deeply, looked at the hundred, then nodded. "OK. Five minutes."

"Get us a booth. I'll be there shortly."

Regan rolled up her window and drove away.

I watched her drive down the street and ran through my assessment. Smart, savvy, and not totally hardened yet to what life had thrown her. She would do.

Regan sat at a rear booth, her back to the wall. Her face and body posture told me trust wasn't big on her to-do list. I slid into the booth. "Coffee?"

"I don't drink coffee this late at night."

"Hot chocolate? Or could I get you something else?" I said.

"You could get me that hundred."

With a smile, I pushed the bill across the table.

She crumpled it quickly, glanced around, then shoved it in her purse. "Ok. What's this all about?"

An old stick-thin waitress chose that moment to wander to our table, pen and pad poised. "Hey, Regan. What can I get you two?"

I smiled up at her. "A cup of coffee, a hot chocolate and a piece of apple pie."

"Gotcha."

Regan held up her hand. "Make that two pieces of pie, Rita."

"You can never resist our pie, can you, honey?" With that, she walked back to the counter.

"Sounds like you come here often, Regan."

She sat back in her seat. "Since you know my name now, what's yours?"

"Jack. Jack Gareth. I'd reach my hand across the table to shake, but I think you'd bite me."

That elicited a snort. "You'd be right. Come on, Jack. What do you want from me if it's not sex?"

"I'm interested in some goings on at the club."

Regan straightened. "You a cop?"

"No."

"If you're a cop you have to tell me."

"Not a cop. Just... just say I'm interested in the business."

"OK. You said you needed help. What kind?"

"The only thing I'd like you to do is note whenever someone who doesn't work at the club goes into the office."

She tapped her fingernail on the table. "Something's going on. I knew it. Salvatore has been real nervous lately. Some of the girls are getting spooked. We thought maybe he had money problems and might not pay us."

"Some of the girls were spooked, but not you?"

Regan opened her mouth then closed it as Rita arrived and plopped our order on the table. She tore off a ticket from her pad and pushed it at me. "You kids dig in."

Regan waited until the waitress left to answer me. "I've been approached by other clubs so I'm not worried."

"A woman like you will always find work," I said, and doctored my coffee.

"Listen, bub." Regan pointed her fork at me. "I dance and strip. I'm not a hooker."

"Never thought you were. By my remark I meant you'd succeed at whatever you do. You're smart, beautiful and exude self confidence. Three advantageous traits."

"Keep your sugar, daddy. What's in this for me?"

I chewed my pie and watched her face and body language. She was nervous, but curious and interested.

"Four hundred a week."

She shook her head. "Six."

"No." I took a bite of my pie. "This is good pie."

"Six is my price."

"No." It was my turn to point my fork at her. "Do you think any of the other girls would balk at an extra four hundred dollars a week just to keep their eyes open?"

"No they wouldn't. But they don't exude self confidence and aren't as smart or as beautiful."

I dropped my fork and laughed. "Five hundred, then. Final offer."

"Deal." She reached across the table and we shook hands.

I released her hand and counted my fingers aloud. "Yep, there's still five."

Regan leaned forward. "How we gonna work this?"

"I'll send you the info via email. I'm sure you have an email account," I said.

"Who doesn't? Write this down."

As I wrote her info down on a napkin she glanced at her watch.

"I gotta get home to my sitter."

"How old's your daughter?"

As a cold wave of frost slammed across the table, I realized I'd fucked up big time. I looked up.

Her eyes were narrow and her fists clenched. "How did you know I have a daughter? Who the fuck are you really and what's this about, Mr. Jack Gareth? If that's your real name." Her eyes widened. "You set this all up, didn't you. The car – everything!"

She was ready to run. I could see it in her eyes. Damn. Damn. Damn.

Honesty had worked with Becky, maybe it was time to ante up again.

"Ok. Here's the real story." I reached into my wallet, withdrew my driver's license and slid it across the table. "Name's Jack Daniels. A woman was killed and my friend is hurting because of it. I'm just looking for answers and closure for her. The club isn't important, only any new people who are coming to see the owner – Salvatore." I sipped my coffee to lubricate my dry mouth. I hadn't had a slip up like that in a long time. "After meeting you at the club I thought you might be able to help me, so I checked you out. That's how I knew you had a daughter."

Regan stared at my license, then looked up. "What else do you know about me?"

I blew out a breath. "You're twenty-six, single, taking online classes at IU, and your daughter's name is Olivia."

"How did you find all of this out?"

"Through the internet. Whatever you put out there is open for the entire world."

She looked to the side. "Damn. So much for privacy." Regan's eyes came back to mine. "This friend of yours – girl friend?"

"Yes."

Her lips twisted. "Figures." She sat silently for a moment. "All right, Mr. Daniels. We have a deal." Her hand flashed across the table and her fingers dug into my arm. "But if any of this comes back to harm me or mine, you're toast." She slid my license back to me then tapped on it. "Remember, Mr. Daniels. I know where you live."

I laughed. "Jack. Call me Jack."

Chapter 56

The intelligence Vega had slipped Sam and Bernie for the last two weeks convinced me that Scarlett's Gentleman's Club was now pushing drugs. She had wanted to email me her report, but I told her to give it to Sam and Bernie. Email always leaves a trace. A scrap of paper with just a date and time was the safest way to pass info. For the last two weeks, every Wednesday promptly at 9 p.m., a gangbanger showed up at the club with a package and left without it. How did drugs tie into Angel's death? Had she innocently run across the drug ring? Maybe, but that didn't explain the brutality of her murder.

I slid into the booth and shoved a pile of tens across the table to Sam and Bernie. "This will probably be your last visit to the strip club. Vega's given me all I need."

"But we can go back on our own if we want, right?" said Bernie.

Sam chuckled. "Bernie's fallin' in love with Vega."

Bernie scowled at Sam. "Naw. She's a sweet kid."

"And a hell of a dancer," added Sam.

"Sorry I missed her act," I said, and glanced up to make sure that Becky was still behind the bar.

"That place has really gone to seed in just the past two weeks," said Bernie. "There's a different crowd in there now. An ugly crowd." He shook his head. "I wish Vega worked somewhere else."

"Drug traffic," I said. "Brings in the dregs."

"Do you know she's close to getting her B.S. in business management?" said Bernie.

I hid a smile. Sam might be right, Bernie was smitten. I stood and they slid out of the booth. "Have a good time, guys."

"Dominique is working tonight," said Sam. "It'll be a great time."

I watched the two old-timers leave and walked to my bar stool. Becky looked my way and mimed drinking. I nodded.

Chapter 57

Becky clicked off the end of the Pistons game and reached for the bottle of JWB . She stopped in the middle of my pour and stared at the front door. Her eyes flashed arctic cold. "Oh no. Not in my house!" Becky slammed the bottle on the bar and started for the pass-through, anger flowing behind her like the wake of a jet ski.

I turned and saw Sam and Bernie walk to their booth as usual. But this time they had Regan sandwiched between them. Regan wore an ill-fitting long trench coat and five-inch gold stilettos. Between the open lapels shone gold glitter.

"Becky. Wait!" I sprung off my bar stool and went after her. She was halfway to their booth when I grabbed her arm. "Hold on, Beck. It's not what it looks like."

She stopped long enough to shoot me a bad look. "No hookers in my bar. We don't serve their kind here."

"Stop making bad Star Wars quotes and hold up a minute."

Becky yanked her arm from my clasp, marched to Sam and Bernie's booth and jammed her hands on her hips.

Her big inhale was cut short by Bernie. "Becky, I'd like you to meet my daughter, Regan."

The air rushed out from Becky like a lit panatela to a child's balloon. "Dau…daughter?"

Regan's eyebrows arched and she stared at Bernie. "Daughter?" Then she looked up at me. "Hi Jack." She gestured with her chin to Becky. "This the girlfriend?"

"Yeah. Hi, Regan."

Regan glanced at Becky, then back to me. "My sympathies."

I slid in front of Becky and leaned on the table. "What's –"

Becky gripped my shoulder and leaned into my face. "You know her?" She gave my shoulder a hard push. "What's going on?"

"That's what I'm trying to find out." I turned back to the booth. "You heard the lady. What's going on?"

Sam grinned. "Big doings, Jack. Big doings." His grin widened as he glanced at Bernie. "Daughter?"

Bernie traced a finger over an old scar on the table. "Could be." His head jerked up and he jabbed his finger on the table. "And I'd be proud if she were."

Regan patted his hand. "My hero." She turned to me. "Club got raided. Big time."

"I'll say," chimed Sam. "Cops in swat gear, people yelling, scrambling for the exits, a few pushy-shovy fights breaking out, tables overturned. I haven't seen that much action since a weekend pass in Saigon. Man, it was really cool." He wiped his mouth with the back of his sleeve. "Bernie, Regan, and I rush to the back door and this six-three, Arnold Schwarzenegger-look-alike guy blocks our way and grabs Regan's arm. 'Nobody's leaving,' he says." Sam shook his head and laughed. "Bernie steps in and throws a haymaker from left field. In a second this guy is flat on his ass with little birdies circling his head."

My eyebrows winged up. "One punch, Bernie? I didn't realize you had that in you."

"Ehh. I had help." He pulled something out of his pocket then opened his hand to show a roll of quarters. "It's for the meter and punching tough guys."

I chuckled, then smacked my forehead. "Oh, crap. I bet he was an undercover cop."

"F 'em," said Bernie.

I sighed. "So then what happened?"

"Nothing. Regan's car was hemmed in, so we ran to my car and skedaddled," said Sam.

"I came with them to get the cash you owe me," said Regan. "They're exterminating at my building and I need to pay for a place to stay for a few days."

The glow of an idea illuminated Bernie's face and he looked at Regan. "You could stay at my place." His eyes lowered to the table. "If you'd want to."

"Yeah," said Sam. "Bernie's got lots of room in that big house." Another grin erupted on his face. "Have you cleaned in the past ten years since Bertha died?"

"Of course, asshole."

"Jarhead."

Regan touched Bernie's arm. "Thanks, for the offer Bernie, but I have a one-year-old baby girl."

The heartwarming look that lit Bernie's face touched all of us. "That would only make it better," he said.

The claw tightened on my arm and I looked into Becky's exasperated face. "Regan is the one who has been slipping us information."

"When you said you had an inside man, I didn't know it was a hook –" Becky glanced at Bernie, then Regan. "An artist."

"Look," said Regan. "I don't hook. I dance and I strip." She tilted her head and stared at Becky. "You got a problem with that?"

Oh crap, I thought. In a minute someone's gonna yell "cat fight."

Becky glanced at Bernie and the fight went out of her eyes. "No. No problem. Can I get you guys the usual and a third glass?"

Bernie looked at Regan. "No. We gotta get Regan settled in – that is, if you're going to stay at my place."

"If it's really no inconvenience, that would be great," said Regan.

I got out of their way as they slid out of the booth. After a round of goodnights, and me slipping Regan the money I owed her, she and Bernie headed for the door.

"You handled that very well," I said to Becky as I slid into the booth. "I was never so proud."

"Oh, screw you, Jack." She rolled her eyes and let out a stream of air. "I over-reacted."

"And looked beautiful doing it."

She placed a hand on my arm and glanced at Sam. "Let me get you two a couple of beers," she said, and headed for the bar.

"Looks like you lost your drinking buddy," I said to Sam.

He looked toward the door. "It's the best thing for him." He turned back to me. "Bernie never had kids. I got four and five grands, but Bernie – most of his relations are gone now."

Sam straightened in his seat. "I'd like to talk to you about Regan."

"Sure. Shoot."

"That dancing stuff. That's no job for a woman like her. She's smart, well spoken and has great curb appeal." Sam sat back as Becky dropped off a pitcher of beer and two glasses, then he waited until Becky left to continue. "With the club closed, her income is nil. I'm pretty sure she's living on the edge as it is." He shrugged. "I know a few people, maybe they can ask around."

Regan's personality certainly inspired loyalty if she could win over two old 'Nam vets – and me. I thought about the problem, then the rolodex in my brain stopped on a name. Roland "Dutch" Dante. I sipped my beer. "Maybe I could do the same."

Chapter 58

Dante DataWare sat a mile off Route 80 in a white collar industrial park. The indistinctive six-story, glass building squatted among the others like one in a row of uneven teeth. I parked in a visitor slot and entered the building. The reception area was the usual chrome and glass, with the receptionist ensconced in a wide glass and chrome desk.

"Hi. I'm here to see Mr. Roland Dante."

She swung to her keyboard and hit a key. "You have an appointment?"

"No, but he'll see me."

"Who should I say is calling?" she asked with tilted head and plastic smile. I was surprised it wasn't made of glass or chrome.

"Tell him Peter Paranoid is here to see if he wants to run another marathon."

Her smile dropped. "Mr. Dante is very busy and –"

I gripped the desk, leaned forward and put on my hard intimidator face. "Do it. Just as I asked."

Her mouth opened and closed, then she raised a phone to her ear. "Yes. There's a Mr. Peter Paranoid here. He said to ask if Mr. Dante wants to run another marathon." She frowned. "Don't shoot the messenger, Helen." She waited on the phone for a minute, then her eyes popped wide. "Oh… Of course. I'll send him right up."

She hung up. The plastic smile returned as she handed me a plastic card. "Please place the key in the slot and the elevator will take you to the top floor and Mr. Dante's office. Have a nice day."

I nodded and headed for the elevator. I didn't think Dutch would mind me asking him for a favor, and even if he couldn't accommodate me, it would be good to see him again.

The elevator doors opened onto a reception area that wasn't glass or chrome. Sage walls and accent lighting gave the area a homey, yet professional, feel. Muted paintings that were certainly originals graced the walls. An older woman, who was probably Helen, sat behind a beautifully inlaid Louis XIV desk.

I walked to her desk and smiled. "Hi."

She peered at me over her half glasses. "Mr. Dante will be –"

The inner door swung open and Dutch stood there wearing a big grin. Styled blond hair sat above a face that could have graced the cover of a romance novel. His gray suit looked impeccably tailored, the crisp lines marred only by the steel crutches on Dutch's arms.

"Jack Daniels," he said. His grin widened.

"Look at you, Dutch. Out of the wheelchair and up on Forrest Gump's magic legs." We walked toward each other and hugged. I stepped back and grabbed his upper arms. "You're looking real good, Dutch!"

"You're not too shaggy yourself. You certainly look better than the last time I saw you in Somalia."

"I was a bit peaked from carrying your fat ass for twenty miles."

"Well, at least you didn't have to carry my legs," he said, and punched me on the arm. "Damn, Jack. It's good to see you. Come in, come in." He turned to the receptionist. "Hold all my calls, and – Jack have you had lunch?"

I shook my head.

"And have Chef make up some sandwiches and coffee."

She lifted the phone. "Right away, Mr. Dante."

Dutch ushered me into a large office that was just as lush and homey as the reception area. We walked to a section with comfy chairs surrounding a coffee table and sat. Dutch took a minute to arrange his prosthetic legs, then settled.

"You have an in-house chef?" I asked.

"Yep. Here and at home. Anything you need is just a phone call away." He sat back and sighed. "It's good to be the king."

"I'm glad to see you're doing well."

"Oh man, Jack. Since we went public, revenue has skyrocketed. I've had nibbles from some conglomerate to buy me out for more money than I could ever spend in a dozen lifetimes."

"You thinking of selling? Let me know so I can dump your stock." I looked around the office, admiring the good taste and comfortable feel. "That little electronic widget you were always playing around with must have worked."

"The Alsdatabot? Yes. I sold that and bankrolled it into several bigger ideas that really paid off." He spread his arms. "Now, Dante DataWare has its fingers in many different pies."

"Glad to hear it."

He stared off to the side and his eyes clouded. I knew he remembered the jungle, the blood and the pain. When they cleared, he looked back at me and smiled. "So, what can I do for you, Jack? Still working the wet end?"

"Nope, retired.   My interests now are only focused on a barmaid."

"So, the same as usual without the gunfire.   You ever get married?"

"No. You?"

"Nooo... I was engaged once, but it didn't work out."

"She found out you had a tiny dick?"

He laughed. "No. Didn't like the idea of a pre-nup."

"Ahh. Good thing you found out in time." I sat forward. "I'm here to ask you for a favor."

"If you need money, Jack, I'm loaded."

"Me too, but my favor is about a friend. She needs a job," I said.

"The barmaid?"

"No, another woman," I said.

Dutch shook his head. "You're playing with fire my friend."

"Don't I know it.   She's twenty-six, pretty, very bright, oozes confidence, and almost has a degree in Business Management."

"What else?"

"She lost her job as a dancer and stripper, has a kid and is struggling to get by."

Dutch sat forward.   "Geez, Jack.   How do you find these people?"

"I dunno, probably the same way I found you when you were working for Van Owen."

With a shudder Dutch held up his hand.   "Don't even mention his name." He tented his fingers for a moment, then nodded. "My VP tells me I should have an intern.   Someone to help with the correspondence and such." He looked forward and tapped his crutch with a fingernail. "Have her come in for an interview. I'll set it up." His gaze slid to mine. "You say she's pretty?"

"Oh, yeah. Very."

"Is she the type to pick my pocket?"

"More likely the type to stand on your balls."

He laughed. "You say she has a kid? She'll really love our in-house daycare center."

"In-house daycare?" I said.

"Yeah.   I've got enough, why not make other folks' lives easier?"

After a knock on the door, it opened and Helen wheeled in a tray loaded with soup, sandwiches, dessert, snacks and drinks.

"So tell me what you've been up to, Jack."

Chapter 59

A week later, I sat at the bar and watched Becky finish loading the cooler, then pick up a rag and start to polish a glass. Her economy of movement spoke of grace, athletic ability, and years of practice. I loved watching her move. Today, she wore her blue, "Taxation WITH representation isn't so hot, either!" T-shirt and her usual tight jeans.

"This stripper, Regan." She didn't look at me, but put the glass in a rack and picked up another. "She a good dancer?"

I almost grinned at her un-subtle fishing expedition. Instead, I slid on my poker face and shrugged. "Don't know. Never saw her act. You'd have to ask Bernie." I held up a hand. "Better yet, ask Sam. Bernie is too attached and protective."

She put down her rag and leaned on the bar. "Is Bernie going to get hurt?"

"Yeah. Probably. He's pretty attached, and attachment always brings pain." I shook my head. "But she's not the type to do any harm purposely. Why do you ask?"

She gestured with her chin and reached for a pitcher. "They just came in. I'll get some beer flowing."

Sam, Bernie and Regan walked to their usual booth and I wandered over. Regan, dressed in a business suit, remained standing. When I neared, she grabbed me in a hard hug. She leaned back while still holding my arms, and stared into my eyes. "The job at Dante DataWare, it's incredible. Thank you so much, Jack."

As Becky headed over with beer and glasses, Regan glanced at her, then kissed my cheek. She looked back at Becky while still holding my arms.

Becky's face could have been the subject for a psychology seminar. Shock, outrage, understanding, acceptance, and relaxation – all in five seconds. She set down the pitcher and glasses, then stared at Regan. "OK. You've gotten me back. Are we even, or do you want to go a few more rounds?"

Regan slid into the booth and shook her head. "Nah. But I really have to thank Jack." She looked up at me. "Not only is the

job super and something that I think I will be good at, but Dutch…"
She closed her eyes and smiled. "Now there's some real eye
candy." She placed a hand on her heart. "I may become a
diabetic."

"Dutch?" I said. "He lets you call him Dutch?"

"Yeah. After I'd been there three days, he said he didn't like me
calling him 'Mr. Dante' and said to call him Dutch."

Huh. No one was allowed to call him Dutch except the folks in
our strike team. They had earned the right and his trust. He must
have fallen under Regan's spell as Bernie had. I should check with
him to see if he wasn't in over his head. On the other hand, maybe
it was none of my business.

"How did he lose his legs?" asked Regan.

"He didn't tell you?"

Regan shook her head.

"It's really Dutch's story to tell, and I'm sure he will when he's
ready."

"He has no legs?" said Becky, voice tinged with sympathy.

Regan's eye narrowed. "He's not a cripple. It's just a minor
handicap, as he'd be the first to tell you."

A smile jumped on my face even as Regan jumped to his
defense. But, it seemed odd to defend a man who could take out an
enemy at seven-hundred and fifty meters with one shot. Seemed
like Regan wasn't the only one who could command loyalty.

"I'm glad everything's working out," I said. "Tell Dutch, 'hey,'
for me when you see him." I grabbed Becky's hand and pulled her
close as we walked to the bar. "That encounter was interesting. It
was fun watching you handle the situation."

"It jumped me for a moment, but I fought it." She squeezed my
hand. "I think it's because of the trust I have in you." She shrugged
and looked forward. "I guess that means I love you."

What?

Wow.

Wow, big time.

A declaration of love from Becky. I watched a flash of red climb
up her neck to her cheeks. I wasn't stupid and knew this was hard
for her. I also knew that I shouldn't make a big deal over it – yet.
"I know. And I love you back, Beck." I released her hand after a
slight squeeze. "How about we say it again in your apartment later
over a glass of Jameson?"

She walked to the pass-through and lifted the divider. "Sounds good," she said over her shoulder. "But you better not let another stripper kiss you again."

Ah... There was my Becky. Her words sounded better than good. They sounded... I had no description for it. I felt joy, elation, fear, and the feeling that I'd just stepped to the edge of a chasm. But nothing could overcome the words she had just spoken.

Cool.

Together, we turned chairs onto tables after closing. We had done this so often, we were almost synchronized.

"What do we do now?" asked Becky.

I looked up. "About..."

"Well, we know Councilman Douglas and the gang are arm and arm in the drug business, but how does that help find Angel's killer?"

"We just have to keep digging... But for tonight, since you told me you love me, let's just spend the time letting me tell you how much I love you."

The chair she lifted halted in mid-air and Becky's face lit with a glow. I saw how deeply my words had touched her and realized they affected me the same way.

She put down the chair. "Let's go upstairs and get started on that."

"Cleanup?" I asked.

"Tomorrow," she said. "Now we have more important things to do."

She reached out her hand, and I held it. It was more than the joining of two hands.

It was a joining of lives.

Chapter 60

The crash of shattering glass from the living room woke me from a sound sleep. I leaped from Becky's bed, naked except for a Sig in each hand. Another crash sounded, then a third.

"What was that?" asked Becky, vaulting out of bed.

"Don't know," I said as I approached the bedroom door. "Dress, and stay behind me."

Becky pulled on jeans and a T-shirt. The smell of gasoline and a flickering light from under the door sent an electric jolt of fear up my spine and banished all sleep from my head. I cracked the door open. Flames engulfed the living room and climbed to the ceiling. I slammed the door.

"Fire. We can't get out that way."

Becky tore the curtains from the window. "Fire escape," she yelled.

I tossed up the sash and stared at the wrought-iron burglar bars over the window.

"Here's the key." Becky thrust it into my hand. I turned the lock and pushed the bars. They didn't budge. A quick shake drew my eye to the shiny new padlock higher up, holding the bars to the wall-mount.

No escape that way.

My thoughts ran on two levels: first, get away from the fire; second, who set us up?

Smoke seeped under the door as I pulled on my jeans, T-shirt, boots and windbreaker. I slipped into my speed-rig in case whoever wanted us cooked had stuck around to make sure we fried.

Becky shook the locked burglar bars. "Jack!"

"There's a way out," I said. "We'll be OK."

Fear etched across Becky's face but not panic. I almost smiled at her courage. If I could think about that during a fire, I was certainly in love. That kind of fire I would never want to extinguish.

I grabbed her hand and pulled her into the bathroom. "Close the door. Wet a bath towel and put it on the floor against the door."

While Becky did as I asked, I wrapped small towels around both of my hands. A quick punch smashed through the glass of the double-hung window. I braced my feet, grabbed the sill and yanked out the window frame. With a crash, I tossed it into the tub.

Becky grabbed my arm. "It's twenty-five feet down to the alley."

"I know," I said, and leaned out the window. "But we're going up, not down." I searched around for the wire I had installed months ago.

And couldn't find it.

Panic and thoughts of an omniscient enemy invaded my mind, but vanished as my hand closed around the wire the wind must have blown free. A quick yank unrolled the short rope ladder I'd installed on the roof. I grabbed the ladder and climbed out of the window and down several rungs.

"Becky. Grab the ladder and climb up. Don't worry. I'll be right below you."

A patina of dread overlaid the stone-hard look painted on Becky's face. I held her steady as she clambered onto the rope ladder. With careful steps, she climbed to the flat rooftop. I was right behind her.

As I hauled myself up, she stared at the rope ladder hanging out of a metal case disguised as a vent. "When did you put this here?"

"After I realized I'd be spending time at your place."

She shook her head and looked at the thick-black smoke billowing up the front of the building. "If the wind changes we're still screwed."

"Got it covered." I grabbed her hand and we ran across the roof to the other side.

Becky's glance lowered. "It's still a long way down."

"We're crossing over to the next building."

Becky stared at me. "Are you nuts? It's at least fifteen feet across. We can't jump that!"

"It's sixteen, and we'll walk." I tossed open another fake vent cover and hauled out sections of bridging. "Help me connect these. They just snap together."

She stared down at what looked like plastic milk carton material. "It's only a foot wide."

"That's enough." I snapped in the last piece, making an eighteen-foot long bridge. I'd used these light-weight military footbridges before and knew their strength was more than up to the task of supporting us. I pushed an end to the raised ledge of the roof then ran to the far end and walked it upright. I let it swing down to the other rooftop and held onto my end.

With a clatter, the bridge fell to the other roof ledge. I stepped onto the bridge and held out my hand. Smoke now billowed toward us making my eyes sting. I shouted over the crackle of the flames. "Come on. The wind's changing."

Becky grasped my hand and took one step onto the bridge. She looked down, yanked her hand free, and stepped back. Fear twisted her face. "It's too high."

I jumped back down to the rooftop and grabbed her wrist. "Then close your eyes and trust me."

"Jack…"

"Trust me." I pulled her wrist over the back of my neck, snaked an arm through her legs and hoisted her in a fireman's carry.

"Jack!"

"Just keep your eyes closed and don't fight me." I stepped onto the bridge and walked across the span to the other rooftop. I lowered Becky to the roof. Her eyes were still closed. I placed a hand on her shoulder. "It's OK. We're safe."

Her eyes popped open. "Oh, Jack!" She launched herself into my arms and held me tight.

"Let's get to the ground."

We ran to the fire escape and climbed down to the street. Sirens screamed down the street before we were halfway down.

The stench of smoke and the sound of dripping water filled the air. The blaze was out. The firemen's masks dangled as they disconnected and rolled up their hoses. We stood on the street in front of the bar. I placed my arm around Becky as we stared at the damage. Tears left trails through the soot on her cheeks. I felt her trembling at the destruction of her home and the memories that had lived in the bar.

The fire chief finished talking to several firemen then strode toward us. "Bad business, this. Bad business," he said. After a glance at the newly painted front window, now shattered by some thug, he turned back to us. "You say you were upstairs, asleep?"

I nodded.

The chief stared up at the second floor. "It's definitely arson. Looks like several Molotov cocktails were tossed through the second-story windows." His gaze met mine. "You don't look stupid enough to start an insurance fire when you're sleeping in the same building, and I know Ms. Quinn well enough to know she wouldn't burn her bar." He looked back at the second floor. "So, I gotta ask. You piss anyone off lately?"

"Who me? No," I said. "Maybe someone thought the beer wasn't cold enough."

He raised an eyebrow. "Yeah. Right," said the chief. He looked at Becky and shook his head. "Sorry about the bar, Ms. Quinn. We'll have Arson here this afternoon." He turned and issued orders to some firemen.

Becky folded her arms across her chest and her head hung in defeat. "Why, Jack. Why?" Her voice was barely a whisper.

"I don't know. But we'll find out, and payback will be hell." I squeezed her shoulders. "I promise you."

One of the firemen walked toward us, yellow coat flapping in the morning breeze. "Hey, Becky," he said. "There's some good news here."

She looked up. "Hi, Billy. I could use some good news." She tilted her head toward me. "We went to school together."

"Of course, you did," I said.

The fireman continued. "The upstairs apartment is gone, but we stopped the fire before it spread to the roof. The building still appears sound." Billy gestured back to the bar. "There's mostly water damage to the downstairs area." He shook his head and smiled. "But the bar itself is untouched. There must have been so much wax on it that the water rolled off it like a duck's back."

I squeezed Becky's shoulder. "That's good news. We can rebuild with the bar as the cornerstone. Thanks, Billy."

He gave a half-hearted salute and left.

"Rebuild, Jack?" said Becky.

I turned her to face me and placed my hands on her shoulders. "Yes. The bar is the keystone of the building. With it intact, we can redo the rest. Some of those booths needed re-upholstering anyway."

She snorted and brushed away a tear, then looked serious. "Won't they just burn us down again?"

The anger built inside me like a red-hot glowing coal, hot enough to torch any enemy.

"Not if we burn them down first."

Chapter 61

I held my gun behind my back as I opened the door for room service. After the bar fire, my paranoia was full blown. I had to have been followed back to the bar. Even with my all precautions, someone got the better of me, and it cost Becky her childhood home. There was no use kicking my own ass. Better to put it aside and plan how to kick someone else's.

Rather than staying at my house, we were holed up in the Mayfair Hotel across town. I was sure the house was still a safe area and certainly wanted to keep it that way.

The gray-haired waiter rolled in a cart and smiled. The heavy tips I'd been giving him made the service quick and the food warm.

"Shall I set up your dinner, Sir?"

"I got it Harvey, thanks." I slipped him a folded twenty. He put the bill in his pocket and left. I locked the door behind him. "Clear," I said.

Becky stepped out from behind the half-opened bathroom door, and lowered her pistol. "Let's eat. I'm starved." She placed her gun on the table and sat while I removed the lids and passed out dinner.

"Grilled cheese sandwich?" I shook my head as Becky took a big bite. "They have some fine entrees and I'm sure they could make you anything you want."

She waved a hand and spoke with her mouth full. "Grilled cheese and fries are comfort food." She looked over at my plate. "Besides, this is the second night you're having Salisbury steak and lima beans. What's up with that?"

"I like their Salisbury steak."

"So shut up and eat."

The destruction of the bar still sat heavy on Becky, but she seemed to have come to an acceptance of the situation. We had entered the building after the firemen left and the interior didn't seem damaged – just wet. That seemed to helped to lessen the trauma for Becky. She hadn't gone upstairs as it was still unsafe, and that kept her from seeing the burned-out rooms. They probably still looked the same in her head.

"This is our second day here, Jack. How do we move forward?"

"Well, I talked the fire chief into letting the restoration company take a quick look at the downstairs area and they said it didn't look too bad." I cut into my steak. "The fire didn't have time to spread down to the bar area."

She nodded as she chewed. "I meant, how do we go about getting the scumbags who did this?"

I put down my fork and sighed. "It's my fault. Despite my precautions, they must have followed me back to the bar somehow." I placed my hand over hers. "Sorry, Beck."

She slid her hand from under mine, picked up a fry and pointed it at me. "Don't even think it. You didn't set the fire. Forget it." Becky tossed the fry down onto her plate and clenched her fist until the knuckles turned white. "I want these bastards. I want them!" she said, her voice turning into a growl. Becky sighed, placed her hand flat on the table and took a calming breath. "Now, what's our next move? It doesn't pay to restore the bar only to have it firebombed again."

"I can't see how this is all connected. There had to be at least two, maybe three men tossing the firebombs. The East Side Dragons? Probably. How does Angel figure into all of this? Don't know. I say we hit Douglas' home and office hard. No more Mister Nice Guy."

"Isn't that what I suggested awhile ago?" she said.

"Shut up and eat."

Chapter 62

"Done? Yeah. Thanks, Reggie." I hung up the phone and turned to Becky. She had just gotten out of the shower and was wrapped in a towel. With a second towel she leaned over and dried her hair. "Who was that?"

"Friend of mine. He's tapped Douglas' home phone for me. We're recording all calls."

She wrapped the towel around her hair and straightened. "Won't they be using cell phones?"

I delayed my answer for a moment and just enjoyed the fact that the towel around her torso wasn't quite long enough. I smiled, then answered. "Most likely, but I'm leaving nothing to chance. We'll let that cook for awhile and hit his office in the Spencer building."

"Douglas is smart. Think we'll find anything there?"

"No. But we might find something that points us elsewhere."

"Spencer Building." Becky's lips pursed. "Same entry as before?"

"Yeah, we'll slip in through the back door. We already know the routine, the timing of the guard, and the layout. We can go tonight."

"Good," she said and walked back to the bathroom. "It's better than sitting around and waiting."

"Nervous?"

She stopped, put her hand on the door jam and turned her head. "No. Just pissed."

We dressed business casual for this insertion, just another couple of office workers. Becky wore a nice pants and shirt we purchased from the hotel galleria, and I wore a dark blue suit minus the tie.

We drove to the back of the Spencer building in the stealth van. Night had just fallen. I had decided to hit the place at seven P.M. It was early enough that we wouldn't look too suspicious, just some people working late.

I peered around the corner to the receiving door, then checked my watch. "Should be just another minute," I said to Becky.

"Now, I'm nervous."

"Don't sweat it. I'm sure Bill's routine hasn't changed."

As if answering my words, the door swung open and Bill squatted, placed a wedge on the ground and let the door swing shut. He walked around the corner and I waited until smoke wafted out.

"Go."

Becky ran to the three-step concrete staircase and vaulted over the metal pole railing. I was right behind her. She swung the door open and dashed inside. I entered, caught the door and eased it onto the wedge. Becky started to run, but I grabbed her arm. "Not like last time," I reminded her. "Now, we're just folks working late."

We entered the elevators and I pushed the button for floor seven.

"Douglas' office is on ten," said Becky.

"Yeah. I don't want anyone seeing us get off at the tenth floor. We'll take the stairs up to ten."

The stairwell on the tenth floor opened onto a hallway lined with government offices. Douglas and Diego Sanchez's offices were separated by the county tax assessor and county clerk's office, Sanchez's being at the end of the hall. It looked to be the size of a closet.

"Search Sanchez's, I'll take Douglas'," I said as we pulled on gloves.

Becky nodded and walked down the hall. I bent and picked the lock on Douglas' door. It gave a slight squeak as I pushed it open.

I glanced over and watched Becky work on her lock. In less than ten seconds she swung the door open. Pride popped a smile on my face as I stepped into Douglas' office and closed the squeaky door behind me. A desk, three chairs and several filing cabinets furnished the small ten-by-ten room painted government beige. A few awards hung on the walls and a wilted plant sat on a three-shelf bookcase. I walked to the desk and plopped in his chair.

The top drawer was locked, but it only took a moment to open it. It contained Post-it notes, paperclips, and the dross of a paper pusher. Three of the other drawers held hanging files in neat alphabetical order. All contained county business.

Filled to the top, the last bottom drawer held a stack of paper tossed loosely together. I lifted out the stack and thumbed through them. Correspondence asking for employment, requests for aid, and other letters from his constituency filled the eight-inch pile. I glanced back at his file cabinets and started to place the pile back into the drawer when something didn't feel right. A twelve inch drawer, filled to the top with an eight-inch pile of paper. Could it be that easy? I felt around until I found the drawer's false bottom and pulled it free. Inside was a thick ledger. "Well, well, well. This is a stupid place to hide something valuable." I chuckled as I pulled out the book. A quick peruse through the encoded ledger told me any info in there had to wait.

I stood, dropped the ledger on the desk, and stepped to a filing cabinet. I had opened the first drawer and scanned the tabs when a squeak reached my ears.

Douglas stood in the doorway, a surprised look on his face. "Hey! What are you doing here?" His gaze dropped down to the ledger on the desk and his eyes popped wide. He dashed into the room, snatched up the ledger and headed for the door. I vaulted over the desk and yanked him by the collar back into the office. He stumbled backward and fell, smacking his head on the corner of his desk. I walked to him, bent down and plucked the ledger from the floor. Douglas was out cold.

When the revolver cocked behind me, I knew I'd fucked up bad.

"Well isn't this cozy. Drop the ledger and put your hands on your head."

I dropped the book, turned and placed my hands on my head. I was so fucked.

Sanchez had a .357 magnum aimed at my chest. He took two steps into the office, glanced down at Douglas, then grinned. He shifted from foot to foot, almost dancing. His eyes blazed with fire as they glared at me. The civil servant mask had fallen off revealing madness underneath.

"Yes, yes, yes. This is perfect. Perfect, perfect, perfect! I'm glad you escaped the fire." His body trembled with excitement.

I braced my legs, ready to leap to the side. I'd never be able to draw my weapon before he pulled the trigger. I had to keep him talking. "You firebombed the apartment? How did you find me?"

"You drove around and made sure you weren't followed, but you never thought about the rooftops." He laughed that sick laugh. "Every time you came into the Dragon's territory we watched which direction you drove away and expanded our rooftop eyes in that direction."

"And you found the bar and set it on fire."

"Me personally?" He snorted. "Of course not. Douglas and I had an iron-clad alibi for that night. I had the boys padlock the fire escape then light up the place."

"You're a member of the gang?"

He snorted again. "No. If I was I could never become the future mayor of this city." His little dance stopped for a moment. "I just have Juan take care of these little problems and bury my little peccadilloes."

"Juan? Juan Cruz Johnson? That's a heavy blackmail club to give to the head of a gang."

The little dance started again. "Juan?" He laughed and shook his head. "I run the operation. I just let my little brother Juan be the one visible."

"Your brother?" I watched the gun lower slightly. Any lower and I might make a dive behind the desk.

"Half brother. We planned this since grade school. I move up through the political ranks, and he supplies the money and muscle."

I gestured down at Douglas with my chin. "He know about that?"

Sanchez sneered. "He's only after money." He glanced at the ledger for a second. "He was too stupid to even use a computer. He's a fool and a tool."

"How you gonna explain shooting me here?" I hoped to put an ounce of doubt in his mind to give me more time for his arm to tire from holding up the gun.

He seemed to read my mind and raised the weapon. His crazed grin came back. "That's why it's so perfect. I kill Douglas with your gun, then I kill you with his. In a week, I'm a hero and the new city councilor."

It was clean, clever and would work. "Who killed Angel? You or Douglas?"

"Angel," he spat. "That red-haired whore! Innocence personified – but it's a lie. She didn't suffer enough!" Spittle flew out of his mouth as his face grew red and twisted into fury. "All those red-haired bitches are lying whores and have to be punished. Punished hard." The gun sagged again.

Self-preservation deserted me. My chest filled with rage at the vision of Angel being tormented under the hands of this insane piece of garbage. "Who was she? Who was the first red-haired whore? Your mother?"

"Shut up! Shut up!" He raised the weapon.

The gunshot roared loud in the room.

Surprised I didn't feel the impact of a bullet, I drew my Sig.

Sanchez staggered, then sagged to the floor, gun slipping from his hand.

Becky stood behind him, her still-smoking .45 aimed at Sanchez.

He looked up at Becky while he clutched his side. "You shot me."

"Yeah," said Becky. "That was for the bar."

"I'll kill you, bitch," he screamed and reached for his gun.

Bang!

Bang!

Bang!

Bang!

Sanchez' body jerked as the slugs tore into his chest.

Becky stared down at Sanchez. "And that's for Angel."

Her face shone with a grim avenger's determination. Her eyes never left Sanchez' body. Her weapon still pointed at Sanchez was rock solid. "You okay, Jack?" she asked.

"Yeah." I stepped to her and took the gun from her hand. "Thanks. Good timing."

She jerked her gaze from the body and looked at me. "What?"

"Thanks. You saved me." I held her shoulders and turned her away from Sanchez. "You did great. You are awesome."

She glanced down at Sanchez then held up a small heart-shaped locket. "This was Angel's. It was in his drawer in a carved wooden box." She closed her eyes as a slight tremor flashed through her. "There are three more pieces of jewelry in there as well."

Anger flooded over me and I wanted me to kick Sanchez' body, but that energy would be better spent easing Becky's guilt. I rubbed my hands up and down her arms. "You slayed the monster, Beck. That scum will never hurt anyone again." I kissed her forehead. "But now we gotta get out of here. Put the locket back where you found it. We'll let the police put the pieces together with a little nudge from us. I'll meet you in the hall."

Becky stared down at the body again and I turned her toward the door. She looked into my eyes for a moment, then left. I rubbed Becky's gun barrel on the back of Douglas' hand, then wrapped his fingers around the handle. There should be enough GSR on his hand now to tag him for the shooting. I picked up the ledger and looked around the room. It needed to be hidden where the police could find it. I scanned the shelf for a book the same size as the ledger. The book, *Thinking Strategically: The Competitive Edge,* fit perfectly. I pulled off the dust cover, inserted the ledger, and put it on the shelf. It had to be kismet – if Douglas had been thinking strategically, he never would have made the ledger so easy to find. I checked Douglas to make sure he was still out cold and left.

I met Becky in the hall.

"Down the back stairwell?" she asked.

"No. We'll go up a couple floors first then take the elevator down."

I stripped off our gloves and shoved them down the front of my pants. After an odd look from Becky I said, "No one will search me there."

"Come on." I grabbed her hand and we ran up the stairwell to the twelfth floor and opened the door into the offices of "Gabers and Smith, Attorneys at Law." The offices were empty. I spied a worn attaché case next to a desk, and picked it up. I grabbed a few business cards from a holder on a desk and stuffed them in my front shirt pocket. "Let's go." With my arm through Becky's, we rode the elevator down to the lobby.

As the doors to the lobby opened, I spied blue uniforms. I turned to Becky as we stepped out of the elevator. "Monday we'll ask the judge for an injunction against the plaintiff's..." I stopped, almost bumping into a cop, then stared at the other half-dozen cops and the milling people who had flooded out of the ground floor's Rose and Crown restaurant to see what was going on.

"Officer, what's happening?" I asked.

"Shots were supposedly heard in the building. You got ID?"

"Shots?" I reached into my top pocket, withdrew a purloined business card. I slid on an anxious face as he plucked the card from my hand. I raised my voice. "Terrorists? Is it a terrorist attack? We have to get out of here." All heads glanced my way. The buzz in the room increased and tension ratcheted up a hundredfold to the edge of panic. I touched the cop's arm, hunched, and moved to stand behind him, swiveling my head in all directions.

"No, sir. We don't have any information yet as to what's going on." He glanced at the card. "This you? Gabers?"

"No. I'm Jacob Smith." I tilted my head to Becky. "My secretary, Janice Newburg." I looked around. "Are we in danger? Can we leave? Is it safe to?"

With a roll of his eyes he moved away from my hand on his arm. "Yes, sir. Just proceed through the front door."

I grabbed Becky's arm and started to run, causing a few others to break into a run as well.

"Walk!" shouted the cop.

I slowed down and we exited the building with a flood of others.

A block away, I released Becky's arm.

"Holy crap, Jack. You even had me believing it was a terrorist attack."

"A raised voice and pulling others into your panic is the key."

We walked another block in silence, then Becky's pace slowed. "I killed him, didn't I."

I placed my arm around her shoulders. "What you did was save other women from the horror that Angel endured."

Becky nodded slowly, then her chin dropped to her chest. "After... He was so... still. So... dead."

"Yes. You ended the corrupted life of madness, leaving only the husk." I squeezed her shoulders. "You saved my life. He was about to shoot me."

Her head came up. "I heard what he said when I came through the door and anger just flashed through my body. I didn't consciously pull the trigger. It just happened."

"And the last four shots?"

"Well... Anger and Angel's locket in my hand had me aiming more carefully."

We turned a corner and walked another block in silence.

"How you handling it?" I asked."

"It's not like I thought it would be." She shook her head. "Not at all. It's surreal. Like a bad movie. But a movie never left me feeling a little dead inside myself."

"That's the shock. It will pass." I leaned in and kissed her cheek. "You saved my life. I owe you a pint of Jameson."

She looked up at me and the first smile since the shooting graced her face. "A pint? More like a fifth."

Her smile faded. "Will I go to jail?"

The question stopped me. "What? No way!" We continued walking and neared the van. "There's no way any of this can come back to you. The gun can't be traced, there are no witnesses. Once Douglas is found to be a drug trafficker, all theories will be that he and Sanchez had an argument. A falling out among thieves is the easiest for everyone to believe."

"He saw your face."

We reached the van and I opened the door for Becky. "True, but from his expression, I'd say he didn't know who I was. Sanchez kept him in the dark about everything except the drugs."

In silence we drove back to the hotel. I stayed quiet, waiting for Becky to open up. This was something you couldn't rush. Becky sat with arms crossed, staring out the windshield.

Her head bowed and her hands dropped into her lap. "I thought I'd feel different," she finally said. "I thought I'd feel relieved, even glad." She placed a hand on my arm. "But the whole thing just makes me wanna cry."

"Yeah. It hurts now, but it will pass." I parked the van and turned toward her. "Tell me about the other jewelry in the box."

Becky looked forward, inhaled deeply and let out a shuddering breath. "Two rings, a necklace, and Angel's locket." She sniffed. "It still held her little bluebell flower. That's how I was sure it was hers." She turned to me. "We must find the others. Their families deserve to know."

"We will." I opened the van door. "For now, let's tighten the noose around Douglas' neck."

It was time to put a flea into the cops' ear about Angel's killer. While Becky took a shower, I called the police on a burner phone. I lowered my voice and put on my Spanish accent. "Hey, man. I got info on why Douglas killed Sanchez."

The operator hesitated a moment, then: "Let me switch you to the detective in charge."

"Detective Rinaldo," said the voice over the phone.

Ah, good. Rocco Rinaldo. The same detective who was handling Angel's murder case. I just got lucky. "Hey. I got info on why Douglas killed Sanchez."

I heard papers rattling. "Who is this?"

"Yeah, like I'll tell you that. Listen. I heard Douglas wanted a bigger cut of the drug money."

"Are you saying Councilman Douglas was dealing drugs?"

"Of course. The street know that, I thought you cops did too, he pay you enough."

"Those are some heavy accusations against the Councilman."

"You don't believe me? Check Douglas' book shelf in his office, that's where he hides his ledger. I seen him put it there." I heard furious writing.

"We'd like to talk with you some more. How about you come in, and we'll talk about it?"

"Are you kidding? With Douglas off the street a new territory just open for me. I'll be way too busy."

"Is there any way we can contact you again Mr. ah... X?"

"Don't need to. Just be glad Sanchez is dead, that way there won't be any more dead red-heads," I said.

Total silence for five seconds. "What are you saying?" asked Rinaldo.

"Nothin'. Sanchez likes to off redheads. The Cruz helps dump the bodies. Everybody knows that."

"Are you talking about Juan Cruz Johnson?"

"Sure. He's Sanchez' brother. Don't you guys know nothin'?"

More paper rattling and Rinaldo's voice rose a half-octave. "Listen, Mr. X. I'd really like you to come in and tell us more about the redhaired women. There's a reward."

"Chump change, hombre. I've said enough. Adios."

I broke the connection.

Becky came out of the bathroom and re-tightened the towel around her breasts. "These hotel towels are too short."

I tilted my head and grinned. "While I, on the other hand, admire their parsimony."

"Humph. Look all you want, but you're not touching me until I've had dinner. I'm starved."

Hunger was another human reaction to killing, but I wasn't going to mention that to her. "More room service grilled cheese and fries?"

"Nope. I want a steak – medium rare, a small salad, and fries. Yeah, fries would be good." She fiddled with the towel wrapped around her hair. "More lima beans for you?"

I rose, held her hands and looked into her eyes. Confusion about the reality of the world still hung back in there, but she was handling it. I kissed her nose. "Your order sounds good. Let's make it two."

Becky finished off the last of her steak. "I heard what you told the cops about Sanchez. Think it will be enough for them to realize he killed Angel?"

"It should be. If not, we'll give them another shove."

"Do we have to stay in this hotel any longer? With him dead it should be okay to go back to the bar..." Her fork stilled and she looked down at her plate. "Oh... I forgot."

"Let's give it another day and see what shakes out. Then we'll do some clothes shopping for you and stay at my house until the bar is rebuilt."

She pursed her lips. "What about the gang. Won't Cruz and the Dragons come after us now?"

"Maybe. With Sanchez dead, Juan Cruz Johnson will be looking for payback. If he thinks Douglas killed his brother, though, he'll forget all about us." I bit into a fry. "Besides, Cruz may think

Sanchez had the bar firebombed 'cause you wouldn't push drugs. I doubt he'd connect it to someone putting five holes in his brother."

The color left Becky's face and her eyes lowered.

Shit. I've got to remember not to be so callous about Sanchez' death. I reached across the table and laid my hand on hers. "Sorry. Didn't mean to be so cavalier. It's just that I've lived my whole life in a gray area. Who's the good guy. Who's the bad. Who knows. Sometimes they're one and the same."

I rubbed the back of her hand. "But Sanchez' death is so clearly in the white that I don't think of it as immoral or sinful. I just think of it as righteous."

Becky let out a big sigh. "And he would've killed again."

"Yeah. For sure. He was a monster."

She flipped her hand over and gripped mine. Eyes filled with doubt and confusion stared at me. "Make love with me?"

I rubbed her hand with both of mine. "I'd love to. But first, you need a good massage. I want you to be a puddle of pretty on that king-size bed before we do."

"As tense as my shoulders feel, you've got your work cut out for you."

I rose and led her to the bed. "I love a challenge."

Chapter 63

Becky's torched apartment was unrecognizable with the exception of the battery run black cat clock on the wall, its eyes still shifting in harmony with its swinging pendulum tail. It was weird how some things were burned black and some small things escaped the heat.

The structural engineer gestured to the ceiling with his pencil. "You'll need to gut everything and replace some bracing right there just to be on the safe side."

I nodded. "Do it."

The man made a note on his clipboard.

"How about the floor?" I asked.

He walked to a blackened area and tapped it with his foot. "A few sections need replacing, but if I had the money, I'd rip it all out and start over. Water damage is a haven for mold."

"Add that to your list then, and have them replace it all. Thanks, Josh." I picked up the wooden box at my feet and headed downstairs.

Becky was wiping down the bar – some things never change. She looked over at me. "Can I go up, now?"

"No, Beck. It's not a good idea."

"But…" Her eyes widened and she stared at the box. "My photo box!"

"Yeah, I found it in the closet. It's in good shape, though I can't say the same for your see-through teddy. It gave its life to save this box."

She pulled the box from my arms, plopped it on the bar and lifted the lid. "They're undamaged!" She lifted up an old black-and-white photo in a metal frame and smiled. "This is me and my dad on Christmas morning."

The picture, taken in front of the bar, showed Becky's dad with his arm around a young Becky and her arm around a new bike. "You're what, nine here?"

"Just shy," she said and grinned at the picture. "My dad was as excited as I was. He knew I'd go on my annual pre-Christmas present hunt, so he stashed it in Mr. Migliano's basement. Had me fooled into thinking I wouldn't be getting the bike at all."

I tilted the picture toward me. "You have his nose."

"Yeah, and his propensity for sticking it where it doesn't belong."

The make-shift door creaked and Ralph walked into the bar.

"Hey, can I get a Coors?"

"Ralph, you nut," said Becky. "We're not open yet."

"I know." He walked to where his usual barstool had stood, patted the bar then walked toward us. "Listen. I was talking to a bunch of the fellas and everybody is ready, willing, and able to come help in any way you need."

"Thanks, Ralph. I really appreciate that." Her eyes narrowed. "How come you're not at work? Your shift ends at two."

"Ahhh..." He looked down at the floor and stuck his hands in his pockets. "Got a two week suspension for drinking on the job."

"Sorry, to hear that," I said.

"One lousy beer. Eh..." He rocked his head back and forth. "Maybe I'll get a new job. Run for office, that way I can drink on the job like they do. We're gonna need a new Councilman, anyway."

This peaked my attention. "What about Douglas?

"Yeah," said Becky. "It's only been four days since the shooting. He can't have been fired yet. The town council will debate a week about when to take a dump."

"Naw, not fired. Dead. Got shived in a detention cell. And funny, no one saw who did it. A cellblock full of thugs and they all go blind at the same moment."

Becky and I exchanged looks. She opened her mouth to say something but I shook my head.

Ralph was looking down at the photo. "Your pops was a good guy. Always willing to help out. Maybe it's our turn now."

Becky's eyes filled. "Thanks. I'll let you know."

Ralph waved a hand and walked toward the door, then stopped and turned around. "This isn't just your bar, Becky. It's ours too." He waved again and left.

"Douglas is dead," she said, her eyes never leaving the front door.

"Looks like Cruz believed Douglas killed him. That means we are free and clear."

"Were we responsible for his death?"

"We are all responsible for our own deaths. Douglas chose his when he started dealing with gangs and drugs."

Becky turned, threw her arms around me and buried her head in my chest. "This nightmare is almost over."

"Yeah, just one more loose end." I held her tight and stroked her hair. "Angel."

Chapter 64

I stared at the coffee maker, willing it to drip faster. Laying off my exercise routine was beginning to take its toll as I found it harder to wake up these mornings. It was good to be home, though, with Becky in my bed. I never thought of myself as the homey type, but I was enjoying pretending to be a typical suburban family man. The word "family" dropped a shitload of ideas, desires, and scary thoughts into my mind.

While the coffee dripped, I slipped two frozen waffles into the toaster, pushed the button down then glanced out the window. It looked like it would be a nice sunny Sunday. Maybe Becky and I could go somewhere different. It'd been eight days since Becky had killed Sanchez, and besides planning the bar re-fit, we were at loose ends.

With a slap of bare feet, the other loose end trudged down the stairs and into the kitchen. She wore the shiny, pink satin pajamas I had bought her. They were a little large, but she said she liked the extra room. She looked like a big yummy piece of Easter candy.

"Hey," she said after a huge yawn. "Coffee smells good." She ran her hands through her hair still scrambled from sleep.

I got down two cups and handed her one. "Help yourself."

Becky sat and gestured to the toaster. "Frozen waffles? You sharing?"

"Sure."

A thump on the front stoop had her jumping in her chair.

"It's OK, Beck. It's just the paperboy with the usual forty-pound Sunday paper. We're totally safe here. Get out some eggs and I'll scramble and burn a couple."

It might take a little while for Becky to stop thinking the police were going to arrest her at any moment.

I walked to the front door, checked the security screen to make sure the area was clear, then opened the door and retrieved the newspaper.

The headlines blared about a new political squabble and I quickly flipped the paper over. A picture stopped me short in the kitchen doorway. I quick-scanned the article and let out a sigh of satisfaction.

"What's up with that satisfied face, Jack?" asked Becky. "Is there a sale on JWB?"

I walked over and plopped the paper in front of her.

Angel's picture stared out at us under the headline, "*Police Solve Local Woman's Murder.*"

Becky slammed her coffee down, heedless of it sloshing on the table. Her eyes lanced down at the article. "They got him, Jack. They got him." She pulled the front section off the pile, folded it, and read aloud. "Evidence found in the home of deceased Councilman's aide Diego Sanchez has identified him as the killer of Angel Anderson. Angel Anderson...blah, blah, blah..."

"Pictures, notes, and a journal found in Sanchez' home have also explained the disappearance of several other area women. Police believe Sanchez abducted and tortured..."

Her voice faded away and her clenched hands crumpled the edges of the newspaper. After a few moments, she put down the paper and looked up at me. "It's over."

Becky lunged from the chair and hugged me hard, her face pressed into my chest. Her body trembled and a tear dripped down her face. I held her and stroked my hand down her hair.

"Yeah. It's over and done."

The smoke beginning to waft from the toaster told me the waffles were done, too..

Chapter 65

With an arm around each other's waist, a feeling of déjà vu swept over me as Becky and I watched Mr. Hennessy finish painting the bar's newest front window. It seemed an unsettled lifetime ago that we had stood exactly like this. A lot of turbulent water had flowed under that proverbial bridge since then, but now the stream was calm.

The window read the same as before but in the opposite bottom corner from "Quinn: Proprietor" a piece of cardboard taped to the window blocked something painted there.

Hennessy stood, dropped his brush into a jar and stepped back to admire his work. "As lovely a job as anyone could ask," he said, and turned to Becky. "You still want that corner spot covered, lass?"

Becky grinned and spoke with Hennessy's Irish accent. "No. If you would be so kind as to remove the cover, Mr. Hennessy, if you please."

Hennessy smiled at me, then walked over and removed the cardboard cover.

Painted in the same gold outlined in black, the words read: "*Now Serving Jack Daniels.*"

Stunned, my mouth dropped open and Becky squeezed my waist. I dropped my arm, walked to the window and squatted. On its own, my hand reached out but Hennessy's warning stopped me. "It might still be a little wet, lad."

I stood and turned to Becky. Surprise and delight had me groping for words. The simple words grounded me, and I felt some of the roots that Becky must feel about the neighborhood. The bar was a place where I could put down my own roots, to grow entwined with Becky's.

She clasped her hands together and grinned. "Whataya, think? See how it works on two levels?"

Like a zombie, I stumbled to Becky, grabbed her in a bear hug and lifted her from the ground. I held on tight as wonder and bliss filled me.

"Seems he likes it, lass," said Hennessy.

I released Becky and stroked her face. "This is…"

"I thought this would be better than branding 'pretzel boy' into your bar stool's leather seat. After awhile your butt would take on the indentation 'yob lezterp.'"

"Beck, you don't know what this means to me."

She held my face with two hands. "Yeah, Jack. I do."

Love flowed through me. Finding Becky was that missing piece I'd unknowingly searched for all my life. My past was just a bad movie I'd seen a long time ago with the images fading rapidly.

With my heart filled, I couldn't help the words that popped out of my mouth. "Becky, will you…" I stopped myself in time. "…pour me a JWB?"

Becky smiled like she knew what I was going to say, but raised an eyebrow and let me off the hook. "Not yet, Jack." With her hand in mine, she pulled me toward the bar's entrance. "Come on, we have an hour before we open and there's still lots to do." She turned to Hennessy. "Sticking around for the grand opening, Mr. Hennessy?"

"Wouldn't miss it, lass. Wouldn't miss it."

The place shone like a bright bubble with new booths, tables, chairs, stools – new everything except the bar itself. Becky turned the new flat screen to a baseball game and muted the sound.

"That's way better than the old set." Wearing her new "*Hope's Province*" T-shirt, she stood, hands on hips, looking like the proud owner of the world's best business, and perhaps she was. After a glance around the room, she squinched up her shoulders and clasped her hands. "We did it, Jack. It's all done." Becky picked up a rag and began to subconsciously wipe down the already pristine bar. I leaned over the bar and slid the pretzel tray on a shelf. Each table held a pretzel bowl twice the size of the old ones – I had insisted on it.

I turned on my bar stool and glanced around the room. "It's a beautiful new baby, but it still has the same aura it always did."

Becky's eyes filled. "Dad's still here. I can feel him."

"Yeah. Maybe you can get him to be pretzel boy instead of me." I glanced at the crowd gathered at the door, then down at my watch. "Time to open."

Becky dashed a hand under her eye to wipe away a tear, and walked to the front door. She threw it open, spread her arms, and raised her voice. "Welcome all to the new Hope's Province Bar."

As the crowd flooded in, Becky strode back behind the bar and started pouring a Guinness for Mr. Hennessy. "First glass for the sign painter."

"I can't thank you enough, Ms. Quinn," he said as he leaned on the bar.

"The first shot goes to Jack Daniels." She filled the glass and with an expert flick of her wrist, sent it sliding down the bar. It stopped right in front of me. I hoisted it up and toasted her. She gave me a quick salute and started drawing pitchers of beer.

Ralph walked in and slid onto the barstool next to me. Becky didn't even look at him but opened a Coors and slid it down to him. He used its momentum to bring it to his mouth and took a long pull. "Ahhh. Now that's what I'm talking about."

"What are you talking about?" I asked.

He waved his bottle around the room. "This. Calm, cool, and Coors." He took another drink. "You guys did a great job on this place."

"You helped," I said.

"Pshaw. The boys and I just did a little hauling and painting. It was a labor of love for all of us." He glanced at the front door. "Oh, God, speaking of labor. Here comes calamity in a miniskirt."

Carli pranced in wearing a low-cut, baggy white satin blouse, the black miniskirt, black stockings, and – I had to look twice, saddle shoes. Her usual teased blonde hair sported a black and pink stripe.

"Shake it up, Carli," said Becky. "You were supposed to be here half-an-hour ago." Becky handed her a tray loaded with a pitcher of beer and four glasses. "Take this to table three."

"Sorry I'm late." She headed out, and over her shoulder said, "I couldn't find this blouse. It's my lucky blouse. I always make more in tips when I wear it."

As she bent over and dropped off the beer, I could see why.

Bernie and Sam piled in and scooted to their usual table. I shot them a wave as Carli walked over to take their order. Since they drank the same thing every night, chances were they would get what they ordered.

For the next few hours, beer was drawn, drinks were served, and toasts were made. Raucous laughter occasionally punctuated the revelry as The Hope's Provence tavern filled with cheer and camaraderie. It was the place to be tonight.

Becky slid from behind the bar and picked up a tray loaded with a pitcher and several bottles of beer. She gestured to me with her head. "Come with me. I'll let Carli take the bar for a while and we'll make the rounds and chat."

Our first stop was a booth with a man and a woman with their heads close together. The man looked familiar and I recognized Ginny Cameron from her red hair and the row of sparkly studs marching down her ear.

"Hey, Billy," said Becky as she placed two Heinekens on the table.

Ah, yes. Billy the I-went-to-school-with-him fireman.

"Hey back, Beck." She turned to me. "Billy and I went to school together."

Keeping myself from rolling my eyes, I just nodded.

Billy reached across the table and held up the woman's hand, displaying another sparkly on her forth finger. "Ginny and I have gotten engaged."

"Congratulations!" Becky turned to me. "Ginny is –"

"I know Ginny," I said. "We went to school together."

Becky's brows clashed and she punched my arm. "No you didn't."

"Yeah, bagel school." I winked at Ginny.

"That's really super, guys," Becky said to the couple. Ginny and Becky chatted awhile about wedding dates, bridal showers and apartment hunting, while I shifted from foot to foot. Billy's vacant stare said he felt the same as I did.

Dwayne's waving hand caught Becky's eye. "Well, good luck, you two," she said to the engaged couple.

I added my congratulations and followed her to Dwayne's table. She plopped down a bottle of Bud Lite.

"Hi, guys," he said. "Great job redoing this place. It's new, but still feels like the old bar."

"Thanks," said Becky. "How's the mail business?"

"Going postal," he said. "For us mail carriers, it's busier than usual. They've given us more area to cover, and there's more retirements happening with no back-filling." He sipped his beer. "Two more years for me, and then I'm out."

"Good for you," I said.

"Yeah. I'll miss the gossip though." He sat up in his seat. "I was delivering to the precinct and talked to Detective Rinaldo. He said that scum Sanchez had a file and pictures of his next victim on his computer."

"That bastard," said Becky.

"Guess who it was?"

Becky closed her eyes and shook her head. Dwayne said nothing, but tilted his head toward Billy and Ginny's booth.

"Ginny?" I asked.

"Yeah. She works over at Cameron's Coffee Shoppe."

"I know." Outrage flooded my stomach and I wished Sanchez was still alive so I could kill him this time. I let the flood of anger go and leaned toward Dwayne. "Rinaldo actually told you that?"

Dwayne peeled a corner off his bottle. "Well, I kinda overheard him when he was talking to another detective."

I straightened and glanced at Ginny Cameron. Another bright flower Sanchez wanted to rip out of existence. My rage evaporated as I remembered Sanchez lying dead on the floor with big holes ripped in his chest.

"Don't mention this to anyone," I said to Dwayne. "No one should live with the nightmare that she was in some psycho's sights."

He nodded. "I only mentioned it to you because..." Dwayne grinned. "Well, you might mention it to that friend of yours, that private eye, Joe Hawkshaw."

I raised an eyebrow and looked down at him.

"I stop at all shops delivering mail. The gossip about you, I mean the P. I., was all over the street."

"I hear Joe's retired."

Dwayne raised his beer. "I heard that too."

I nodded to Dwayne and pulled Becky away from his table. "It's a good thing Sanchez's dead."

She closed her eyes a moment, then opened them and nodded. "It's a good thing."

I squeezed her shoulder and directed her to Bernie and Sam's table.

"Ah," said Bernie as Becky put the pitcher on their table. "Glad you brought another. I've got a bigger thirst these days."

"And a smaller bladder," said Sam.

"Asshole."

"Jarhead."

Sam looked over Bernie's shoulder and out the window. "Hey, Becky. It looks like Hope's Provence is pulling in some high-class customers."

A long black limo had pulled to the curb. The chauffer walked around the car and opened the back door.

Regan stepped out, wearing a dark blue paisley dress that didn't cling, but didn't hide her curves, either. Perched on her hip was a very pretty baby, with dark hair the same color as her mother's.

The chauffer cocked his arm and a man inside the car held it and stood. The chauffer reached into the car and handed him two steel crutches.

"Whoa," said Becky. "Who's that with Regan?"

I had to smile. "That's Roland Dante."

Becky stared at him as they walked in the door. "He *is* some serious eye-candy. If I'm dreaming somebody pinch me."

I pinched her hard.

"Hey!" Becky rubbed her arm. "What was that for."

"Just fulfilling your dreams."

Becky didn't have time to answer as Regan and Dutch walked over to the table. As soon as little Olivia spied Bernie, she let out a squeal and held out her arms. Bernie sat her on his lap and she made a grab for his beer.

"Should I bring another glass, Bernie?" said Becky with a laugh.

Bernie grinned. "She's my little sweetheart. I'll share."

"She's certainly a chip off the old block," said Sam.

I turned to Dutch. "Slumming?"

"Are you kidding? I heard that tonight this bar is the most happening place in the state."

"You got that right," said Becky. She smiled at Dutch. "Hello. Becky Quinn, proprietor."

Dutch held out a hand and Becky took it in both of hers and stepped closer, almost touching shoulders. "Welcome, Mr. Dante. Can I get you anything special?" She smiled up at him and batted her eyes.

"Oh, please," said Regan. "That has to be the lamest come-on I've ever seen." She turned to me. "Step closer, Jack and I'll show her how it's done."

I held up my hands. "I'm so not going there."

Dutch gave me a puzzled look. "What...?"

I pulled a chair over for Dutch. "Just sit and watch the show."

"Wanna see the knockout punch?" said Regan. She stuck out her arm and waved her left hand under Becky's nose. A diamond the size of Pittsburg sparkled on her forth finger.

"Holy hell, Dutch," I said. "Are you two getting married?"

Still grinning, Regan slid into the booth next to Bernie and Dutch lowered himself into the chair.

"Yep," said Dutch. "I asked, she said yes, done deal."

Congratulations rang around the table.

I leaned over and whispered to Dutch, "Pre-nup?"

Regan must have good ears as she looked up at me. "No. He didn't want one." She placed a hand over his. "But I insisted."

"This calls for champagne," said Dutch. He looked up at Becky. "What's your best vintage?"

"Probably Miller," said Regan. "It's the champagne of beers."

Becky ignored the remark as a smirk popped on her face. "I have several bottles of a 1995 Clos d' Ambonnay in the back."

Dutch's eyes widened. "A '95 you say? That's..."

"The best there is," said Becky. "And a bargain at only twenty-eight hundred dollars a bottle."

I stared at Becky and she turned to me and grinned.

"Dad knew someone who had few bottles. He bought it twenty years ago as an investment."

"Dust one off," said Dutch. "I can't think of a better occasion to open a bottle."

Becky turned to me and placed a hand on my shoulder. "I can only think of one other occasion that might be better. Can you, Jack?"

I looked into her eyes and felt the rest of the past I hadn't given up fall off me like a heavy overcoat. The future shone ahead with no baggage to tote, no what ifs. From here on it was Becky, the neighborhood, and our lives together.

"I bet we're thinking of the same occasion." I wrapped my arms around her waist and pulled her close. "Let's talk about it later tonight."

Love beamed from Becky's face. "Over a glass of Jameson?"

"That'd be perfect, Becky. Perfect."

John Migacz was drawn at an early age to stories of action, adventure and inspiration, and he began searching for a medium for his overactive imagination. Misguided youthful exuberance interrupted this pursuit as he volunteered for the US Army, where he served with the 198th Infantry Brigade in Vietnam. After detours into the fields of photography, painting, and filmmaking, he discovered his passion for writing during his tenure as a computer administrator for a major telecommunications firm. When not writing, John spends his time indulging his grandchildren and annoying their parents.

John has written several novels, and numerous short stories and essays. John can be reached at: www.johnmigacz.com.

www.ingramcontent.com/pod-product-compliance
Lightning Source LLC
Chambersburg PA
CBHW050505260626
47157CB00004B/1195